A Rob W
First published in Great Britain in
United

Copyright @

The right of Rob Wyllie to be identified as the author of this work has been asserted by him in accordance with the Copyright, Design and Patents Act 1988

All rights reserved. No part of this publication may be reproduced, stored in a retrieval system, or transmitted. in any form or by any means, electronic, mechanical, photocopying, recording or otherwise, without the prior permission of the copyright owner.

All the characters in this book are fictitious and any resemblance to actual persons, living or dead, is purely coincidental.

RobWyllie.com

# The Ardmore Inheritance

Rob Wyllie

# Chapter 1

*Polymath.* There was no doubt about it, that's what he was, although he'd only come across the word a couple of days previously, in some podcast or other he'd been listening to on the train. *A person of wide knowledge or skill.* That's what it had said when he'd googled it, and yeah, that's what he was, too bloody right. And wasn't that rather marvellous for this Geordie lad, and only thirty-one years old too? He learnt the basics when he was in the Navy, but since he'd came out, he'd done well. *Bloody well.* Street artist and master hacker, those were now his core skills and where it had all started. But then pretty soon afterwards he'd added a third, a skill that was a bit more old-school, but no less satisfying. *Cat burglar.*

It had been a bloody long journey, trekking up the M1 and the M6, and when he'd got to Glasgow, four hundred miles and seven hours later, and in the pissing rain too, the sat-nav was telling him he'd still got another fifty-seven miles and an hour and half to go. But he'd pushed on, and now he was parked up in the big Q7 in a little inshot right alongside the loch, no more than fifty metres from the gates to Ardmore House. As he jabbed the stop-start button to kill the engine, he reflected how much he loved his wicked Audi SUV, kitted out with every option in the catalogue, and acquired only three months earlier. How many lads his age could afford a motor like that, bought and paid for all perfectly legit from the proceeds of his very lucrative business activities? Yes, all perfectly legit, apart from the cloned registration plates it was running on, keeping him free from both speeding tickets and detection. He allowed himself a smile of satisfaction as he zipped up the dark bomber jacket and taking the black silk balaclava and matching silk gloves from its pocket, slipped them on. Cartoon burglars always had a bag slung over their shoulders, labelled *swag*, but he didn't need one of those, labelled or otherwise, because the items he was planning to nick, two of them if he got lucky, would comfortably fit in a back-pocket.

The late April sun had long since dropped behind the craggy mountain ridge to the west, but the moon was up, reflecting hazily in the lapping waters of Loch More. He had no definitive idea of what hours the family kept, but it was now half an hour past midnight so it had to be a good each-way bet that all four would be safely tucked up in bed, if in fact they were all at home. He knew the twins would be there, at least according to that morning's barrage of Instagram posts, and of course that was why he'd made the bloody expedition in the first place. As to the father and their older brother, he didn't know their movements but he'd just have to play that one by ear and deal with any difficulties that might arise as and when.

The house was equipped with one of these wireless alarm set-ups that could be armed from a smart phone, and they'd also gone to the trouble of installing a few cameras around the place that allowed their home to be monitored remotely, no matter where in the world they were. But luckily they hadn't gone to the trouble of protecting the system with a fit-for-purpose usercode and password combination, which is why for the last two days he'd been able to case the joint whilst supping a cold beer and lounging on his comfortable sofa back in his Battersea flat. For the usercode, his old mate Commodore Roderick Macallan (retired) had chosen his personal email, r_macallan@supermail.co.uk. Not exactly difficult to crack, even if it hadn't been in the public domain, which it was. And then the password? Obviously, the Commodore wanted something nice and easy to remember. So naturally he'd picked the birth-date of his beautiful twin daughters, Pixie and Posy. And finding *that* date wouldn't have taxed even his ninety-year old granny, given that the influencer twins were determined to play out every second of their lives on social media.

He'd been worried the 4G signal would be a bit patchy up here but in the event it was more than acceptable, allowing him to do a final remote sweep of the house and grounds on his smartphone before leaving the car. There was a camera covering the front gates, but it was too dark to make out whether they had been left open or not, although his earlier surveys had suggested they never bothered to close them. Too much of a pain when driving in and out, he assumed. The cameras in the house were confined to the hallway, kitchen and upstairs landing, but he saw that all the lights were off and so it was reasonable to assume that everyone had retired for the night. *Time to go in*. With a deft swipe he disarmed their alarm system, then tucked his phone in an inside pocket and got out, quietly closing the driver's door behind him. He didn't bother locking it, smirking as he weighed up the chances of two thieving bastards being active in this remote neck of the woods at the same time. Two-thirds of not very much at all.

He'd noticed during his on-line surveys that the floodlight which illuminated the gate area was aligned with a bias to the rightmost gate post, a bit of sloppiness on the part of the installation guys that he meant to exploit. As he reached the entrance to the driveway, he took a quick glance round, then sprinted to the other side of the road, staying out of range of the gate's proximity sensor. A few steps took him past the opening, allowing him then to re-cross the road so that he was standing alongside the left-hand gate post, noticing at the same time that the gates had, as he expected and hoped, been left open. If everyone was safely tucked up in bed, it was unlikely that they would notice the light coming on in any case, but he didn't intend to risk that. Crouching down, he crept forward, keeping his shoulder tight against the post, and then edged alongside the open gate. *In, no problem.* Now his eyes were adjusting to the moonlight and he could see the old house looming ahead, shadowy and imposing against a dark-navy sky. He'd done a bit of research and found it had been built in the eighteen-eighties by Sir Archibald Macallan, a prominent Glasgow shipbuilding magnate, and had been one of the first houses in Scotland to be equipped with both electricity and hot and cold running water. He'd also read that the guy was a right bastard, treating his workers like shit and with a reputation for cheating his suppliers out of their due. But it hadn't stopped him getting a knighthood and amassing a fortune, most of which disappeared after the second world war when competition from overseas crushed the Clydeside yards, with their arcane trade-union demarcations and prehistoric equipment, out of existence. The Ardmore Estate was about all that survived, passed down the male line until it came into the possession of the current Laird, Sir Archie's great-great-great grandson Roderick. *His pal, the Commodore.*

Underfoot, the driveway was tarmaced and smooth, obviously well-maintained and a pointer to the piles of cash that the estate must be raking in from their hunting and fishing operations. Nice, but he wouldn't have swapped his business for theirs. Too much like hard work for a start, and besides, he couldn't see how anyone could shoot one of these magnificent antlered beasts without wanting to puke. It was about a two-minute walk to the front door, where the drive opened out into a large gravelled forecourt. Three cars were parked neatly end-on facing the house, suggesting that all the residents were present and accounted for. A ten-year old Discovery, which he knew was the Commodore's. A battered long-wheelbase Land Rover, which looked like the typical estate hack, probably the wheels of Peter Macallan, the son who ran the estate on a day-to-day basis. And then the transport of one of the Poxy twins, as the tabloids had disrespectfully named them, a top-of-the-range hot hatchback, courtesy of a marketing deal they had cut with the German manufacturers. Sleek black metallic he recalled from the pictures he'd seen on their Instagram, although it was impossible to make out in the semi-darkness. Matching motors with matching personalised number plates. *Naturally.* He assumed one of the cars would have been left back in London, the twins travelling up together to what they called their Highland retreat. At least he hoped that was the case, so as to give his mission a reasonable chance of success.

But of course he wasn't going in the front door, that was far too risky, even with his bravado. Instead he'd identified a ramshackle porch on the south side of the house, which an old photograph of the place he'd found on the web revealed as constructed in timber with a corrugated tin roof. He'd sketched out an internal plan of the house based on his on-line surveillance and although he couldn't be sure, he figured the porch led into a boot room or something of that sort, directly adjacent to the large farmhouse-style kitchen. Its door might be locked or it might not be, but he didn't expect it to present much of an obstacle to his bunch of skeleton keys if it was. Which left only the bloody dog to worry about.

He'd caught it on camera a day or two earlier, lounging in the kitchen in its bed-basket whilst chewing a bone, an ancient golden retriever or labrador, seriously overweight and very definitely looking as if it was not long for this earth. That was his hope anyway. He'd brought some doggy treats and some chocolate buttons too, proper milk chocolate ones which he knew they loved but weren't supposed to eat. Hopefully they would do the trick, but if it didn't and it started sounding off, he'd just have to leg it and have a re-think. But he was an optimist and of course he was a polymath, wasn't he, so how hard would it be to calm some old moth-eaten mutt? Pretty soon he was going to find out.

Skirting round the edge of the forecourt, he took care to give the house a wide berth in case he triggered any security lights, creeping along the lawned verge to avoid his steps crunching on the gravel beneath his feet. Reaching the south wall he spotted the porch, still just about standing, and even in the moonlight he could tell it hadn't changed much from that old photo. He tiptoed across the wide path that he guessed ran all the way round the house, and slipped under the rickety roof. Fumbling in an inside pocket, he withdrew a powerful LED torch and shone it towards the panelled door which guarded the entrance to the house. At first sight it looked sturdy and appeared to be secured by twin mortice locks, which would have presented a worthy challenge to his lock-picking skills- if not for the fact that it stood partially ajar. Handy, that. And then when he got closer and gave it the gentlest of pulls, he saw why. After years of exposure to the prevailing south-westerly rainstorms, it had swollen to such an extent that he doubted if they'd been able to close the thing even once in the last ten years.

Smiling to himself, he pushed it open and slipped through.

As he had suspected, the door led into a small cloakroom, a half-dozen or so outdoor jackets hanging on hooks, and several pairs of walking boots arranged neatly on a low shelf, none of which he could imagine belonging to the glamorous twins. And then he heard it, coming from the direction of what he surmised was the kitchen. A low snuffle and a louder yawn, then a slow pad-pad-pad as the old labrador wandered over to greet him. *Silently.*

'Good boy, good boy,' he whispered, gently patting the animal on the head and scratching under its chin. The dog gave a sigh and nuzzled its nose against his jacket pocket, evidently detecting the receptacle that held the treats.

He kneeled down, taking a crunchy bone-shape biscuit out of his pocket, then held out his palm. The labrador picked it up with surprising delicacy then flopped onto his stomach as he turned his attention to despatching it. Whilst the animal was distracted, he took out the chocolate buttons, burst open the pack and spread a generous quantity on the flagstone floor. The dog looked up momentarily but continued working on the biscuit.

'Good boy,' he said again as he edged his way into the kitchen, closing the door behind him. The dog, trapped in the cloakroom, made no sound of protest, evidently looking forward to his date with the chocolate buttons. The intruder killed the torch, the room being adequately illuminated by the silver glow from the clocks of the oven unit and microwave. He'd prepared a sketch of the place, roughing out the location of each room, but now that he was in the house he was able to visualise the layout quite clearly in his mind. On the ground floor was a grand entrance hall with four or five doors leading off, which he guessed would include a couple of living rooms, if that's what they were called in this kind of place, a big dining hall and maybe a study or a library. All of which was completely irrelevant, because neither of the social-media-obsessed twins would have left their phones downstairs when they went to bed, not in a month of Sundays. Which meant if he wanted to steal them, which was the whole point of his mission, then he was going to have to go upstairs and exponentially raising the risk factor, slink into their rooms and snatch them away whilst they slept. He could feel the adrenalin start to surge, his face beginning to redden as he psyched himself up for the most dangerous part of the operation. In his mind, he ran through the sequence of events once again. *Creep into the hall, tiptoe up the stairs, slip into each bedroom in turn, pray the phones have been left lying on a bedside table, do the snatch, beat it.* It had all seemed perfectly straightforward when he'd mentally rehearsed it on the way up the motorway, but now, on the ground, doubts were beginning to surface, the principle one being, what if one of them was awake, or woke up as the theft was in progress? The problem was, both women boasted a feisty reputation, and he didn't think it likely that either would just lay down supinely if they found an intruder in their bedroom in the middle of the night. He didn't like violence but he didn't want to get caught either, which presented a dilemma.

He was just about to make his move when he thought he heard movement upstairs. Damn, but perhaps it was just one of them popping up to visit the loo. So what if he had to give it five or ten minutes for them to drop off again? He had plenty of time. But then suddenly, he heard a shout, the voice muffled but just loud enough for him to make it out. A voice which definitely seemed to emanate from an upstairs bedroom. *What the hell are you doing?* And then a loud crack, which could only be a shot from a gun, followed by a blood-curdling shriek of pain. And then, no more than a few seconds afterwards, another shot rang out. *Shit shit shit, this wasn't part of the plan.* Momentarily frozen to the spot, he tried to weigh up his options, rapidly concluding that there was only one. *Get the hell out of here, and fast.* But then he heard something else. The thump of footsteps banging down the stairs and then the squeak-squeak of a pair of sneakers skittering across the varnished parquet flooring of the great hall. Then a grating creak, which he assumed was the heavy front door being dragged open, but with no corresponding bang of it being closed behind the escaper. As his composure began to return, he slunk over to the door that led to the hall and edged it open. Through the gap, he heard the rah-rah-rah of a starting motor turning over, followed by the distinctive rasp of the hot-hatch's powerful engine firing into life, shooting up a shower of gravel as the driver sped away, foot nailed to the floor.

Now the house was deathly silent, and for the first time he noticed the quiet tick-tick of the roman-numeralled clock mounted next to the hob. *Twelve forty-seven.* Feeling calmer now, he reappraised the situation. It would be a shame to leave the place empty-handed, especially when he knew that knowledge was power and could be turned into money too, a mountain of the stuff. If he'd learnt anything in the two years he'd been in the hacking business, it was that. So it would definitely be worth spending a few more minutes here. It was mission creep for sure, but the original mission brief was surely now out the window. So that was it decided. Nip upstairs, have a quick sniff round, take a few snaps, then scarper.

But he'd need to be bloody careful not to leave any trace, because there was something he definitely didn't want to add to his impressively poly-mathematical skill-set. *Murder suspect.*

## Chapter 2

*It's a rather complicated matter.* That's all Asvina had given away to them when she'd phoned with a brief trailer for what was to be their next case. Which meant that it was going to be an absolute bitch, because Miss Rani, London's premier family-law solicitor to the rich and famous, never passed them the nice easy straightforward ones. That wasn't a problem for Maggie, because after all, if the matters were easy and straightforward, Asvina wouldn't need the services of her firm. *Bainbridge Associates, Investigation Services to the Legal Profession.* That was their tagline, summing up rather neatly what they did. Checking identities, uncovering dodgy bank accounts, verifying personal back-stories. In other words, all the grubby stuff that the fancy twelve-hundred-quid-an-hour lawyers felt was beneath them.

Maggie had arranged to meet Jimmy at the exit of the Docklands Light Railway station in Canary Wharf, just a stone's throw from the gleaming glass palace that housed Addison Redburn, the prestigious law firm where Asvina was a half-a-million-a-year partner. And as usual when he was meeting with Asvina, he'd made a special effort to spruce himself up. Hair washed and tied back in a neat pony-tail, a freshly-pressed blue shirt with a button-down collar, smart black jeans, polished tan cowboy boots. Maggie had known her Scottish assistant barely two years, but already they were like an old married couple and mostly, in a good way. The relationship was characterised by mutual respect and an ability to disagree on how a case should be approached without sulking, which, when she thought about it, perhaps stretched the marriage analogy too far. Maybe she would be best to reserve judgement until they bumped into the mythical seven-year-itch. Then again, her own actual marriage had only made six years, so maybe she was being optimistic in thinking they would still be working together by then.

'Any idea what this is about boss?' he asked, shooting her a smile. 'Although to be honest, I don't really care. It'll just be great to be back in the saddle again.'

He was right, because it had been a while since they'd had a nice big juicy one to get their teeth into. Her little firm was doing ok now, their reputation having spread as a result of cracking a couple of very high-profile investigations in the past year, but much of the recent work had been pretty dull and routine. This one however had every prospect of being anything but.

'Not much. It's a complicated inheritance matter I think, with a ton of money involved. Not exactly sure what it is she wants us to do, but you can imagine it won't be a walk in the park.'

Asvina's PA Mary had met them in the reception atrium where they had been issued with passes then escorted to the high-speed lift that delivered them up to Miss Rani's glass-walled corner office, an impressive south-west facing suite on the second-highest floor, commanding a view in one direction over the river to the picturesque Royal Borough of Greenwich, and towards St Paul's and the City in the other.

She greeted them warmly, embracing Maggie in a suffocating hug then shaking Jimmy's hand.

'Thanks for coming in guys,' she said. 'Mary will be in with the drinks in a moment. But I'm a bit pushed for time so I'll get straight on with it if you don't mind.'

Maggie gave a wry smile. Her best friend was so ridiculously successful that for her, time literally was money. One occasion during an idle moment she and Jimmy had done a rough back-of-a-fag-packet calculation, revealing that Asvina was bringing in not far off a pound a second. So it was understandable she didn't like to waste any of those seconds on non-billable small-talk.

'I don't know if either of you remember the Macallan incident? About six months ago. Up in your neck of the woods Jimmy I think it was.'

'How could I forget?' Jimmy said. 'The Ardmore mystery, that's what the media called it. The father blew his son's head off and then shot himself, but no-one's ever worked out why. So it's that, is it? That's what we're going to be working on?'

Maggie caught the look of disquiet on his face, and she could hear it in his voice too. It seemed he knew something of this matter, although she was puzzled as to what it might be.

'Yes, that's it, and it was the most dreadful family tragedy, wasn't it?' Asvina said. 'And now of course, there's the horribly mundane matter of sorting out the estate, which as you may now have guessed has fallen to our firm, in our role as executors. And hence on to me personally.'

'Well of course we'll be happy to help in any way we can,' Maggie said, at the same time wondering what they were letting themselves in for. 'But I think you said it was a rather complicated matter?'

Asvina nodded. 'Well, yes you could say that. First of all, there was the little matter of establishing whether the document that was vested with us was still valid.'

'There was some doubt about that?' Maggie asked.

'Only in so much that the father, that's Commodore Roderick Macallan, had been having some correspondence with a local solicitor about changing the terms of his will in the months before he took his own life. But in the end, we concluded those discussions were only exploratory, and since they had never been formally written up or witnessed, we took the view that they could be ignored.'

'And that was the complication?' Maggie asked.

Asvina shook her head. 'I wish I could say it was only that. The fact is, there are some peculiarities in the provisions of the existing will that makes it rather a bugger to execute, not to put too fine a point on it. Although it's not a particularly large estate in terms of absolute value.'

Maggie shot Jimmy a half-smile, who returned a look suggesting he was thinking the same thing as she was. *Not a particularly large estate.* In Asvina Rani terms, that probably meant no more than nine or ten million pounds.

'And who benefits from the will?' she asked. 'There are twin daughters I seem to remember?'

'Yes there are,' Asvina said. 'And they're identical twins too. Pixie and Posy. Not their given names by the way, but ones they adopted several years ago when they began their careers in the public eye.'

'Elspeth and Kirsty,' Jimmy said, his voice signalling disapproval. 'That's their real names.'

'Do you know them then?' Maggie asked him, surprised.

'I've met them,' he said. 'Once.' By his expression, it was evident he didn't mean to give anything else away.

'That might prove useful,' Asvina said brightly, not giving Maggie the chance to ask the obvious question, being *how* he knew them. 'There is also Roderick Macallan's estranged wife to be considered too.'

'That's the twins' mother?' she asked.

'No,' Asvina said, 'Alison Macallan is the Commodore's second wife. I should have said that his first wife, the mother of his three children, died in very tragic circumstances. But I guess you'll know all about this Jimmy?'

'Aye, I do,' he said. 'Although it's pretty much in the public domain, courtesy of the twins. They mention it a lot on their channels.' From his tone, Maggie guessed that once again he didn't approve.

'Their mother died in child birth,' Asvina explained. 'This was in Canada, where their father was on secondment at the time, somewhere over on the West coast, Vancouver I think. So as I understand it, the first twin was delivered perfectly normally. But then there were terrible last-minute complications with the second baby, something about how she was lying in the womb I believe. So as a result, the doctors had to do an emergency Caesarean, but the mother had already lost a lot of blood and they were terribly worried about the outcome. I think in the end it may have come down to them choosing between saving mother or baby. Whatever the truth of the situation, they managed to deliver the second twin about half an hour later, but sadly Phillipa Macallan died on the operating table.'

'God, how horrible,' Maggie said. 'But you say his second wife Alison is estranged from the Commodore? Does that mean they're not divorced?'

'Not yet. The break-up was acrimonious, let's put it this way, and we had only recently started with the formal proceedings before he died. Which of course, just adds to the complexity of the matter, as I've eluded to already.'

'It does sound very interesting,' Maggie said. 'So you mentioned some peculiarities in the will. What are they all about?'

Asvina smiled. 'Yes, as I said, it's all rather complicated. In fact it goes back to late Victorian times, when one of Roderick Macallan's ancestors built the Ardmore estate. Sir Archibald made his fortune in shipbuilding and more or less invested all of it in building the house and laying out the grounds. I think it was true to say it became the love of his life. Which brings us to the covenant in the will.'

'A restricted one I'm guessing?' Maggie said, nodding sagely. In her days as a trainee solicitor, immersed in the mundane conveyancing work that was the lot of the junior, she'd come across many of these clauses and knew what a pain in the backside they could be. Which was of course the intention when they were drawn up in the first place. They weren't called restricted for nothing.

'Yes, exactly,' Asvina said. 'As I said, it had been the love of Sir Archie's life and so he took precautions to ensure it could not be sold off and broken up once he'd passed away.'

'And that's what the covenant tries to enforce?'

'Yes, it does. It lays out that in the event of the death of the current incumbent, it must pass, *intact*, to the oldest offspring- the oldest surviving issue in lawyer-speak. Specifically, it states that the estate must not be sold off in order to split the proceeds between the surviving beneficiaries. Over the years of course there have been attempts by the family to have the covenant overturned, but the courts have always held firm. And as the house and grounds have been listed for several decades now, it makes it even more unlikely that it could ever be successfully challenged.'

'I understand,' Maggie said, thinking out loud. 'So I think I begin to see the complication. Because this time, the next in line to inherit happens to be twins, and I'm guessing that eventuality was never considered in the original provisions.'

'Well no, it wasn't,' Asvina said, 'that's true, but in fact that in itself isn't a problem. Legally speaking, the estate would be inherited by whichever of the twins was first-born. And it's *that* which is providing our current little complication.'

'How do you mean?' Maggie asked.

Asvina gave a wry smile. 'Each of the twins is claiming it is she who is the first-born, and we are finding it impossible to verify the truth one way or the other.'

'What?' Maggie said, puzzled. 'But surely there must be records? You know, birth certificates and the like? Particularly since they were born about half an hour apart, which must be unusual for twins.'

'Well yes I guess it is, and yes there are records of course. But in Canada at that time, the register of births only stated the date of birth, not the time. We checked that.'

'But what about family?' Maggie asked, then remembering that both their parents and their older brother were dead, she realised it was quite conceivable that the truth had died with them. Changing tack, she asked. 'Are there no aunts or grandparents who might know?'

'Roderick had an elder sister, and we were able to get in touch with her but she didn't know. She's nearly ninety and said she had always been confused over which girl was which. As I said, Elspeth and Kirsty are identical twins so I suppose you can understand that. And Roderick and Phillipa were both the children of older parents, so it's not surprising that both sets of grandparents are now dead.'

Maggie gave Asvina a sympathetic smile. 'Yes, I think I can see now what you meant when you said it was a complicated matter.'

'And that's not the half of it,' Asvina replied. 'You see, Alison Macallan has now formally decided to contest the will too.'

'Can she do that?' Jimmy asked, breaking his silence, a silence that Maggie had noted with some anxiety.

'Yes, of course,' Asvina said, 'although whether she will be successful is another matter altogether. When they split up you see, the Commodore changed the terms of his will rather rapidly to exclude her from inheriting anything. But it's normal for a spouse to have rights over the estate of their deceased partner whatever the state of the relationship at the time of death, so a family court may feel that the will is very unfair to her. That's just my opinion, but it wouldn't surprise me if they looked at her case with some sympathy.'

'And do you think it's harsh?' Maggie asked Asvina.

'I think so, and it's made more complicated by the fact that since she and the Commodore split up, she's been living in a gate cottage owned by the estate, near the village.'

'Lochmorehead,' Jimmy said morosely.

Maggie gave him a quizzical look but made no comment. Instead she said, 'So don't tell me Asvina. Mrs Macallan could be evicted, if whichever twin inherits the place doesn't want her around?'

Asvina nodded. 'Yes, that's a distinct possibility. So as you can imagine, she's rather sore about the whole thing. That's understating it actually. In fact, she's absolutely livid, mad as hell. The whole thing's a bit of a mess.'

'And you want us to sort it all out is what I'm guessing?'

'Yes please,' Asvina said, laughing. 'Shouldn't be too difficult. No seriously, I know it's going to be quite a challenge to say the least. But I think the mission is quite straightforward to define if not execute. You either need to somehow find out which of the twins was born first- and god knows how you're going to do that - or you need to broker some sort of a settlement between them, which will probably have to include the estranged wife too.'

Maggie raised an eyebrow. 'Bloody hell Asvina, even by your standards this is a challenging one. But of course, we'll do our best, won't we Jimmy?'

'What?'

She shot him an admonishing glance. He was staring at the floor, seemingly lost in his own thoughts.

'We'll do our best, won't we Jimmy?'

'Aye, sorry boss,' he said, forcing a half-smile. 'Aye we will.'

'Great,' Asvina said briskly. 'That's it all arranged then. Brilliant.' Furrowing her brow, she gave her watch an extended look, a look Maggie calculated had cost her friend about thirty quid. 'So if you don't mind guys, I've got some folks coming to see me in a couple of minutes.' Politely but firmly, she ushered them towards the door. 'Keep me informed of progress if you would.'

In the lift on the way down, Maggie had tried to make conversation with Jimmy, which shouldn't have been exactly difficult given how much they now had to talk about. But he seemed distracted and disengaged, his mind elsewhere, his answers terse to the point of rudeness. And it was so completely unlike the Jimmy she had come to love that she now knew, if she hadn't before, that there was something badly wrong.

'Jimmy,' she said quietly. 'What is it? Is there something you're not telling me?'

He gave her a half-smile. 'Look, I'm sorry Maggie, it's just all come as a bit of a shock. You see those twins, Elspeth and Kirsty Macallan. My wife Flora was at school with them, and with that woman who was murdered four years ago too, Morag Robertson. The damn place is cursed I tell you. And now it seems I'm bloody well going back there.'

## Chapter 3

DI Frank Stewart smiled as the high-tech vending machine delivered him, as ordered, a steaming Americano fortified with double Espresso. He picked it up and then with a jaunty step schlepped over to the adjacent machine, swiped his debit card across the contactless reader, then punched in the code number he knew off by heart. Six-one-six, sending a Twix King-size tumbling into the receptacle below. Things were looking decidedly up at this moment in time, that was his opinion, mainly because his sleepy wee department had, much to his surprise, gone viral. At least, that was the term his mate Eleanor Campbell had used to describe the sudden and unexpected explosion of interest from across the whole UK policing community. And it was all down to his boss Jill Smart, who had recently spoken at a national police leadership conference up in Birmingham.

'We've got this small department,' she had told an assembly of a couple of hundred of her Detective Chief Inspector colleagues, 'hidden away in a dump of an office just off the Uxbridge Road. We call it 12B, I've no idea where that name came from, but that's what it's called. It's been up and running for a couple of years now, and we in the Met find it's a very handy facility for the sort of matter that doesn't quite fit into our conventional teams. Cold cases, early-stage investigations and the like.' Very handy for tidying away big embarrassing screw-ups too, was what she hadn't gone on to say, although everyone in the room took it as read. And since every force in the country had a ton of *them*, Department 12B was suddenly in demand.

The first one he was turning his attention to had come in from Greater Manchester Police. *We think it's probably some sad geeky teenager. Take a quick look, see if there's anything to worry about.* That was the terse instruction that got Frank onto what would become known, obviously, as the *Geordie* case. And when Jill Smart had fleshed out the detail, he could see why they were so keen to get it all wrapped up and locked away out of sight.

He found Eleanor at her adopted desk, and surprisingly for once, the forensic officer wasn't on the phone to her on-off boyfriend.

'How's Lloyd?' he asked guilelessly.

'He's a pig.'

Resisting the temptation to ask for further explanation, he shrugged and said, 'Aye, all men are. Comes with the territory. Anyway, work to do, let's get on.'

Generally speaking, there would be a bout of tense negotiation required before she consented to do even the most trivial of tasks, principally because Eleanor Campbell was a stickler for doing things by the book. Meaning in practical terms she always wanted to see a bloody case number, whereas Frank would go to any length to avoid having to attach that bureaucratic limpet to anything he was working on. The reason being that once an investigation got a case number, it became visible to the brass, who had a nasty habit of asking awkward questions, like why are we spending so much on this stupid case, and worst of all, when are we going to solve it?

But this time he didn't have to worry about any of that, because Eleanor was fully on board with the project.

'You got it then I hear? You got DCS Barker's phone?'

'I got it,' she said, 'at least I got WPC Green to get it for me. She hates him way more than I do.'

'Aye, not surprising that, because she has to work with the arse five days a week. But anyway, nice work wee Eleanor. So anyway, just run it past me again, what are we going to do?'

She gave him a look of mock disgust. 'I've explained two-factor authentication to you a million times.'

'Three times I think you'll find, if we're being strictly accurate, and that was quite a while ago to be fair. But that's what this guy Geordie's doing, do you think? The two-factor stuff?'

'Defo. That's why he breaks in and steals their phones. And by the way it might not be a guy, in like a man.'

'You mean it could be like a woman?' He found it hard to resist a spot of gentle mockery of the way she spoke, and he knew he usually didn't have to worry about causing offence because generally she never noticed. Evidently she assumed that everyone spoke that way, even oldies like him. But she hadn't missed it this time.

'Are you taking the piss?'

'No no,' he said hurriedly. 'When I say this *guy* Geordie, I mean it in a strictly gender-neutral sense of course.' *Gender neutral.* That was a phrase he'd learnt on a course, and he'd found it went down well with millennials like her.

It seemed to satisfy her. 'Cool. So how did we get on to this dude in the first place?'

That was a question he wasn't fully at liberty to answer. Because it was an Assistant Chief Constable, the high-profile high-flying Katherine Frost of the Greater Manchester Police, who in desperation had brought it to the attention of Jill Smart after learning of Department 12B from one of her DCIs. 'This will ruin my entire career and reputation if it gets out, you must understand that,' she had said to Jill, 'I need to know I can count on you. On your absolute discretion and that of your team.' And afterwards he could see why she was so exercised about it. Because if like her you were on a career fast-track, with every prospect of making Chief Constable before you were fifty, but you also liked to be chained to your bed by the wrists whilst being orally pleasured by another woman, and you liked to take a video as a souvenir too, then you would, quite naturally, insist on discretion. So Smart had given her the assurances she needed before passing it on, smirking, to Frank Stewart, who had laughed uncontrollably and promised to guard the secret with his life. But he had to tell Eleanor something.

'It came from the Manchester boys, or to be more accurate, a Manchester girl. Seems as if our guy Geordie broke into the pad of one of their top brass and has been indulging in a spot of blackmail ever since. Highly embarrassing for the officer in question.'

'Sweet.'

Frank chuckled. 'Aye, you could say that. So obviously the mission is to catch this hacker guy before he does any more damage.'

Having been tipped off by the Manchester affair, Frank had put out some feelers courtesy of his good mate DI Pete Burnside, and found out that Geordie had also been active across London and the South East for at least a year, and always with the same MO. Break into someone's pad, nick a phone or a computer and then leave a signature example of his graffiti artwork on a wall or in some cases, on the front door. The guy was talented, there was no doubt about it, although he'd read a critic in the *Guardian* complaining that most of his work was highly derivative and he'd blatantly copied the style of his obvious inspiration Banksy. Which had made Frank laugh, because it wasn't as if the street artist was some sort of modern-day Robin Hood. He was nothing more than a common criminal and with an ego the size of St Paul's Cathedral to boot, an ego that Frank predicted would surely be his downfall. It had to take five minutes minimum to do one of these paintings and that made it odds-on that one day he'd be caught in the act.

But it was what he did afterwards that intrigued Frank the most. Because no more than a few hours after the physical break-in, Geordie would follow it up with a skilled cyber attack, granting him unhindered access to the victim's private documents, photographs and god knows what else besides. At least a couple of celebrities had been done, and a week or two later some rather embarrassing photographs had mysteriously appeared in the seedier tabloids, which had caused their publishers to have some awkward questions to answer as to their source. However as far as Burnside knew, none of the victims known or otherwise had yet lodged a formal complaint. But as Pete said, you wouldn't, would you? Kick up a fuss and you could expect the scumbag to tell the world your most precious secrets, which was the last thing you'd want. That was until ACC Katherine Frost had been targeted and had decided to put her faith in Department 12B.

And now wee Eleanor Campbell was going to demonstrate how it was done.

'So Barker's phone,' Frank said, giving her a quizzical look. 'I assume it's got a password or a pin or whatever you call it?'

'That doesn't matter,' Eleanor said. 'It'll come through as a text notification and we'll be able to see it anyway.'

'It?'

'The authentication code.'

'Aye sweet,' he said, risking mimicking her again. 'But tell me young Eleanor, what's brought on this recent and much welcome hatred of DCS Barker on your part?'

'He tried to make me look stupid in a meeting. In front of lots of my colleagues. Nobody does that and gets away with it.'

Frank liked that. Hell hath no fury like a geeky forensic officer who's been made to look stupid by a fat-arsed Detective Chief Superintendant.

'Fair point well made wee Eleanor,' he said. 'So what's the plan?'

'We're going to hack into his iCloud account. Zak's given me an app to help.'

He remembered Zak from his Aphrodite investigation, a capable lad from the Met's Maida Vale labs who was even younger-looking and geekier than Eleanor herself, if that was possible.

'And this app is legit?'

She shrugged. 'Suppose. It came from GCHQ or MI6 or somewhere, that's what Zak says.'

Frank doubted that anything that came from either of those sources was in any way legitimate, morally or otherwise, but he didn't say so. And he wasn't bothered either.

'Ok, right, let's go.'

She punched a string of text into her keyboard, bringing up a login screen for the iCloud website.

'So first we need like a user code and a password. User code is easy, it's always their email, and we know his. Password is more difficult,' she said, frowning, 'but not *that* difficult. Not when we have Zak's password generator app. It's well wicked. It uses artificial intelligence all through it. A-I. It's way cool.'

Frank had listened to her explain A-I to him many times before but couldn't remember a thing about it, which would no doubt displease her. So he decided against asking for a refresher, instead allowing her to continue uninterrupted.

'So you can program it with personal stuff,' she said. 'Stuff you know about the mark.'

'Mark? That's what you call them do you, the victims?'

'Yeah, as in a con-artists mark. So as I said, we can program Zak's app with stuff you know about the mark. Like for example, we know Barker supports Spurs.'

'Arsenal actually,' Frank said, shaking his head with mock disgust.

'Whatever. I can easily change that.' She furrowed her brow then hastily banged something into her laptop. 'So it also knows his date of birth and the street where he lives and where he works and where he went to uni and his school and where he was born....'

'Aye, I get the picture,' Frank said wryly, 'but can we get to the point?' He knew from experience that when Eleanor went off on one of her long technical explanations, you were best to set aside the rest of the day.

'You *don't* get the picture,' she said, evidently intending to ignore his interruption, 'so from that, Zak's app can web-crawl onto like mega-tons of other databases, like the electoral register, the register of marriages, deaths and births, the land registry....'

'Eleanor....'

'...and stuff like that,' she said. 'It's wicked.'

'Eleanor, where's this all going?' he said, struggling to hide his impatience.

'So from that information it can narrow it down to a short-list. Nearly everybody chooses passwords based on stuff they know, don't they, because it's easier to remember? Stuff like their favourite football teams or players, or kids names or birthdays, or your old school, or your granddad's name blah blah blah. So by knowing all that, it massively cuts the number of possibilities the app has to try. As I said, it's super-cool artificial intelligence.'

For the first time, he began to understand what she was talking about.

'Aye I see that, *very* clever, very clever indeed. So what do we have to do to kick it all off?'

'We just have to click on this button that says go,' she said matter-of-factly, pointing to the screen. 'But of course before we do all of that, we always try the obvious one first.'

'Which is?'

She looked at him as if he was an alien from another planet, which he might as well have been, given how little he understood of what she had been talking about for most of the morning.

'Doh, *password* of course. P-a-s-s-w-o-r-d,' she said, spelling it out. And a few keystrokes later, they were rewarded by a message. *Usercode and Password accepted.* There was no doubt about it, DCS Colin Barker was a genius.

'So this is the wicked bit now,' she said, picking up Barker's phone in response to a discreet *ping,* then rotating its screen to face him. 'Now we have the authentication code, we've got admin rights to his account.'

She punched in the code then navigated her mouse to a link labelled 'Account Settings.'

'See?' she said, smiling triumphantly. *'Change authentication phone number.* Give me your phone number Frank, will you?'

'What, are you kidding?' he said, shooting her a smile. 'I'd lose more than my pension if Barker ever found out about this. But seriously, I think I'm seeing how this Geordie goes about his business.' He wasn't sure if he did, but he wasn't going to admit that to Eleanor. Luckily she was ready with an explanation.

'Yeah, so immediately after he steals their phone he goes on to their cloud account and diverts the authentication phone number to one of his own phones. That means that even if the mark reports their phone missing and blocks it, he's got as long as he wants to take whatever he needs from their cloud drives. I mean, nobody checks their cloud drives, or at least hardly ever. So he could have access for weeks and weeks before his marks realise they've been hacked.'

A thought came to Frank, and even although he knew it would make him look stupid, he asked the question anyway.

'But what about that password stuff? How does Geordie get round that? Because I don't suppose he has Zak's wee app, does he?'

She gave him a pitying look. 'Old-school hacking. It's not as clever as Zak's but it uses the same sort of techniques. And also, there's mega-tons of hacked personal data for sale on the dark web and people often use the same passwords across all their sites. Which is a mistake. That's why two-factor authentication was invented.'

'Because it's now so easy to crack a usercode and password?'

'Exactly,' she said, her expression betraying disappointment that Frank had worked it out for himself. 'As I said, that's why he has to steal their phones.'

It was all completely fascinating, but he wasn't sure if it actually helped at all with the main objective, which was uncovering the identity of the slippery artist-hacker.

'So how do we set about catching this guy?' he asked. 'Any ideas?'

She gave a grimace. 'He's one capable dude, so I don't think we could track down his IP. That'll be cloaked behind some weapons-grade firewalls on the dark web.'

'This dark web again?'

'Yeah, it's standard for these hacker guys.' She made it sound as if everyone should know that.

'So what's the answer?'

'Difficult,' she said, giving a perplexed frown. 'There might be something around the triangulation of his mobile phones, but I'd need to think about that.'

He nodded slowly. 'Aye well that's fair enough Eleanor. Take as much time as you like. You've been an amazing help, you really have.' He was just about to get up to leave when she gave him a pained look.

'So aren't we going to look at Barker's iDrive? Now that we're like in?'

His face broke into a wicked smile. 'Of course. It'd be rude not to. Now that we're like in.'

Which is how they came to know of Barker's big secret, something that might help to explain his inexplicable rise through the ranks and also explain how he'd inexplicably held onto his job for so long, despite his demonstrable and abject uselessness.

And it also explained that dodgy handshake too.

***

Now there was some movement on the Geordie case, Frank could turn his attention to the other matter that had come into the department as a direct result of its new-found fame. A matter that was showing every prospect of being an absolute belter. A gory double murder, a prisoner who had hanged himself in his cell and the subsequent revelation of a massive miscarriage of justice. No wonder Police Scotland had sent the case scuttling down the M74 faster than a hot potato on a hot tin roof, if that wasn't too much of a mixed metaphor.

Now he was looking forward to his regular Thursday evening couple of pints with his brother in the Old King's Head. And another encounter with the vision of forty-two-year-old loveliness that was Maggie Bainbridge.

## Chapter 4

For a while it had been touch and go in his mind but on balance he was glad he'd gone through with it in the end. Pulling on one of these old jackets and grabbing a pair of the walking boots, that had been a smart idea, but then he was full of smart ideas, wasn't he? The old labrador hadn't batted an eyelid bless him, when he'd slipped back into the boot-room to collect them, and for a moment he'd considered taking the mutt with him when he left. It got a bit lonely living on your own, and he had a notion a dog would be an amiable companion, not that he'd had any experience of them to judge that. But on second thoughts, they could be a bit of a tie, so he'd quickly expunged the idea from his head.

As he'd sprinted up the stairs, he'd tried to prepare himself for what he might find. He'd not expected it to be pretty, but the scene of carnage that awaited him in Roderick Macallan's bedroom was like something from a horror movie. For a moment he thought he was going to throw up and *that* would have been a frigging disaster, spraying a shed-load of his DNA about the place. But he just about held it together, long enough to take some photographs, not that he saw himself looking at them any time soon. *No way.*

It was the son Peter who was the real puke-inducing mess, the side of his face having being blown off by the sawn-off shotgun that now lay cradled in his father's arms, finger still on the trigger from when he had shot his own brains out. There had been blood all over the floor but he had been super-careful not to have trodden on any of it, not that it mattered since he'd already figured out that these boots and jacket were going into the middle of the loch as soon as he was finished here. And he'd rapidly resolved not to hang about a second longer than was absolutely necessary.

But then just as he'd been about to disappear, he'd made a spur-of-the moment decision. Now that he was there, it would have been a shame not to at least try and complete the original mission, not that he'd thought there was much chance of success. But nothing ventured nothing gained, that's what they said, wasn't it? So he'd turned his back on the horror show and crept along the upstairs landing, trying each of the twins' bedrooms in turn. He hadn't been sure which one was which, not that it had mattered. A quick scan of the first one had drawn a blank, pretty much as expected. Nothing on either bedside table other than a glass of water and a crumpled fashion magazine, the bed not slept in. Shrugging to himself, he'd crossed the landing and cautiously pushed open the second of the bedroom doors, and there it had been. A top-of-the-range iPhone 12, sleek and expensive. He'd covered the short distance from door to bedside in just three strides before slipping it into his pocket and retracing his steps down the stairway and into the kitchen. Opening the door to the boot-room, he'd called quietly to the labrador, not that there was anyone around to hear them. The dog had given a muffled bark and padded through to him, nuzzled his head against his leg, then flopped down in his bed-basket.

Back in the Audi, he'd quickly fired up each of the Macallan twins' iCloud accounts, expecting one of them to deliver an authentication code to the phone he had just nicked, so that it could be diverted to one of his burners kept specifically for the purpose. He waited expectantly for at least five minutes, figuring that the slow delivery could well be down to the variable 4G signal, but nothing came through. *Shit*. So this must be someone else's phone. A minor set-back, but perhaps he would find a way to profit from it nonetheless, when he was back in his London flat and had time to think it all through.

He'd taken the boots and coat off before getting in, obviously, not wanting to risk depositing any fibres or suchlike in his nice motor, and now they needed to be safely disposed of. He'd jumped out and wrapped the boots in the coat, bundling them up as tightly as he could. And then he'd sprinted across the road, leapt the low crash barrier and made his way down to the water's edge across the pebbly beach. It wouldn't have been enough to just throw them in from there, he'd already figured that out, so after first removing his wicked Nike Air Max's, he'd waded in, wincing as the icy water sent shivering spasms through his body. And then when it reached his waist, he'd began to swim. It had brought back sweet memories of his brief sojourn in the Special Boat Service, before

Commodore Macallan had bankrolled that smooth and lucrative transfer to civvy street. He'd swam for a few minutes, covering a couple of hundred metres before pushing the bundled coat and boots under the surface, watching for a moment as they began to sink. And then he'd broke into a smooth front crawl and headed back to the shore.

Setting the powerful heater to maximum, he'd blasted off along the lochside and in no more than an hour he'd been cosily warm and dry again. It was a couple of hours later, just as he was crossing the border into Cumbria, when it had suddenly come to him, something he hadn't registered at the time. That just before that hot hatchback had roared off into the night, he was now pretty sure he'd heard *two* car doors slamming. A rather interesting fact, which he could see opened up a fund of fascinating business opportunities. Especially since he, better than anyone, knew the precise motive for the murders of Roderick and Peter Macallan.

# Chapter 5

Thursday night had become their night, Maggie, Jimmy and Frank, and for the eighteen months or so it had been extant, their get-togethers had followed a strict routine. No matter how early Maggie and Jimmy arrived at the Old King's Head from their tiny serviced office on Fleet Street, Frank would already be there, and no matter how much progress he'd made with his first pint, he always instructed his younger brother to head to the bar and get another round in, the instruction generating first complaints and then grudging compliance.

But since their earlier meeting with Asvina Rani, Maggie had been observing her partner's mood, and the cloud of dark foreboding that had enveloped him did not seem to have lifted appreciably. She knew that getting back together with Flora meant everything to him, and so she would have expected that an opportunity to be working so close to where his estranged wife lived would have raised rather than dampened his spirits. But she suspected she knew what it was. His affair with the irresistible temptress Astrid Sorenson, the beautiful Swedish country music star, had broken Flora's heart and she knew that the shame and regret lived with him constantly. And today, rather than being buried deep in his brain in a file labelled *too difficult*, it had been brought to the forefront of his thoughts.

'How's it going wee brother and Maggie?' Frank said, as they settled down at the table he had bagged for them.

He telegraphed a glance at his half-empty glass. 'I was just hoping you were on your way to the bar Jimmy mate.'

'I'll go,' Maggie said quickly. 'It's got to be my turn for once.'

'No no,' Jimmy said, forcing a half-smile. 'Mustn't break with tradition. Two Doom Bars and a large chardonnay?'

'What's bugging him?' Frank asked Maggie as Jimmy left to battle his way through the crowded bar-room. 'The dog ate his lunch or something?'

So she told him a bit about that morning's meeting with Asvina, and the likelihood of her or Jimmy having to visit Loch More in the near future.

'Loch More?' he said, giving her a curious look. 'Well it's a small world so it is.' She waited for him to elaborate but he didn't say anything more.

At least the awkwardness between them, the result of that horrible occasion several months ago when she'd had to turn down his invitation to dinner, seemed to have softened noticeably in recent weeks, and now she entertained hopes that one of these Thursdays he'd ask her again. Or maybe if he didn't, she might ask him instead.

'Do you know the Loch More area then?' she asked him.

'Nah, I don't but *he* does,' he said, nodding in the direction of his brother who was approaching with the drinks. 'And listening to him go on about it, I don't think he likes the place much.'

'I gathered that.'

'What did you gather?' Jimmy asked as he laid their drinks on the table.

'Nothing mate, nothing,' Frank said unconvincingly.

'I was just telling Frank about the Macallan case,' Maggie said, 'and how complicated it is.'

'Aye, it sounds messy right enough. I've seen these lassies on You Tube by the way. Pretty girls, the pair of them.'

'What, Frank Stewart's been on You Tube?' Jimmy said, giving a laugh. 'What's the world coming to. You'll be sending emails next.'

'I was watching some old Scottish football clips,' he said, returning his brother a friendly one-finger salute. 'Ally's tartan army from way back in the seventies, that magic game against Holland. The Macallan girls came on before it, advertising some wee electric Toyota.'

'Yeah that's what they do,' Maggie said. 'They call them brand influencers, or brand ambassadors, I'm not sure what the difference is. But it seems to make them a lot of money whatever it is.'

'Aye, but it doesn't seem to have stopped them getting in to a punch-up over the Ardmore estate, does it?' Jimmy said. 'You'd have thought they already had plenty of money.'

Maggie was glad to see him something more like his old self. Now she wasn't sure whether to raise the question that had been intriguing her, but finally decided that it might be easier in this more convivial setting, and with Frank present to lighten the mood, as he invariably did.

'I hoped you don't mind me asking Jimmy,' she said uncertainly, 'but do you know the twins?'

He shrugged. 'Well I wouldn't say I know them exactly. I only met them once, at a do up in Lochmorehead a few years ago. It was a weekend when I had a seventy-two hour leave from Helmand I think. It was Flora's dad's sixtieth birthday bash and they were there. As I told you, they were at school together, my Flora and the twins. There was only about half a dozen girls in the wee village school and they were all pretty close as you can imagine. And there was that other girl, Morag Robertson, the woman who was murdered by her husband. She was there too and I met her just to say hello to. It was just a couple of months later that she was killed.'

Frank shot his brother a look of astonishment.

'Bloody hell, did you say Morag Robertson? This is just bloody ridiculous, so it is.'

'What do you mean?' Maggie asked, perplexed.

'Look, I can't really tell you too much right now,' Frank said. 'It's just something that's come into the department in the last day or two. I don't know if there's any connection to what you guys are working on, but it would be nuts if there was, let's just say that.'

'And you're not going to tell us anything else?' Jimmy asked, smiling. 'Us, your bestest mates in the whole wide world?'

This is more like it, Maggie thought, relieved. It seemed as if his sense of humour hadn't completely deserted him.

'Sorry, can't,' Frank said with an apologetic expression. 'It's not that I don't want to, honestly. It's just that I've not even opened the bloody file yet, let alone looked at it in any detail. And not just that, I've still not come up with a name.'

Maggie smiled to herself. She'd come to learn of the importance Frank gave to christening his investigations, and not with just any old name, it had to be the right one. *Operation Shark, the Leonardo Murders, the Aphrodite Suicides*. They'd all been huge cases that had started with nothing more than a snappy sobriquet. But once it had a name it seemed to galvanise him, the matter rapidly snowballing until he felt he was able to take it to his boss DCI Jill Smart, and ask for that official seal of approval that came with the allocation of a case number.

'Anyway, enough of all that, we're all here to have a bit of a laugh, are we not? So here's something that'll amuse you and I guarantee it,' he said, wearing a wicked expression. 'Obviously I'm not supposed to tell anyone, but this is an absolute cracker. Something else me and wee Eleanor have been working on. I can't name any names mind you, and you'll soon understand why that is, believe you me.'

Maggie gave him a fond smile. He was a good person, Frank Stewart, and he would have been only too aware how talking about his estranged wife caused his brother pain. So it was all credit to him for introducing a change of subject.

'What, handcuffs?' she laughed after she'd heard the tale. 'And do you think they were official police issue?'

'Oh aye, they were that alright,' Frank said, 'def-initely. Even the top brass like her get issued with a pair. Hers were probably gold-plated too.'

'What about the other woman?' Jimmy asked. 'Is she a cop as well? Maybe the other pair of cuffs belonged to her?'

'Can't tell,' Frank said sardonically. 'We can only see her arse in the photo.'

'So how come it's landed with you?' Maggie asked, still smirking at the image Frank had painted in her mind. An image which, much to her consternation, left her moderately aroused too.

'Good question. It turns out our reputation goes before us and we're now attracting stinky manure from every force in the land.' His manner was matter-of-fact, but Maggie could detect the pride in the way he said it. 'Seems like there's a lot of crap out there that needs a bloody big carpet to be swept under, and well, you can imagine why they want to get *this* one tidied up pronto. You know, before the tabloids sink their teeth into it.'

'And what did you say this guy was called?' Jimmy asked. 'Georgie?'

'Geordie. You know, a bit like Banksy. That street artist guy from Bristol.'

'I guess you're anxious to track him down,' Maggie said, 'assuming it is a *him* of course.'

Frank laughed. 'Aye, wee Eleanor pointed that out too. That it might not be a him I mean. But when our boys and girls do the psychological profiling in this sort of case, nine times out of ten it's a him we're looking for. Some spotty teenager with no mates, stuck in his bedroom with nothing else to do, that's my guess. But I'm sure we'll figure it all out soon enough. Eleanor's on the case, which is good news for me.'

Maggie nodded. 'Yeah, she's a clever lady. But anyway, how about we give talking shop a rest and have another drink instead? I could really do with one.'

'I'll go,' said Jimmy and Frank in unison, causing them to burst into laughter and then exchange a high-five. And then simultaneously they reached into a pocket and took out a coin, sparking further merriment.

'Best out of three then mate?' Jimmy said, winking at his brother. 'Heads or tails?'

Not for the first time, Maggie reflected how fortunate she had been that the Stewart brothers had come into her life just when she needed them the most. It was no exaggeration to say that Jimmy in particular had saved her life, and it was a debt she fully intended to repay.

And she was going to make a start by sending herself up to Lochmorehead to interview Mrs Alison Macallan, leaving Jimmy safely four hundred and fifty miles away here in London. With the beautiful and dangerous Macallan twins.

## Chapter 6

It had made sense to travel up to Scotland in her old Golf, because it had allowed her to fit in an afternoon visit to her parents in Yorkshire *en route*. It had been lovely as usual, her mum fussing over her like she was still five years old, and what had made it even better was that she had caught her dad on one of his good days, a day when he could remember both her name and who she was. Naturally they had been disappointed not to see their adored grandson, but it was already half way through the Autumn term, and with all the trauma Ollie had been through in the last two years, he needed the solid anchor of school in his life. So he had remained back in Hampstead under the care of their treasured nanny Marta, and could look forward to staying up late, watching inappropriate TV, and stopping off at the corner-shop for sweets on the way home from school. In fact, Maggie doubted if he would miss his mummy at all, but in any case she only intended to be away for one night, a punishing schedule that would involve a four-hundred and fifty-mile slog back to London when her business in Lochmorehead was complete.

The little hotel was splendid, old-fashioned but cosy and comfortable, and furthermore she had been allocated a room with a stunning view of the loch. It was close to eight o' clock when she'd arrived, the setting sun blasting a beam of shimmering purple through a gap in the mountains, the reflected hues dancing on the water surface. It was a magical landscape, which made it all the more difficult to reconcile with Jimmy's description of it. *The damn place is cursed I tell you.* But maybe Mrs Alison Macallan would be able to shed light on that when they met later that morning. After a hearty cooked breakfast of course.

'Full Scottish madam?' She had ordered the heart-attack inducing feast without thinking, but now that the elderly waitress was preparing to place it in front of her, she was beginning to have second thoughts. The fact that it had had to be wheeled out on a trolley rather than carried in on a tray was a pointer to its wholesomeness.

'Yes please,' she said, the arresting aroma rising up from the platter instantly blowing away her reservations.

'I'll just bring you your toast madam. Back in a moment.'

Maggie gave a grunt of acknowledgment through a mouthful of sausage, before turning her thoughts to the morning ahead. The objective with regard to Mrs Alison Macallan was relatively clear, but the chances of the mission being successful were rather harder to calculate. Asvina had said Mrs Macallan was very bitter about the way she had been treated by her husband, and Maggie knew from her own personal story how difficult that often made it to approach a situation rationally. When the motive escalated from justice to revenge, that's when it was most difficult in her experience, but with Alison's husband dead more than six months, and that death being so tragic, maybe her bitterness would have dissipated somewhat. She wouldn't have long to wait before she found out.

But now she had to admit to herself that Alison Macallan wasn't the only reason she had decided it should be her and not Jimmy who made the gruelling trip northwards. In fact, she wasn't even the main reason. The friendly waitress had now returned with her toast and Maggie smiled up at her.

'Excuse me, but is there an outdoor store nearby? You know, where I can get some hill-walking gear. And also, is there a doctor's surgery?'

The waitress smiled. 'Yes madam, there's Active Outdoors just a couple of miles along the road, heading up towards the Rest and Be Thankful. Out of the car-park and then turn right and then it's on the left, you can't miss it. They've got a good range and there's a wee cafe up there too. They do a nice coffee and a scone, so they do.'

Maggie gave an inward grimace at the thought of more food, but still managed to shoot the kindly woman a smile.

'Thanks, that sounds absolutely perfect. And the doctor's?'

'We've still got a wee surgery here in the village. Doctor McLeod and his daughter. They're very good.'

Doctor McLeod and his daughter. *Dr Flora Stewart.* That was assuming she was still using her married name. Now all she had to do was make up an ailment and book an appointment.

Having given a good account of herself in the battle with her breakfast, she refilled her coffee cup and spent a leisurely ten minutes admiring the view, before completing the check-out formalities. She had decided to postpone her visit to the outdoor store until after her meeting, and since it was a lovely morning she resolved to walk the three quarters of a mile to Mrs Macallan's home.

The cottage was on the main road, if it could be called that given the sparsity of traffic, and was designed in what she thought was called Scottish baronial style. Clearly a former gatehouse or lodge, it was constructed in stone with an impressive covered porch and a fairy-castle turret. It guarded a set of ancient-looking wrought-iron gates, secured by a rusty chain and padlock which suggested that this had not been the principle entrance to Ardmore House for many years. To her surprise, she found the front door slightly ajar, and was just about to call out when an overweight labrador squeezed out through the gap and gave a muted woof, which Maggie took to be a friendly greeting. The dog snuggled up against her leg and gave another bark, just as the door was opened.

'Hello, you must be Miss Bainbridge I take it? Don't mind Flossie, she's very friendly.'

Alison Macallan was approaching fifty, but looked older, her hair greying and unkempt, her face bereft of makeup. She was dressed in salmon jogging bottoms which had clearly seen better days, and a shapeless cream Arran pullover. But despite her unprepossessing appearance, Maggie could see that under the surface an attractive woman was struggling to break out. But that's what it did to you, the killer combination of tragedy and despair, when fear of the future stalked your every waking moment and stopped you from sleeping too. She remembered it only too well, and when she was at her lowest, she wouldn't have dared look in the mirror. But maybe their shared experience might help the mission.

'Maggie. Please, it's Maggie. I hope you're still ok with this Alison?' She bloody hoped she was, because she couldn't very easily nip back another day.

'No no, it's fine,' Alison said, although the tone was guarded. 'Come through.' She led Maggie through a tiny kitchen into a dark sitting room, furnished with two floral-pattern armchairs that, like the Arran pullover, could count their best years behind them. A pile of magazines was strewn across a small coffee table, upon which stood in addition to the reading matter, a bottle of supermarket own-label vodka, three-quarters empty, and a solitary glass. She gave Maggie a wry smile.

'It's from last night, honestly. I know I shouldn't, but I find it helps.'

'No need to explain Alison,' Maggie said, as she took her seat. 'Been there, done that. A dozen bottles of cheap chardonnay a week was my average, and that was just when I was trying to cut it back. You see, my husband and his lover were murdered in front of my little son, and he was only six at the time. And she was raped too.'

'Good god,' Alison said, looking aghast. 'I'm sorry.' For a moment Maggie wondered whether she had been right to tell her, but she knew she had to, if she wanted to have any chance of building a bond with this woman.

'No, I'm sorry too, I didn't mean to upset you. I only shared this because my story's *so so* similar to yours. The fact was, my husband Phillip was a pig, but it was still a great shock when he died.' In truth, and to her eternal shame, she had felt nothing when he had died, but there was likely to be little profit in sharing this with Alison Macallan.

'Yes my husband turned out to be a pig too,' she said. 'Worst than that, a complete bastard. But I loved him once. And yes, it was still a shock when he died, especially in the circumstances. I assume you know all about it?'

Maggie doubted if there was a person in the country that didn't know about the Ardmore shootings.

'Yes, of course, it was never off the news was it? Such an awful thing, a man killing his own son. So yes, I can totally understand it must have been utterly devastating to you Alison. Unimaginably so.'

But then she had to ask the question that the entire nation had been asking these past six months.

'Do you know why Alison? Why he did it?'

She shook her head sadly. 'Of course I've asked myself that again and again, but I don't, not really. I know that Roderick found Peter incredibly frustrating, and there were always arguments. Both of them had been drinking that evening and all I can imagine is that their emotions boiled over.'

Maggie gave her an inquisitive look. 'You say arguments? What did they typically argue about, if you don't mind me asking?'

Alison shrugged. 'I don't mind. The running of the estate, mainly. Obviously Roderick could not give much attention to the day-to-day affairs when he was in the Navy, so he handed that job over to Peter quite a few years ago. And it was doing extremely well financially, I know that. But they often had disagreements about how it should be run. As I said, there were lots of arguments.

Especially after Roderick retired, when he had time on his hands.'

'I can understand that, generally speaking,' Maggie said, 'but there must have been something particularly serious to lead to the events of that terrible night, surely?'

She shrugged again. 'I really don't know. I know that Peter was very committed to the conservation movement and he became passionate about marketing the estate on that basis. In particular, he wanted to stop offering deer hunting as a sport. I'm not sure Roderick saw eye-to-eye with that.'

'But I assume that it made up quite a large proportion of the revenue?'

'Yes, I think so, although I'm hopeless with money so I never really got involved in Roderick's business affairs.' Which made Maggie smile to herself, having seen the detailed documents Alison's solicitor had prepared in support of her claim against the deceased's estate. 'But I think he was very much against the plan, and not just on business grounds. Roderick saw stag hunting as very much part of the estate's traditional heritage, and preserving that heritage was very important to him.'

'Did you like Peter?' Maggie said quietly. 'Because you were his step-mum. I'm sorry but I'd quite forgotten that.'

'I did,' Alison said, giving a sad smile. 'He was just six when his mother died and he was terribly traumatised by it of course. He never really got over it to be honest. That's why he liked animals much more than people. In the years before he died I often thought Flossie was his only friend.'

'She was Peter's dog?'

'Yes, and much loved. Of course, there was no one to care for her after the... well you know... so I brought her here.'

Maggie saw the chance to steer the conversation back towards the main objective of her visit.

'And so when you married Roderick, you took on his children too. That must have been difficult for you? Particularly with the twins having never known their mother.'

Alison looked at her sharply. 'I did my best, but I was young when Roderick and I got together and I was terribly naive about what being a step-mother involved. And the twins were difficult. Particularly Elspeth, or Pixie as she now ridiculously calls herself.'

'How old were they, when you first got together with your husband?'

'Just four years old. And to be honest, they had been allowed to run wild. Roderick had been really struggling to come to terms with Phillipa's death, and what with his naval career and everything, they never really got the attention they needed. So when I came along, they were rather resentful to say the least. We even thought about sending them to boarding school. It was affecting our marriage you see.'

Poor things, thought Maggie, denied a mother's love then facing the prospect of being shunted off to an institution when they got in the way. It was little wonder they'd turned out the way they did. But now it was time to get down to business.

'So I hope you don't mind Alison, but I want to talk about this legal challenge of yours. About your claim against your late husband's estate.'

Her face suddenly hardened. 'You can talk all you like, but I won't be persuaded to drop it. I won't.'

'No no,' Maggie said, giving an understanding smile, 'and that isn't my instructions from the executors, far from it. But you see the difficulty from your standpoint is that the provisions in the will are quite specific, and the change to the will which made that provision was added less than two years ago. I'm sorry to be blunt, but it says you were to inherit nothing and by implication it means that you can no longer live here in the lodge. And because the change was made so recently, it will be impossible to argue that this is anything but the clear intention of your late husband. It's very harsh, I totally agree with that, but it's also completely unambiguous, I'm sorry to say.'

'But my solicitor says it's totally unreasonable and there's a very good chance that a family court will overturn it.'

Maggie allowed herself a wry smile. Yes, her solicitor would say that, and then many thousands of pounds of fees later, would apologise profusely for the unreasonableness of the judge in seeking to rule in favour in the provisions of the will, irrespective of the moral justice of the document.

'Well I was a lawyer myself,' she said. 'Still am in fact, technically-speaking. And in my experience, a negotiated settlement always wins over conflict. Every time, hands down. And I really do think there's an opportunity for you, given the dispute over the main provisions of the will.'

'What do you mean?' Alison asked, visibly softening.

'You know the estate and Ardmore House must pass to the *eldest* surviving offspring, and that the remaining assets are to be split between *all* the surviving offspring? So that would mean that either Pixie or Posy gets the house and the estate, and the remaining assets are split between them.'

'Nearly three point seven million in cash and investments.'

'Exactly,' Maggie said, reflecting that this woman was remarkably clued-up for someone who professed to be hopeless with money. 'But I wondered, you must surely know which of the twins was first-born?'

She answered quickly. 'I don't, as it happens. It never came up and it never ever occurred to me to ask. I'm sorry.' Was it just Maggie's imagination, or was the answer just a bit too off pat?

'Well that's a pity,' she said, screwing up her nose. 'But now both are claiming it's they that's the elder, which makes the whole thing a bit of a mess.'

'But you said there was an opportunity for me?' Alison asked, evidently keen to pivot the conversation back on herself.

'Well yes I think there is. We've been asked to try and establish which twin is the rightful heir, but between you and me, I think there's two-thirds of no chance at all that we can do it. They were born over thirty years ago, and in Canada too, and even if we were lucky enough to find say a nurse or a midwife who was present at their birth, would they be able to say which one was which, after all this time? I very much doubt it. So I'm certain the only way forward is a negotiated settlement.'

She gave Maggie a doubtful look. 'They both hate me, so I would be very much surprised if they agree to anything that benefits me.'

'Hate you? I wasn't aware of that,' Maggie said, surprised. 'But irrespective of that, it's still in everybody's interests to come to an amicable settlement.'

'But they'll never agree to that,' she said, her tone betraying further scepticism.

'Well, that's to be established. But if I was to put it to the twins that a family court might for example rule that you as Roderick's wife was entitled to half his estate, *and* that you should be allowed to live in Ardmore House until your death, well that might get them around the negotiating table, don't you think?'

Her eyes brightened. 'Do you think a judge might say that?'

Maggie frowned. 'No, that's on the improbable side of improbable. But it's not totally impossible either, so it might focus the twins' minds on the risk to them of letting your legal challenge go ahead.'

'So what are you suggesting?' Alison asked.

'I need a proposal from you. In other words, what you would accept in return for dropping the formal claim.'

It didn't even take a second for her to reply.

'I want this place. And outright ownership too, not just to live in. And I want an annual income of forty grand from the investments. For life. Inflation-proofed.'

Maggie had to hand it to Mrs Macallan. She really had it all worked out.

'Well, it's a good starting point, thank you. My colleague is meeting with one of the twins today, Posy I think it is. After that meeting we should have a better idea of the prospects of a settlement. But yes, this has been very helpful Alison, it really has.'

Flossie the labrador had sidled into the room unnoticed and now flopped down at Maggie's feet before looking up at her expectantly.

'Sorry missy,' she said, patting her on the head, 'if I'd known you'd be here I'd have kept you a sausage and a bit of haggis.'

And now it was almost time for her doctors' appointment. But first, a quick visit to Active Outdoors beckoned.

\*\*\*

'Mrs Brooks is it? Mrs Magdalene Brooks?'

The young receptionist called out her name, loud enough for everyone in Lochmorehead to hear. Maggie assumed that everyone knew everyone else's business in this lovely little village, obviating the need for privacy and discretion.

'Yes, that's me,' she replied brightly, even if she was not being quite truthful. But she *had* been Mrs

Magdalene Brooks once, and as far as she was aware, there was no law against using your old married name even if you were now both divorced and widowed.

'D'you have any underlying health conditions or are you on regular medication?' She didn't have and she wasn't, but had she been so, everyone for thirty miles around would have got to know about it. It had been a similar story up at the outdoor store, where the sales assistant had greeted her like a long-lost friend, and in addressing her as *miss* rather than *madam*, had instantly gone up a notch in her estimation. He looked no more than eighteen years old, but was already built like a lumberjack, the effect accentuated by the full red beard and thick checked shirt.

'You'll be a fell runner I'm guessing from the accent,' he had said pleasantly. 'Yorkshire isn't it? I love the Dales, from what I've seen on telly.'

She hadn't wished to disappoint him.

'Was once,' she had said, lying. 'But it gives the old knees a pounding, doesn't it? So I've switched to hill-walking, although I'm still relatively new to it.' As in, never having done it before in my life.

'Well that's no problem, we can get you kitted up with everything you need,' he had said, before immersing her in an enthusiastic barrage of techno-speak which seem to involve base layers and wicking performance and breathability ratings and a hundred other things she didn't understand.

'Actually, I really just wanted a jacket,' she had said.

'Ah, outerwear. Of course. Get that. So if you'd just like to come with me miss.......'

Which is why she had left the store wearing a down-filled, three-layer, fully-wind-and- waterproof item of leading-edge mountain technology, in a fetching shade of royal blue. An example of which, according to the young lumberjack, had already been up Everest, which would at least make it a talking-point the next time she saw Jimmy and Frank in the pub. And she had gained a hat too, which had come free with the jacket, perhaps poor compensation for the two-hundred-and-fifty quid she was down on the transaction.

'Definitely not on any medication?' the young receptionist shouted, sounding slightly disappointed.

'No, none.'

'Ok, Dr Stewart will see you now,' she said, pointing behind her. 'Room two, just along the corridor there.'

Reaching the half-closed door, Maggie knocked then tentatively poked her head through.

'Come in please.'

Dr Flora Stewart was standing by her examination bed with her back to her, about five-eight, slim but broad-shouldered, with striking flame-red hair braided in a French plait and reaching down almost to her waist. Having completed the rearrangement of the bed which was the task that been occupying her, she turned and smiled at Maggie. *And god, she was beautiful.* Piercing blue-green eyes, a wide mouth and perfect pale skin, sparingly freckled in harmony with her colouring. And in that moment, she understood why winning back this woman had become Jimmy Stewart's life work.

'Take a seat please Mrs Brooks. What can we do for you today?'

So Maggie related the elaborately made-up story of splitting from her husband and taking up hill-walking in way of catharsis and the fainting turns she had experienced these last three days and not wanting to venture into the hills if it was likely to endanger her own life and that of her rescuers. Doctor Stewart had taken her blood pressure, her pulse and her temperature, asked her about her lifestyle and how often she exercised, before concluding that there was nothing really to worry about, but that she should perhaps start with some gentler challenges before she went Munro-bagging.

Maggie thanked her as she closed the door of the consulting room behind her, feeling slightly ashamed of her subterfuge but elated that she had finally been able to meet the woman of whom she had heard so much.

*Emma* was her favourite Austen novel, and if the experience of its heroine Miss Woodhouse had a lesson for the world, it was that if you started to meddle in the love affairs of others, it was liable to all go terribly tits-up. But there and then she resolved to do everything in her power to get Jimmy and Flora Stewart back together.

She just had to make sure he never *ever* found out.

## Chapter 7

He was grateful to Maggie that he hadn't been asked to make the trip to Scotland, but that didn't mean that he was much looking forward to this assignment either. It had been a toss-up which of the twins to see first, Posy or Pixie, but in the end only one of them was in town, the other apparently in sunny Mallorca doing a shoot for another car company, this time Japanese. So he would start with Pixie, internet research confirming her to be Elspeth, whom he vaguely remembered to be the quieter of the twins, although that might be because he hadn't really spoken to her at his father-in-law's birthday do, unlike her sister, with whom he'd had way too much interaction, thank you very much.

They'd arranged to meet at a tiny studio off Old Compton Street where Pixie was making a video blog for a fashion brand. Looking it up on the map, he saw it was located in what used to be, and might well still be for all he knew, Soho's red-light district. The place was called Excelsior Media Centre, and he wouldn't have been surprised if it had once been the sort of seedy den where they produced old-school top-shelf magazines, a business now long since made defunct by the explosion of on-line porn. In preparation for the meeting, he'd dug into the twins' history, finding out that they were sufficiently well-known to merit their own individual Wikipedia profiles as well as one dedicated to their joint activities. Spotted by a modelling agency when they were just sixteen, they had been a fixture on the front covers of the teen magazines before spotting the opportunity afforded by the emerging social media explosion. Before long they were brand Posy and Pixie, lending their beauty and sass to sell everything from high-street cosmetics to take-away pizzas. Until this case had emerged, he had been only vaguely aware of the world of influencers, but it was bloody astonishing how much money they could make from it. It was all about building up a giant online following, an army of devotees who could be trusted to allow their buying decisions to be influenced by the attractive twins. He'd learnt that their combined following had reached over two million worldwide, making them the hottest of hot properties in the fast-moving market space they occupied. And he'd learnt what was apparently the phrase of the moment, from watching a dozen or so of their impressively glossy videos. *On point*. It seemed that for any product or service to have any merit, it had to be on-point, and only the Macallan twins were qualified to bestow that coveted accolade.

She came out to meet him in the little reception area, smiling a greeting which was warmer than he'd expected, given the frostiness of their earlier phone-call, when she had seemed reluctant to agree to the meeting. He'd guessed it was just that she was always busy. She was smaller than he remembered too, no more than five-foot-three, but perfectly proportioned, with slim hips and a full bosom which he seemed to remember reading had been expensively and expertly enhanced. She was wearing a figure-hugging black knitted dress and silvery stiletto sandals, with a string of glimmering white pearls setting off the look of high-priced sophistication.

She gave him an appraising look from top to bottom then nodded almost imperceptibly. He hoped he'd passed the test.

'Pixie,' he said, shooting her his beaming smile and holding out a hand. 'I'm Jimmy, Jimmy Stewart from Bainbridge Associates, working with the executors of your father's will. It's so good of you to agree to meet me.'

Delicately, she shook his hand then said, 'That's all right Jimmy, it's very nice to meet you.' If she remembered their previous brief encounter at his father-in-law's party, she wasn't letting on for now. 'But I'm not Pixie.'

'What?' For a moment he was confused, thinking that somehow he must have managed to get the sisters mixed up.

'Pixie's dead and buried. I'm Elspeth now. What I mean is I'm Elspeth again.'

He gave her a perplexed look, she responding with a laugh.

'Don't worry Jimmy, I'll explain all. Look, there's a nice cafe next door, you can buy me a coffee and we can talk about what you came for.'

They found a table by the window, and a few seconds later a young waitress glided over, smiling an embarrassed smile which suggested that she recognised the Macallan twin. Although he wondered if she knew which of them it was, a doubt confirmed by her opening words.

'What can I get for you? It's Miss Macallan isn't it? Posy?'

Elspeth seemed unconcerned by the misidentification, not bothering to correct her. Jimmy ordered a tall Americano, she a skinny decaf which for some reason he had predicted would be her choice.

'It happens all the time,' she shrugged. 'We're identical twins. It can be quite funny sometimes. And useful too, if we're feeling mischievous.'

'Aye, I can imagine,' Jimmy said. 'I've got a brother, but nobody would ever mix us up, I can tell you that. But anyway, the demise of Pixie. I'm interested to know more.'

She smiled. 'This dress I'm wearing, it's Dior. I assume you've heard of them? They're very famous. And really back on point at the moment.'

'Vaguely,' he said, suppressing a smile, 'but I'm afraid fashion's not my thing. You can probably tell, looking at me.'

He noted, mildly offended, that she didn't demur.

'This dress is six grand, the pearls the same. The shoes are nearly two grand. You see, that's the market we're working in now. It's not the teenagers spending their pocket money anymore.'

Although he was no marketing expert, he could see the sense in it. The twins were now entering their thirties, their loyal cohort of followers presumably growing older with them, and now they were selling an altogether more lucrative lifestyle centred around luxury designer brands and the essential bling that went with them. Big cars, fancy hotels in Davoz and the Caribbean, watches, jewellery, cosmetic surgery. All the essentials of the jet-set and their wanabees, driving a ton of cash into the coffers of the newly-sophisticated Macallans with every click.

'So I'm now brand Elspeth Macallan,' she said. 'It sounds nice, don't you think?'

'Yes it does,' Jimmy agreed. 'And what about your sister? Is she planning to re-brand too?'

'We do everything together business-wise, so yeah, I expect so,' Elspeth said. 'But of course that was before all of these horrible things came into our life.'

He wasn't sure whether she was referring to the terrible death of her father and brother, or her falling-out with her sister over their inheritance. Or maybe even to that other thing he'd discovered just as he was leaving the office to come to the meeting. But that's why he was here, to find out.

'I'm sorry for your loss,' Jimmy said. 'I know it must have been terrible for you and Kirsty.'

'Do you think so?' she said, her face suddenly hardening. 'I loved my brother of course, but my father was a hateful man. He liked to get his own way you see. He was just so used to being able to order all these men about in the Navy. So he thought he could behave the same with his own family and everyone else around him. To be honest, I don't mourn him one bit.'

Her venom shocked Jimmy, but then he remembered having encountered plenty of guys like her father in his army days. Mostly they were inadequate characters who would have been nobodies without their rank, and he wondered if Commodore Roderick Macallan had been the same.

'And Kirsty? What about her?'

'Kirsty hated them both, more than me I think. She hated Peter for being so useless and she hated our father for letting the estate get so run down and for everything else he'd done. I love my sister of course but she's money-obsessed. That's why she's trying to take my rightful inheritance away from me.'

*I love my sister.* From where he was sitting, it didn't sound much like it.

Smiling, he said, 'Well of course that's why I'm here Elspeth, to talk about the terms of your father's will. Well, at least to understand if there's any possibility that we could arrive at a settlement that everyone can agree on.'

'Settlement?' she said, her tone sharp. 'Why should there be a settlement? I'm the oldest and that's all there is to it. I get Ardmore House and the estate and half the money. That's what the will says. It couldn't be clearer.'

He'd thought it was going to be a difficult meeting and so far he hadn't been wrong. But the fact was, Elspeth Macallan wasn't seeing things straight, and now it was his job to put that right. Diplomatically, if he could.

'Look Elspeth,' he said softly, 'I can see where you're coming from, honestly I can, but well, I think there's a couple of obstacles that might arise before we can put this thing to bed. Going forward that is.'

He winced inwardly at the sound of the ghastly corporate-speak emanating from his lips, but it did seem to have succeeded in its objective of softening the blow.

'What do you mean, obstacles?' she said in a quieter voice.

He gave a concerned smile. 'You'll know your stepmother is intending to contest the will. We've heard from her solicitor that she will be claiming half the entire estate. And it's not impossible that she might succeed. She was his wife for over twenty years.'

'Alison's a fool,' Elspeth said, spitting out the words. 'Daddy hated her and wanted her to get nothing. That's why he changed his will. It was quite clear.'

'Hated her? Why was that?'

She shrugged. 'Daddy had moved on with his life and she was being simply tiresome.'

He took that as code for *daddy had found a new woman and wanted rid of the old one with as little fuss as possible.* But he opted against sharing the thought with her.

'Well that may be Elspeth, but if a court were to take her side, that would have a big effect on you and your sister's share. So it might make sense to work out something that would persuade Alison to drop her challenge.'

'No, absolutely not,' she said. 'Never. Daddy wanted her to get nothing and that's what I want too.'

He allowed himself a wry smile. At least he couldn't fault her for her clarity. So with that out of the way, now was the moment to bring up the elephant in the room and see where that ended up. Crushed underfoot would be his forecast.

'Well that's fair enough,' he said, smiling, 'if that's how you feel about her. But the other thing I need to ask is, is there any way you can prove that it's you that was the first-born? Because I'm afraid if this goes to court, they won't just take your word for it.'

It sounded blunt but there was really no other way of saying it. And as predicted, it didn't go down well.

'I love my sister, but she's lying when she says she is the oldest. Everybody knows that it's me. Everybody. I don't know why she's doing this.'

*I love my sister.* There it was again. He didn't like to think what relations would be like if she hated her. 'The thing is Elspeth, the executors made some investigations before my firm got involved and they couldn't find anybody who seemed to know for certain. Even your old aunt, your father's sister, didn't seem to know.'

'Well Aunt Grace is rather old and doddery, so that's no surprise. Although she is lovely.' It sounded like exactly what it was, an afterthought for his benefit.

'Look, I don't want to press you on this,' he said, which was precisely what he was doing, 'but is there anything or anyone you are aware of that could support your claim? It's really important Elspeth I'm afraid. Really important.'

'It's not a *claim*. I've *told* you already, I'm the eldest.' For the first time, Jimmy detected an element of doubt buried beneath the petulant tone.

'Well, of course I have to take your word for that,' he said, trying not to sound disrespectful, 'but it's going to be difficult to prove, that's all I'm saying. So is there really no way you could come to an agreement with your sister? I don't know the place of course, but I'm guessing Ardmore House is big enough to be divided into two very acceptable homes, and the grounds are lovely too. And that shouldn't breach old Sir Archie's covenant because the house and the estate would remain in the family. And wouldn't it be quite nice to live in such a beautiful place with your sister?'

She gave him a contemptuous look. 'Do you really think I would want to live next door to *them*? Her and Mr Perfect with their perfect loved-up life and their perfect little brat?'

If her bitterness left him temporarily speechless, he recognised instantly what had prompted it, something he hadn't previously considered to be a factor in the twins' relationship. *Jealousy.* For unlike her sister, Kirsty Macallan was married, to a handsome ex-international rugby player, and they had a daughter, a two-year old sweetheart blessed with the perfect genes of her parents. All of this was, he suspected, absolute gold-dust from a business point of view, taking Kirsty into areas where her sister could not yet venture. Now in his mind, he was already rehearsing what he was going to say when Maggie asked him how the meeting had gone, and finding himself unable to decide between a simple *not well* or a more accurate *total disaster*. He hoped to god she had fared better with Alison Macallan, otherwise the case was dead in the water before it had even got properly started.

'Well, I really don't know where we can go with this Elspeth,' he said, giving a sigh, 'but we're duty-bound to continue our investigation and see where it leads.' Nowhere was what he suspected, but he couldn't really say that to her.

She gave him a piercing look, then suddenly said, 'I remember you. I didn't say before but I do. You were at that party in the village hall, for Dr McLeod's birthday. You see, I watched you and Flora all night. Every second.'

It was an odd thing to say and he wasn't sure where she was going with it. But it didn't take long for him to find out.

'And now you're not together any more, that's what I've heard?' she said.

'No. No, I'm afraid we're not.' They were just a few words, but they didn't convey how bitterly he regretted the fact they were true.

'Things change. People change.' She looked into his eyes, holding a steady gaze. 'So I was wondering, will you have dinner with me? I'm sure we could have a lot of fun together.'

What sort of fun she had in mind, she didn't say, but at least she'd been rather more delicate in her proposition than her sister had been all these years ago. Then, Kirsty Macallan had asked him, quite outright and quite shamelessly, to make love to her up against the wall of Lochmorehead's old village hall, although she'd expressed it rather more agriculturally. Shocked, he'd said no, but that didn't mean he hadn't been tempted.

But now Elspeth was staring at him impatiently, her lips shaping into a seductive smile.

'So come on Jimmy Stewart, what do you think? It'll be fun, you know it will.'

And then, unthinking and probably without malice, she plunged the metaphorical knife into his heart.

'I don't know what's stopping you. After all, Flora's seeing someone now, isn't she? And I've heard it's quite serious.'

# Chapter 8

Now that he'd set wee Eleanor Campbell off and running at the tricky Geordie case, Frank could finally turn his attention to the other equally perplexing matter that had recently thumped into his in-tray. The one that had been sent down from the north side of Hadrian's wall in an armoured security van guarded by a squad of armed officers in full riot gear, battering down the M74 with sirens a-wailing and lights a-flashing. At least, that was the comic vision that had immediately filled his mind when his boss DCI Jill Smart had, with exaggerated subterfuge, handed him the single sheet of paper containing the case briefing. A case briefing so sensitive that she had determined it had to be delivered in person, causing her to battle through the frightful early-morning London traffic between Paddington Green nick to his own wee Atlee House office. A case briefing she considered too toxic to trust to either the internal post or to e-mail.

'This is one-hundred-percent weapons-grade dynamite Frank,' she had said, giving her little speech before handing over the sheet of paper, as if still uncertain whether she was doing the right thing. 'Even by the standards of epic cop screw-ups, this is the dial turned up to eleven.'

*The dial turned up to eleven*. He smiled to himself as he acknowledged the cultural reference to *Spinal Tap*, definitely one of his favourite films of all time. A cultural reference that could now enjoy the accolade of having entered the vernacular whilst most lay people remained unaware of its source. He wondered if Jill herself knew, because somehow he didn't see her as a rock chick.

'So this is serious shit is it ma'am? Sounds like it to me.'

'Yeah, serious shit,' Jill had said. 'That's why they've sent it over the border to us, to keep it out of sight of the local media hacks. So we need to treat this with kid gloves, understand?'

'Why ma'am? he'd asked guilelessly. 'Why the big secrecy?'

'You'll find out soon enough,' she'd said, without giving anything more away.

'And you can't tell me anything else?' What he'd meant was, you won't.

'It's a double murder case and a pretty shocking one too, that's all I've been told. Anyway, Police Scotland have assigned a liaison officer to help you with anything you need. She's based at a station in Glasgow. New Gorbals I think it's called. Do you know it?'

Did he know it? He'd spent the first eight or so years of his not-so-glittering career in that manor, making first detective constable and then detective sergeant after a three-year stint pounding the beat. It had been mainly low-key stuff, dealing with the sad losers and deadbeats who had simply just been unlucky to be born in what was still one of the most deprived areas of his home city. Petty burglary, pimping, supply and possession of Class A drugs, that was how they eked out a pathetic living, a living which earned barely more than they were getting from their benefits. And not being the brightest sandwiches in the picnic, they invariably would get caught at some point, giving them the chance to sample the delights of Her Majesty's Prison Barlinnie, better known to the locals as the Bar-L. The place was an infamous Victorian hell-hole, where well into the twenty-first century the in-cell bucket-as-toilet routine known as slopping out was still in practice. But at least the sad bastards granted temporary residence within its forbidding walls were guaranteed three meals a day and a warm place to sleep, which made it understandable why many of them opted to go straight back so soon after their release. Now Frank was getting the chance to go back too, to re-visit some of his old haunts for the first time in quite a few years. But unlike the locals, he would be able to leave again anytime he wanted. At least he hoped so.

The liaison officer went by the name of Constable Lexy McDonald, which gave a good indication as to how seriously the local force were taking the investigation. He'd expected as a minimum a Detective Inspector like himself, or at a push, an experienced Detective Sergeant who'd been round the block a few times and knew what was what. Instead he'd been allocated the lowest form of police pond-life. A constable, and a uniform too, not even a DC. And in this most misogynistic of outfits, a girl to boot. *Priceless.*

Swearing under his breath, he picked up his phone and dialled the number he'd been given. A bright voice answered on the second ring.

'Police Scotland, Constable Lexy McDonald speaking.'

Mildly amused at the formality of the response, he noted the lilt in her voice that betrayed the distinctive musicality of the Western Isles. A voice that sounded about sixteen years of age.

'Hi, this is DI Frank Stewart with the Met. I've heard you're to be my go-to guy up there in my homeland. Good to make your acquaintance.'

'Thank you sir, I was expecting your call. My sergeant's told me I've to help you in any way I can sir. With the case I mean.'

'Aye well that's really good to hear Constable MacDonald,' he said pleasantly. 'So has this wee case of ours got itself a name yet?'

'Not yet sir, at least I don't think so. I was just told it was one of the Whiteside cases.'

'*One* of the cases eh? That's interesting. So we'd better get ours a name sharpish, don't you think? Oh aye, and on the subject of names I'll call you Lexy from now on, if that's ok.'

*'That's no bother sir. And I'll call you sir, shall I sir?'*

Frank let out an involuntary guffaw. Like himself, it seemed PC McDonald had a sense of humour. Instantly he knew they were going to get along just fine.

'Aye, well I'll take Inspector Stewart as well, that's my Sunday name. But before we get started, I was going to ask you how long you've been on the force.'

He was pretty sure of the answer he was going to get, but he thought he'd better check just to be sure.

*'I've just finished my two years' probation sir,'* she said, with obvious pride. *'This is only my fourth day in an operational role.'*

He allowed himself a wry smile. The brass were taking this so seriously that they'd allocated him a liaison who counted her length of service in days.

*'But I'm really keen to get stuck in sir,'* he heard her say, as if reading his mind. Of course she was. They all were, when they were only four days into their careers.

'So am I Lexy, so am I,' he lied. 'But come on, tell me what you know. About these Whiteside cases, if that's what they're called.'

*'Ok sir. So Professor Geoffrey Whiteside was the chief forensic pathologist back in the days when we were still Strathclyde Police.'*

'Aye, that's what it was when I worked up there.' He still had his old warrant card with their logo and the photograph of a young and keen PC Frank Stewart, all revved up and ready to eliminate all traces of crime from south of the river. Somehow it hadn't quite worked out as he'd envisaged.

*'Yes, it's been Police Scotland for nearly ten years now I think,'* Lexy said, instantly ageing him. *'But anyway, Professor Whiteside was of course brought in for all the high-profile cases and that meant he was involved in nearly every murder investigation on the patch.'*

'Including our one?'

*'Yes, including our one, but I'll get to that in a minute. So the professor left the forensic service four years ago and it was quite a sad story I suppose. He got cancer of the liver and had to take early retirement, but the treatment wasn't successful and he died not long afterwards. He was only sixty-three.'*

'Aye, that's tragic right enough,' Frank said, sensing where the conversation was heading. He was no medical expert, but he knew what was the number one cause of liver trouble, having been warned plenty of times of the dangers by his own GP. 'So was he a drinker then, our Dr Whiteside?'

*'Yes sir, it seems so. My sergeant says everyone knew about it at the time but it was just brushed under the carpet.'*

'But now I'm guessing it's come out from under the carpet, am I right?'

*'Yes sir, you're right. There was a case up here, before they started looking at all the other ones he had been involved in, and that's where it all started. A woman called Senga Wilson was sent down for murdering her lover mainly on the forensic evidence of Dr Whiteside. On the basis of the time of death and also some of her DNA which was discovered at the scene of crime.'*

'Yeah, I think I remember the case vaguely.' It wasn't the case he remembered, but the name. Senga, that peculiarly Glasgow epithet immortalised in Billy Connelly's classic comic song. *Three men frae' Carntyne and five Woodbine and a big black greyhound dug called Boab.* It made him laugh out loud just thinking about it, and he wondered if Lexy, a generation and a half younger than him, knew of it too. He doubted it, and he wasn't going to embarrass them both by asking.

'Aye, Senga Wilson, that's right,' he said. 'She battered him senseless then cut off his todger, is that the one?'

He heard her laugh. *'Yes that's the one sir. It was in all the papers up here. But she'd always claimed she'd been at home with her husband at the time of the murder. The trouble was, he wouldn't corroborate the alibi, obviously because he thought she'd been shagging around and he was pretty sore with her.'*

'Understandable,' Frank said, laughing. 'But something's happened I'm guessing, to bring it onto our radar?'

*'She took an overdose sir. In Cragton Valley.'*

Frank knew all about Cragton Valley prison, the principal place of incarceration for women offenders in Scotland, having sent quite a few of his customers there in the past. It also held the unenviable record of having more of its inmates commit suicide than any other jail in the UK, a record which a succession of governors seemed unable or unwilling to do anything about.

'Dead?'

*'Yes sir. They couldn't save her. She had three children too sir. Poor wee things.'*

He sighed. 'Aye, they always have. Kids I mean, and I expect they're in some god-forsaken care home somewhere. With their mother having been in jail and all that.'

*'Actually no sir, they're still with their father. In Sighthill. He's got a wee council flat up there.'* Frank knew the place well. Leafy Surrey it wasn't, and he feared for their life chances growing up in a dump like that.

'Fair play to the guy then. But I'm guessing he's got some involvement in our wee story, right?'

'Yes sir, he has. You see, these flats are all stuffed with CCTV aren't they? So he knew they could prove his wife had been with him on the night of the murder, and he'd gone to the trouble of getting a DVD made, from the security guy who was a friend of his. It showed her coming home from work at about half-past six and then not leaving again until seven the next morning.'

'And this didn't come up at the time?' Frank said, struggling to hide his disbelief. 'What I mean is, the investigation team didn't look at the CCTV?'

'I don't know sir. I've not really had time to look thoroughly at the file. It's quite thick. But no, maybe when Kenny Wilson trashed his wife's alibi they didn't think to look.'

Couldn't be arsed to look more like, he thought, especially when they already had the word of the country's top forensic guy that she had done it. Why look any harder? But he knew it was easy to be clever in retrospect, and what was it they said about people in glass houses shouldn't throw stones? He'd been there himself, burying the private doubts and throwing a case over the wall for the CPS and the jury to sort out later. Although of course it was the Crown Office of the Procurator Fiscal up there, not the CPS. Same difference.

'Aye, I guess that's it,' he said. 'So what changed?'

'Well sir after his wife died Kenny Wilson had a change of heart. His local MP runs a surgery in the community centre once a fortnight and he went along to one of her sessions with his DVD and his story.'

'And then I'm guessing that's when the shit really hit the fan?'

'Well, sort-of sir,' she said, sounding unsure. 'His MP went straight to the Procurator Fiscal's office but apparently she had quite a job to get them to re-look at the case.'

That didn't surprise Frank. In his experience the prosecutors on both sides of the border weren't interested in justice. They were only interested in statistics, and re-opening a case that had already been neatly shut down screwed up their spreadsheets and so was something to be resisted at all costs.

'That figures,' he said. 'But I assume they must have agreed in the end?'

'Yes sir. They sanctioned a review of the evidence first of all as I understand it.'

'Aye, they would do that,' he said, smiling to himself. 'Lexy, you must promise me you won't turn into a grizzled old cynic like me, but you know why they did that don't you?'

'No sir I don't.'

'It's because they wanted to make sure it wasn't *their* screw-up before they broke cover. You know, check if they'd been sloppy with the evidence at the time. Covering their arses in other words.'

*'I think you're right sir. But eventually they decided to look again at the forensic evidence in particular. Because obviously if the forensics said she was there at the scene and she definitely wasn't then it had to be the forensics that were wrong.'*

Frank laughed. 'I tell you what Lexy, for someone who's only been on the job thirty-two hours by my calculation, you know a lot about this stuff. I'm impressed.' And he wasn't flannelling her, he *was* impressed.

*'I stayed up to two o' clock last night sir,'* she said, her voice oozing enthusiasm. *'I just got really interested and couldn't leave it alone.'* He knew it wouldn't take long for that to be knocked out of her, but right now it was going to be a massive benefit to him on this case.

'So I'm assuming our good professor cocked something up big-time? Something like that is it?'

*'Yes sir, he did. It was the time of death. I don't understand the technical details, but when the Procurator's forensic team looked at the photographs of the scene they worked out that the victim must have died at least eight hours earlier than what the professor said. Something about foaming and skin pallor, but as I said I don't understand the details.'*

He was conscious that the victim was as yet un-named, an oversight he mentally kicked himself for not asking. The dead deserved at least that respect, no matter what kind of person they had been in life.

'That's interesting Lexy. And our victim, what do we know about him?'

*'Thomas Johnstone's his name sir. Forty-one years of age and with a string of convictions on his record. Drugs and petty larceny, but mainly living off immoral earnings.'*

Having worked his Gorbals beat as long as he had, the revelation didn't come as a surprise to him. Senga Wilson, with her three young kids and a deadbeat husband, had trodden a path that he'd seen a hundred other poor women like her being forced to follow. A path that led her first to Cragton Valley and then to despair.

'It's a bloody tragedy so it is, but it'll not be the last time we see it I'm afraid. But I interrupted you, sorry. You were telling me about the time of death.'

*'Yes sir. So as I said, it looks like the time of death was about six to eight hours earlier than Professor Whiteside said. And that meant that Senga couldn't have done it, because she worked on the checkouts at Tesco and she'd been on a long eight-to-six shift that day.'*

And now he began to see it, the outrageous miscarriage of justice unfolding before his eyes. The investigation team would have had their prime suspect and of course it would have been no trouble to scrape up a bit of her DNA at the scene. Tommy Johnstone was her pimp and lover and no doubt abuser too and she'd have been at his flat plenty of times. His place would be awash with the stuff. The only problem was, Tommy-boy had been killed whilst Senga was busy swiping the barcodes at her local supermarket. A minor difficulty for the senior investigating officer that could easily be solved by applying a wee bit of pressure on the distinguished forensic pathologist who'd turned up pissed at the scene. *No one needs to know about this prof. Our little secret. Just fix it*. It made him sick at the thought of it.

'So what are they going to do about it? The Procurator Fiscal I mean?'

He already knew the answer. The murder of a low-life pimp and the tragic suicide of a desperate mother who was just trying to make ends meet wasn't going to keep anyone in authority awake at night. This was going to be swept back under the carpet.

*'They're doing a case review I think sir, but my sarge says it'll get dumped in a filing cabinet in some basement and never see the light of day again.'*

'Aye, smart guy your sarge. So come on, let's get on to our case shall we. I hope you've been up all night on this one too.'

*'I was sir,'* he heard her say earnestly. *'Three o' clock the night before.'*

'Ok then Lexy, tell me all.'

'All right sir. So this case concerns the murders of Mrs Morag McKay and her two-year old daughter Isabelle.'

'Christ, I didn't know there was a toddler involved,' he said, taken aback.

'Yes, I'm afraid so sir. It was a terrible thing altogether. It happened about four years ago at the naval base up at Ardmore. I don't know if you know of the place, it's on Loch More.'

Frank knew of the place all right but not as well as his brother. Or his former sister-in-law Flora, who'd grown up there. Actually, he wasn't sure if former was the right term, maybe it should be estranged sister-in-law, not that it mattered. He hadn't got to know her that well, it was true, but it had been well enough to know she was smart, funny and beautiful. What he did know for certain however was that Jimmy had been a right arse to lose her.

'Aye, I know it. So this one involved our Professor Whiteside too I'm assuming?'

He already knew the answer but he asked the question anyway. After the Senga Wilson case had inconveniently reared its ugly head, there would have been a panicky review of every case that Whiteside had been involved in, in a desperate attempt to make sure the bodies, both metaphorically and physically, remained buried.

*'Yes sir, and it was the same problem. He got the time of deaths wrong again, meaning the man who was convicted couldn't possibly have done it.'*

'Another cast-iron alibi then I'm supposing?'

*'Yes sir. You see her husband Lieutenant McKay was still at sea at the time of the actual death. In fact, he was under the sea sir. On board a nuclear submarine. Thirty miles off the Scottish coast. They were just coming back to port after a seven-month training voyage.'*

'Well well,' Frank said, laughing, 'that *is* a cast-iron alibi. And it was him that got done for the murders was it?'

*'Yes sir, it was.'*

'And so where's he being held? Doing life somewhere I guess?'

*'He was in Low Moss sir, and you're right, he got a life sentence. But he took his own life four weeks ago. In his cell. He slashed his own wrists.'*

'Christ, another one? So what's the Procurator Fiscal's office saying this time?'

*'I don't know sir. I asked my sarge and he said they'd put it in the hands of these boys down in London. I assume he meant you sir.'*

Yes, but why? What was so different about this one that it had to be shunted off to a department four hundred miles away, a department that nobody had heard of? And why had the prosecutor's office come direct to them rather that routing it through the Police Scotland hierarchy? Experience told him that this kind of thing only happened when there was the need for a massive super-sized cover-up. But the question was, who was it that both wanted and needed to keep this under wraps?

On a hunch he said, 'Lexy, does the file say who the senior investigating officer was on the case?'

*'Yes sir,'* she replied brightly, *'It was a DCI Pollock.'*

'Fuck's sake,' he blurted out, immediately apologising for the profanity. 'Not Brian Pollock?'

*'Yes it was sir,'* she said, sounding perplexed. *'Do you know him sir?'*

'Aye, I do,' he said. 'And so should you. I expect he did a wee speech at your passing-out parade.'

*'Not Chief Constable Pollock sir?'* He could hear the disbelief in her voice.

'The same. Chief Constable Sir Brian Pollock. The guy with more letters after his name than a box of Scrabble.'

And now he understood what Jill Smart had meant when she'd described the case as weapons-grade dynamite. And it was a stick of dynamite that was liable to blow up in the face of anyone who got too close to it.

*'Are you still there sir?'* PC McDonald asked.

'Aye sorry Lexy, I was just thinking.'

And when he thought about it, he knew exactly what he had to do. This was a matter that could destroy wee Lexy's career before it even got started, and he didn't want to be responsible for that, no way. And that nice friendly sergeant of hers, you could bet your arse he would be reporting everything that was going on back to the brass. So for now he'd need to tell her a wee white lie, but one that he would put right in the future. He adopted what he hoped was a disappointed-sounding tone.

'I'm really not sure there's much my department can do about this one Lexy. I'll obviously give it some more thought and I'll talk to my guvnor, but maybe you should ask your sarge to find you something else to look at in the meantime. Sorry. But let me have your mobile number just in case.' That was so if he needed anything from her, he wouldn't have to call her at the station.

So what a turn-up for the books this was. *Brian Pollock, would you believe it?* He knew the guy from way back, and he'd been a complete and utter shite then. Now Frank was going to take great pleasure in destroying the bastard's career. But first, their case needed a name. He pondered for a minute and then gave a half-smile.

*The Ardmore Cover-Up*. Not one of his best, but it would have to do for now.

## Chapter 9

They'd agreed to meet once again at their local Starbucks, the establishment conveniently located just a stone's throw from Riverside House, the shared office suite housing the investigative powerhouse that was Bainbridge Associates. In truth it wasn't much of an office and it wasn't by the side of the river either, nowhere near it in fact, but 238A Fleet Street EC4 was the sort of address that gave Maggie's embryonic firm the aura of solidity and professionalism that it needed to prosper. Nine other start-up firms shared the accommodation, their administrative needs catered for by the feisty Miss Elsa Berger, a capable young Czech woman who also happened to be deeply in love with Jimmy Stewart. It was a love that as far as Maggie was aware was currently unrequited, and if she knew anything about her colleague, it was destined always to be so. Regardless of that, the coffee-house had become their go-to meeting place ever since they had discovered it as a result of one of Elsa's clandestine schemes to get up close and personal with Jimmy.

'The bloody coffee machine's run out of beans again,' Jimmy would say, making no attempt to hide his annoyance, and unaware that Elsa had deliberately engineered the shortage. 'I'll need to go to bloody Starbucks again, and the drinks cost a bloody fortune in there. I mean nearly four quid for a latte, it's ridiculous.'

'I come with you, bring petty cash,' Elsa would pipe up in her appealing Eastern European accent, and then twenty minutes or more later they would return with the drinks, invariably giggling over some private shared joke. Maggie always found that mildly irritating, but only in the same way as when you weren't invited to a social occasion that you'd never wanted to go to in the first place. But today Elsa had been excluded from the visit on account of the phone call Maggie had received earlier that morning from Frank.

'Got a bit of a business proposition for you guys,' he had said mysteriously. 'I've not properly run it past Jill yet so I've asked her to pop along to our meeting as well.'

Jill and Frank had got there before them, which surprised Maggie because Frank was generally only on time if they were meeting in the pub. She assumed his prompt presence could be accounted for only because his boss had commanded him not to be late. So what of DCI Jill Smart? Overall, she thought she quite liked her, the senior policewoman being smart, efficient, professional and occasionally quite witty, characteristics that she would normally find endearing. But there was an enigmatic quality to her bearing that meant you were never quite sure if you were seeing the real woman beneath the super-smart exterior. And if Maggie was being honest with herself, she recognised the hint of jealousy she felt towards the woman, mainly on account of her annoying slimness, the result of a maniacal devotion to the gym, but also because of something else she had observed that last time they'd met, when they were in that restaurant celebrating the successful resolution of the Aphrodite case. *DCI Jill Smart had a thing for Jimmy.* But then, what woman didn't? No-one she'd ever met, that was for sure. It wasn't as if she had a thing for him herself, she was fairly sure of that. Sure, he was good-looking, outstandingly so, but she was nearly ten years older than him for a start, not that that need be an insurmountable obstacle. The truth was she simply felt possessive towards him, protective even, because he'd single-handedly rescued her when she was at the lowest point in her life. No, she didn't want Jimmy for herself, but she wasn't going to hand him over to just anyone either.

Today however she had resolved to push all that to the back of her mind.

'Hi guys,' she said, more brightly that she felt, 'have you ordered?' It had been nearly two in the morning before she had got back from her Scottish trip, and she had found Ollie wide awake and anxious to share the minutiae of his day with her, a request she could hardly refuse.

'Aye, the usual poison,' Frank said, smiling. 'Just waiting for them to shout my name then you can wander over and collect them wee brother.'

Jimmy shot him a look of mild disdain but didn't say anything.

'So how's tricks?' Frank continued. 'Making any progress on your Macallan thing?'

'I'm not,' Maggie said mournfully. 'I wouldn't say my trip north was a complete waste of time but no, I wouldn't say we've made much progress either.' In fact, the only reason the trip hadn't been a complete write-off was because of her very satisfactory meeting with Flora Stewart, but she couldn't very well reveal that in the presence of his brother. 'I'm just hoping Jimmy's got something positive to report.'

They heard a barista bellow *'two americanos, a skinny latte and a cappuccino for Frank'.*

'That's us,' Frank said, nodding towards the serving counter. 'Nip over and fetch them and then we can hear all about it when you get back.' With a resigned shrug, Jimmy got up and shuffled off as instructed, returning a couple of minutes later with the drinks, secured in a sturdy cardboard cup-holder. As he set them down on the table, she noticed Jill reach out and almost imperceptibly, slide a finger across the back of his hand, he reacting with the faintest of smiles.

'So Jimmy,' she said, trying to erase the image from her mind, 'how did you get on with the Macallan twin? I can't remember which one you were seeing, Pixie or Posy.'

He smiled. 'Well actually it was neither. What I mean is they're re-branding, as they call it. They're going back to their original names. So it was Elspeth Macallan I saw yesterday.'

'Frank told me a little about your case,' Jill said, 'so I googled them. It must have come up with about a million pictures of them. They're pretty girls, but a bit in your face for me.'

'Yeah, they're everywhere,' Maggie said. 'As Jimmy said, it's all about brand Macallan.'

'Sounds like it should be a make of whisky,' Frank said, smiling.

'It is one already,' Jimmy said straightforwardly. 'No connection though, at least I don't think so. But anyway, coming back to my meeting, well to be honest I got precisely nowhere. In a nutshell, Elspeth Macallan insisted she was first-born and she gave me the metaphorical two fingers when I suggested a compromise might be a good idea.'

'Yeah, I got pretty much the same treatment from Alison Macallan too,' Maggie said, frowning. 'She's pretty sore about the way her husband treated her and she's willing to take her chances in front of a judge.'

'See you in court?' Frank said, shooting Maggie a sardonic look. 'The only guys that'll profit from that are you lawyers. No offence of course.'

'None taken,' she said, smiling. 'We'll just have to hope we get on better with Posy, the other twin.'

'Kirsty, you mean,' Jimmy said. 'She's rebranded, remember? But there *was* something else that came out of my meeting with her sister. Something I need to run past you Maggie, to see what you think about it.'

'What was that?' Maggie didn't know how or why, but she thought she knew what he was going to say.

'She asked me out. To dinner.'

She smiled, pleased that her intuition had proved accurate. But then again, you didn't need to be Sherlock Holmes to predict what would happen when any woman was within touching distance of Jimmy Stewart.

'So what did you say?'

He laughed. 'I sort of said maybe. That I'd let her know when we'd decided about the case. I think I gave her the impression that I had to get your permission first.'

'Quite right too,' she grinned. 'I'm not having you cavorting with beautiful young women on company time.'

'Certainly not boss, I wouldn't dream of it,' he said. 'So I'll give her a buzz some time and let her know we'll take the case, and then maybe suggest just a wee low-key lunch at some point. I suppose it might come in useful, having at least a friendly relationship with her.'

'Brilliant,' Maggie said, before turning her attention to Frank. 'So this business proposition you mentioned on the phone. Are you going to tell us what you have in mind? Something legal I hope.'

She saw him give Jill an enquiring glance, as if seeking permission for what he was about to say.

"Oh aye, perfectly legit in every way, more or less. We're the cops, remember? But anyways, to business. Now you know we don't often use private investigators,' he continued, sounding as if he felt the need to justify what he was about to say, 'but there's this brand new case that's recently come in to our wee department, one that you could call hyper-sensitive, not to put too fine a point on it. Would you agree with that description ma'am?'

Jill Smart smiled at Maggie. 'Yes, I described it to Frank as dynamite and I've heard nothing to change my mind since I said it.'

'And of course when I found where the scene of the crime was,' Frank said, nodding in Jimmy's direction, 'well I thought it might fit in pretty well with your wee Macallan matter.'

Jimmy gave him a sharp look. 'God's sake, you can't mean Lochmorehead? That would be just too much of a coincidence.'

'Nearly right. Two miles away. On the Ardmore naval base, in one of the tied houses there. A wife of one of the sailors was murdered. The poor woman was stabbed to death and her two-year old had her throat cut. It was an absolute tragedy so it was. Bloody horrific.'

'No way, we're not getting involved in this,' Jimmy said, raising his voice. 'No way.'

Maggie looked at him, alarmed. 'What's the matter Jimmy?' Then she remembered once again what he'd said about the place being cursed. And she remembered the other thing he'd said too, about the woman who'd been murdered, the woman who'd been at school with Flora and the Macallan twins.

'Is it Morag Frank?' she asked quietly. 'Morag Robertson. Is she the woman you're talking about?'

He nodded. 'Aye. Morag McKay was her married name but yes, it's her. But listen, it was only an idea. Don't worry if you'd rather not do it. I'm sure we can work out a plan B.'

'No no, it's no problem, honestly,' Jimmy said, giving his brother a half-smile. 'It just came as a bit of a shock, that's all. I met her the once, at that party, and it was only a few months later when she was killed. She seemed a really nice lady, really friendly and she was looking forward so much to her husband coming home. Her murder really shook the community as you can imagine. A terrible thing.'

'I can understand that,' Maggie said, relieved that her colleague seemed to be feeling better about the matter. 'Frank, we'll do what we can to help of course.'

'Well that's great,' he said. 'To be honest, I've not completely worked out what I need you to do. It's just that there's a bit of a half-cocked idea forming in my mind, something that we cops definitely couldn't do ourselves.'

Maggie smiled. 'I'm intrigued.'

'Aye, well careful what you wish for,' Frank said, then gave Jill Smart another enquiring look. 'So ma'am is it ok if we agree a budget now? I thought maybe thirty or forty hours max should cover it with these guys. We might not use all of it, but I'd like to get it in place, just in case.'

Maggie shot Jimmy a knowing smile, a smile he returned with interest, signifying he was thinking exactly the same thing as her. If there was already a budget, there must be a case number, and knowing how much DCI Smart guarded the release of that most precious of administrative devices, and how much Frank Stewart coveted them and how hard he usually had to fight to get one, it could only mean one thing.

This case must be bloody serious.

## Chapter 10

Kirsty Macallan had returned from her video shoot in Mallorca, the assignment being for a Japanese manufacturer of sport-utility vehicles who was about to release a ground-breaking pure electric version onto the market, a vehicle that promised to lay down a new marker for the sector by offering double the range over the competition, eliminating range anxiety in a single leap. At least that's how she described it to Maggie and Jimmy as they sipped coffee in the expensively-equipped kitchen of her Fulham mid-terrace home.

'I'm impressed,' Maggie said smiling, 'by your technical knowledge I mean. I know where to put the key in my old Golf and that's just about it. '

'I memorised the press release,' Kirsty said in way of explanation. 'I've always found it pays to have some empathy with the product set you're working with. And it shows respect for the customer, don't you think?'

Maggie couldn't help noticing that whilst she was addressing both of them, her eyes were continually wandering in Jimmy's direction. And then she remembered that Jimmy Stewart and Kirsty Macallan had previous, albeit unrequited.

Kirsty gave a fond smile as she saw her husband wandering in with their little daughter in his arms, the child giggling as he nuzzled his stubble against her cheek.

'Come and join us darling, won't you?'

'Yeah sure babe. Did you tell these guys that they're loaning us a top-of-the-range one for a full year and putting in a fast-charging adaptor too? Wicked, isn't it?'

Rory Overton was tall and muscular with chiselled good looks that somehow had remained unblemished despite nearly ten years as a professional rugby player. 'He was a winger,' Jimmy had tried to explain to her on the way over, she knowing next to nothing about the game, 'lightning fast, about the quickest in the premiership. He could do the hundred metres in ten seconds and you wouldn't have wanted to get in his way if he was coming straight at you.'

'So you guys are the detectives, right?' Overton said, smiling. 'Going to sort out this mess for us I hear. I'm Rory by the way, Kirsty's husband. Although you've probably worked that out already, being detectives. And this is our darling Esme. Esme, say hello to the nice lady and gentleman.' The toddler gave a coy smile then turned her face away, placing a comforting thumb in her mouth.

'She's shy,' Maggie said, fondly remembering how her son Ollie had been exactly the same at that age. That was just six years ago, but it seemed like more than a half a lifetime away given everything they had been through together in that time.

Kirsty got up and walked over to her husband, wrapping an arm round his waist and gently brushing back a wisp of her daughter's hair. In an instant, Maggie could see why this power couple were in such demand. Young, successful and ridiculously good-looking, it was hard to think of an aspirational brand that wouldn't want to be associated with this perfect family. But Jimmy had told her about his one previous meeting with Kirsty Macallan, when, seemingly unconcerned at the presence of his wife, she had shamelessly delivered a proposition that most men would have found impossible to resist. And then there were the photographs from her father's funeral, images she had not yet seen but whose contents she was aware of. Once on a popular chat-show, she had heard a well-known actress lament what she described as her out-of-control libido, and if this was an affliction shared by Kirsty, then perhaps not everything in the Macallan household was as rosy as it looked at first sight. Or at least if it was, it wasn't likely to stay that way for long.

'You know why we're here, I assume?' Maggie said quietly. 'And forgive me, but I should have said sorry for your loss. It must have been terrible for you.'

'Yes, we're so sorry,' Jimmy added. 'Such an awful thing.'

'Yes it was awful,' Kirsty said, her eyes moistening. 'I still can't believe it happened, it still seems like a dream. But life must go on of course. And I'm so lucky to have these two. They're everything to me.'

Rory Overton gave his wife an affectionate kiss on the cheek. 'We'll be fine. And it'll get better in time. You know it will babe, trust me.'

'But I loved them both so much and I miss them terribly.'

Maggie gave Jimmy a wry look, remembering him relating what her sister Elspeth had told him. *Kirsty hated them both, more than me I think.* Whether that was true or not would no doubt emerge in due course. But right now she had to ask the question, insensitive as it unarguably was.

'I don't really like to ask, but have you any idea why he did it? Your father I mean.'

Overton shot her a sharp look. 'I don't see how that's any business of yours.'

'It's ok Rory, really it is,' his wife said. 'The fact is, we don't know. And we'll never know the truth now, will we?'

'Kirsty's brother was useless,' Overton said, interjecting. 'And darling, before you say anything, you know it's true. I know you shouldn't speak ill of the dead, but Peter was nice but seriously dim, not to put too fine a point on it. I think it frustrated the old man, how his son was making such a botch of running the estate. My belief is they were having a big argument about it and the Commodore just lost it.'

'I shouldn't have asked, I'm sorry,' Maggie said, pondering on Overton's words. It seemed just so implausible, this hugely-senior ex-naval officer losing his cool and murdering his own son in cold blood. But he was probably right, it wasn't any business of theirs.

'So Posy's dead and buried then?' Jimmy said, evidently deciding a change of subject was called for. 'I was talking to your sister the other day and she told me about your rebranding and all that stuff.'

'I'd have done it at least two years ago,' Kirsty said, a hint of bitterness in her tone, 'because once I got all *this* then it made sense to leave the teenagers behind. But Elspeth couldn't see it, no matter how hard I tried to convince her.'

'She's still jealous babe,' Overton said. 'That's what it is. Jealous of me and jealous of Esme.' There was a horrible coldness to his tone that caused Maggie to bristle.

'And how did you two meet then?' Jimmy said out of the blue.

Maggie saw the Overtons exchange a knowing look as if to say, shall we tell them or not?

'A case of mistaken identity,' the husband said, smirking.

'He came up behind me at a party and put his hands on my boobs,' Kirsty giggled.

'Thought it was Elspeth of course,' he said. 'Easy mistake to make, isn't it?'

'So you were with Elspeth before?' Jimmy said, asking the question Maggie was about to float herself, and evidently struggling to hide his surprise. 'Wasn't that a bit awkward?'

'It was just a casual thing with me and Elspeth, always was. She wasn't looking for any commitment and that suited me fine at the time. But then I met Kirsty and everything changed.'

Maggie wondered if he really meant it, or whether he was saying it for his wife's benefit. She also wondered how Elspeth Macallan would feel, hearing their relationship so callously dismissed. She'd known Rory Overton for barely ten minutes but already she'd decided she didn't like him at all. Too smug and too smooth by half. But the fact was, it really was irrelevant to the matter in hand how she felt about Kirsty's husband, the matter in hand being the last will and testament of Commodore Roderick Macallan RN.

'Obviously we're here to talk about your father's will,' she reiterated, 'as agents of his executors Addison Redburn.'

'The provisions are quite clear,' Kirsty said sharply. 'I'm the elder twin and Ardmore House and the estate comes to me and my family.'

Jimmy gave her a quizzical look. 'The problem is your sister says exactly the same thing, she told me herself. So I'd be interested if you've got any suggestions as to how the situation can be resolved.'

'Resolved? There's nothing to resolve. I'm the oldest and that's all there is to say about it.'

'Aye, but can you prove it, that's going to be the issue,' Jimmy said. 'Can you prove it.' His tone was much blunter than Maggie would have dared to employ, and smiling to herself, she realised what he was doing. It was the old good-cop-bad-cop routine. They'd employed the technique in the past and it hadn't failed yet. And it seemed to have worked again, as the wind quickly went out of Kirsty's sails.

'Well I don't know,' she said. 'Why should I have to prove it, when everybody knows it's me that's the oldest?' She gave her husband an uncertain look. 'That's right Rory, isn't it?'

But it seemed that some of Rory Overton's self-assurance had temporarily evaporated in the face of Jimmy's inexorable logic.

'I don't know babe. Maybe these guys are right.'

'But you *know* it's me darling, you've always known.'

'Yeah babe, but I only know because you told me.' Maggie watched him shuffling uncomfortably, holding little Esme tighter to his chest and gently rocking her to and fro, even though she was perfectly content.

'Jimmy's right I'm afraid,' Maggie said quietly, gratefully assuming the good cop role, 'and of course it's not that we don't believe you Kirsty. But I hope you can see the difficulty.'

'But I've *always* known,' she replied, but this time there was resignation in her voice. 'So, what do we do?'

'There's only two options I'm afraid,' Maggie said. 'We either need to find proof that you are indeed the elder, or we have to agree a settlement between all three parties.'

'What do you mean, all three parties?' Overton said sharply.

'I met with Alison a couple of days ago, and I'm sure you won't be surprised to hear that she's also preparing a challenge to the will. The thing is, I can see her being treated with some sympathy by a family court.'

'That's bollocks,' Overton said, swinging from his previous uncertainty to naked aggression. 'The will was quite clear. She gets nothing. Nothing at all.'

'Aye, but the thing is Rory,' Jimmy said in a mollifying tone, 'she was married to your father-in-law for over twenty years and she helped to bring up his kids. That's the sort of thing the court might see as a significant investment in the marriage, and so there's a pretty good chance that will be recognised.'

'And what makes you qualified to say that?' Overton sneered.

'Woah, don't shoot the messenger pal,' Jimmy said, spreading his arms in an apologetic gesture. 'I'm only repeating what Asvina Rani told us. It's up to you whether you believe her or not, but I would if I was in your shoes.'

'It's all right Rory,' Kirsty said. 'I think they may have a point. Especially if Alison tells them how my father treated her in the last few years. I don't think he would come out of it very well.'

'What do you mean?' Maggie asked softly. She thought she already knew what Kirsty Macallan was going to say.

'He...he was having an affair, we were pretty sure of that. All of us. Elspeth and Peter too.'

Maggie gave her a sympathetic look. 'And do you know who the other woman was?'

Kirsty shook her head. 'No, we never found out. Someone from the village or the base I expect.'

'What about Alison?' Jimmy asked. 'Do you think she knew?'

'She knew he was having an affair,' Kirsty said, frowning. 'That's one of the reasons the marriage broke down. But I'm not sure if she ever found out who it was with. It obviously didn't come to anything, whoever it was. I mean, my dad didn't run off into a glorious sunset or anything like that. I guess it just fizzled out like all the others.'

*Like all the others.* Maggie smiled to herself, thinking how that might play out in front of the sort of prim magistrate that often presided in the family court these days. It wasn't likely to deliver a good outcome for the Macallan twins, that was for sure.

'Look, there is a way out of this,' Maggie said, adopting a serious tone. 'Alison gave me a proposal of what she would accept in way of settlement, and I would thoroughly recommend you and your sister should try and come to an amicable agreement with your stepmother. Because if you don't, there's a risk of the court making an award that neither of you would like. To be honest, what she's asking for is a bit over the top, but I think there's room for negotiation. I suspect if you made a counter-proposal that lets her stay in the lodge, then she'd probably accept.'

Jimmy nodded. 'Aye, I'd do that if I were you two. You and Elspeth I mean. It just takes any risk off the table. Smart move in my opinion.'

'No way, absolutely no way,' Overton said, shaking his head. 'Forget that. We get the house, we get the estate, we get half the money. That's what the will says and that's what we want, isn't it babe?'

It's actually Kirsty that would get it all, not you, Maggie thought, but she knew there would be little to gain in pointing this out. Rory Overton was hostile enough and she didn't want to throw any more fuel on the fire.

'Very well then,' she said, giving a sigh. 'It doesn't look as if there's anything more we can do for you.' She smiled at Kirsty. 'But let me ask again, just before we go. Are you absolutely sure there's no-one who can vouch for you being the elder?'

She gave a resigned look. 'I don't think so. I thought there might be some records at the hospital where we were born, but it closed ten years ago. Well, not actually closed, but they moved the old maternity unit to a new general hospital somewhere else in Vancouver. And they seem to have lost track of the births that happened before the move. I don't know if...'

'Right, I think we're done here,' Overton said, cutting his wife short. 'We'll be in touch if we think of anything.'

Maggie knew they wouldn't be.

\*\*\*

'Nice guy, eh?' Jimmy said, as at a leisurely pace, they made their way back to Parsons Green tube station. *'Not.'*

'Never meet your heroes, isn't that what they say?' Maggie said, laughing.

He shot back a sardonic smile. 'Can I just remind you he played for England, so he's no hero of mine. But yeah, he's really up himself, no question about it. Horrible guy altogether.'

She nodded. 'He is. And god, he really wants the house and the estate, doesn't he? More than she does, it seems to me.'

'That doesn't surprise me,' Jimmy said. 'I read an article about him in a rugby magazine a few months ago. He's really into his shooting and fishing, big-time. So I'm thinking this is probably his wee retirement plan, now that he's given up the game. I guess he needs to find something else to do with the rest of his life.'

'Yeah, there's something in that,' Maggie agreed, then giving him a mischievous smile she continued, 'And what did you think to Kirsty? Because she was certainly interested in you if I'm any judge. She hardly took her eyes off you for a second.'

'Aye maybe,' he said, shrugging, 'but I don't think she remembered who I was, did she? From that party I mean.'

She laughed. 'She probably asks so many men to sleep with her, she's lost track.'

'Yeah, I expect that's it,' he agreed, evidently unconcerned. 'But there was one thing I did pick up on actually. And I wondered if you'd noticed it too?'

She gave him a puzzled look. 'No, I don't think so.'

'I'm surprised,' he said, not bothering to hide an annoyingly smug expression, 'please don't tell me you're losing your touch.'

'Don't be so bloody cheeky,' she said, trying hard not to laugh, 'or I'll have you court-martialled.'

'I'm not in the army now,' he said, deadpan, 'in case you'd forgotten.'

'Come on then smart-arse. Tell me what you've got. I haven't got all day.'

He gave her a look of mock superiority. 'Aye, I will then. So what I was thinking was, if Kirsty Macallan is so damn sure she was the first-born twin, why's she suddenly so interested in her old maternity records?'

## Chapter 11

Frank's train trip up from London had been both convenient and comfortable, the four-hour-something journey time allowing ample opportunity to down a couple of beers from the service trolley and to ponder how he would handle the delightful act of serendipity that had parachuted Brian Pollock back into his life. To tell the truth, it had been a bit of a shock at first, being more than ten years after he'd last had the displeasure of working with the shit-faced bastard. Back then, the newly-promoted Inspector Pollock had waltzed into New Gorbals station from a previous fast-track assignment somewhere in the north-east, the jungle drums sending the message in advance that he was a complete prick and needed to be handled with great caution. Frank had not long turned thirty, and had banked a solid two years as a hard-working and street-smart Detective Sergeant. All things being equal, there was a fair chance he would make Inspector before too long, such was the regard for him amongst the brass. That was until Pollock turned up to screw all his carefully-laid career plans.

The case had been relatively routine but high-profile. An ex-footballer turned pundit had been accused of raping a woman he had met in a Glasgow bar. After sharing a few drinks together, they had taken a taxi back to her flat, where the offence was alleged to have taken place. So far, so normal, but what had made this one more complicated than it needed to be was that the woman had waited more than three weeks before reporting the incident to the police. Nonetheless the station DCI had reviewed her complaint and satisfied that it was credible, allocated the case to DI Pollock. Frank hated these cases with a passion, because he knew that some poor wee lassie was going to be asked some horrible questions about this most private and intimate aspect of her life. And it didn't matter how sensitively you tried to put it, there was always that elephant in the room. *Prove to us you didn't say yes.* He'd had to do it a couple of times in the past, and he had no desire to do it again. Which is why when he was rostered to the investigation and told by Pollock he had to interview the woman, whose name was Sharon Thomas, he called up a favour and brought in a woman DS from Paisley whom he'd met on a course, and whom he knew was Renfrew district's go-to officer for these sort of cases. Meanwhile Pollock was all over the media, predicting a swift resolution to the investigation. A forty-one-year-old man was in custody and was helping with enquiries he told them, and they were expecting him to be charged soon.

Except that DS Priti Chowdray of Renfrew division wasn't convinced. First of all, the victim had steadfastly refused to allow the police doctor to examine her. Secondly, gentle but persistent questioning had uncovered some inconsistencies in her story, the woman first claiming the rape had happened on a sofa in her living room whilst later she remembered it had actually taken place when they were in bed together, sleeping off their over-indulgence. As DS Chowdray had explained to Frank, this seemed like a classic case of post-coital regret and so should be treated with caution, she recommending a more thorough investigation of the alleged facts before charges were brought. Not to justify or excuse the actions of the guy, she made that clear, a man who in her opinion had cynically set out to take advantage of the woman's inebriation, but simply in the interests of justice.

But Pollock wouldn't have it. All he could see was another collar and a high-profile one at that, another step on his way up the promotional ladder. So Sharon Thomas was coerced into tidying up her recollection of events, on the pretext that a man like that would probably do it again if he wasn't put away for a good spell. Suddenly, she remembered the night with crystal clarity. After arriving back at her flat, she'd poured them each another drink and then they'd sat on the sofa, where they'd held hands and kissed before it all started to get out of hand. She said no, of course she had, but he had ignored her, reaching up under her skirt to tear off her knickers, then lying on top of her and forcing her to have unwanted intercourse. With that version of events, the Procurator Fiscal had little option but to proceed with charges, even although Frank knew they harboured doubts at the time.

And then two days later, the accused's lawyers released a series of explosive texts, first to the press and then to the prosecutor's office, which turned the spotlight on what had really happened that night. A barrage of messages had been sent by the alleged victim to the accused, lascivious in nature and thanking him for the wonderful time she had had, and looking forward to seeing him again as he had promised. At first ignored, there was eventually a single response from the former footballer, terse and brutal, thanking her for being a great shag, his exact words, but that he wasn't planning to see her again anytime soon.

With the case blown out of the water, Pollock had embarked on a damage-limitation exercise, played out principally on Scotland's broadcast media. An exercise that laid the blame for the foul-up squarely on the shoulders of the Detective Sergeant who had been working on the case, a DS whom in Pollock's words, had displayed repeated lapses in both judgement and endeavour. The brass knew it was all bollocks of course, but no-one wanted to be the one who stood in the way of golden-boy's career. So Frank had been bought off with an offer of instant promotion to Inspector, providing he took up a new post in the Metropolitan Police, and with immediate effect. Meanwhile the inexorable rise of Brian Pollock continued unchecked. It seemed that every time he screwed up, he was shunted upwards until eventually, and against all notions of natural justice, he had ended up as Chief Constable of Police Scotland, with the obligatory knighthood that came with the job. For Frank, London had worked out fine, but unlike plenty of his colleagues, he hadn't ever wanted to make the move south. But the incident had seared a burning injustice in his heart which he knew would not be erased until he got even with the bastard who had caused it. And now finally here was his chance, and the elevated status that Pollock had somehow attained was going to make his fall from grace even sweeter.

The train had arrived into Glasgow's Central Station bang on time, and the weather being reasonable for his home city, that is not totally pissing down with rain, he decided to walk the one-and-a-half miles to the New Gorbals police station.

'I'm here to see PC McDonald and her sergeant,' he told the duty officer on the desk. 'I'm DI Frank Stewart.'

'We've got three PC McDonalds,' he answered, Frank noting the unhelpful tone and the absence of a 'sir' in his response. But then he'd forgotten they didn't like outsiders up here, even if they spoke with a Glasgow accent. In fact, *especially* if they spoke with a Glasgow accent.

'Lexy,' he said, 'PC Lexy McDonald. And by the way, it's sir to you, ok pal?' He thought it wouldn't do any harm for word to get round the place that Frank Stewart had turned into a right tosser since he'd joined the Met.

'Oh aye, I'd forgotten about her *sir*,' he said, unchastened. 'She's new. Wait a minute and I'll get her to fetch you through.'

A couple of minutes later he heard the buzz as the automated access door was unlocked, then watched it opening outward into the entrance area. A small and pretty freckled-face constable in an obviously brand-new uniform materialised from behind it, beaming a wide smile.

'Welcome to the New Gorbals sir,' she said. 'Welcome back that is.'

*Welcome back.* The truth was, it was quite nice to be back, even although the manner of his leaving still rankled.

'My sarge wants to sit in with us sir, if that's ok,' she said, as she led them across to the small interview room which was apparently to be his temporary base whilst he was in town.

'Sure. What's his name?'

'Sergeant Muir sir.'

'Jim Muir?'

'Yes sir.'

So they'd finally made old Jim a sergeant. He'd been a DC when Frank had made DS, the guy already in his mid thirties with a career that was slowly going nowhere. But whilst a lot of guys were quite content to see out their service on the coal-face, Muir wasn't, and even ten years ago he was bitter about it. But rules were rules, and if you couldn't pass the sergeants' exam then it was no dice. But fair play to the man. Better late than never, even although he guessed the reason for his unexpected and undeserved promotion was the same one that allowed Colin Barker of the Met to cling to his unmerited DCS role. The old dodgy handshake routine. But maybe he was just wearing his cynicism on his sleeve.

'Jim, good to see you again,' he lied, extending a hand. 'Keeping well?'

'Mustn't grumble,' Muir replied. 'I'd get you a coffee but the machine's bust again.' So much for the warm welcome.

'No worries Jim, I had a couple of wee cans of Tartan on the way up on the train. It's not often we get a wee day out, is it?'

'Are you staying up here long?' Muir asked, his eyes narrowing. Again, no *sir*. But Frank wasn't bothered.

'Me?' he said. 'No, just the one night I think. I want to pop over to Shettleston to see my mother and father, and then I'll be away back down the road tomorrow.'

He saw Lexy giving him a surprised look, having told her he would stay for as long as it took. But he didn't want Jim Muir knowing that.

'So this case Jim,' he started, adopting a matey tone and deliberately ignoring PC McDonald, 'it looks like a right heap of shite to me. It's my DCI's fault, Jill Smart you know. She's got this megalomania to extend my wee department across the whole of the UK and between you and me, I can't be arsed with it. Way too much work if you know what I mean.'

Without waiting for him to answer he continued,

'So to be honest, I can't see the point of this whole shebang, can you? We can't bring back the woman and the kid that was murdered and now the guy who was supposed to have done it has gone and topped himself. So what's the point of opening it all up again, that's what I say. Complete waste of my time and everybody else's. It's not as if there's not enough new cases to be going on with, is it?'

Muir nodded. 'That's the view over at HQ I think.'

*Aye, I bet it is*, Frank thought to himself. From the Chief Constable downwards.

'So maybe I'll just spend a few hours with Lexy this afternoon taking a quick surf through the file. Just so we can tick all the right boxes and make everybody happy, right? Then we can shove it back in its dusty old filing cabinet, and no harm done. You're welcome to sit in if you want Jim, by the way. Many hands make light work and all of that.'

Frank knew he wouldn't. In fact, he was counting on it.

'No that's fine Frank,' he said, grimacing. 'You carry on with Lexy. I've got plenty to be getting on with.'

He shot Muir a smile. 'Great. So I'm planning to knock off early anyway, about half three, so I can get over to Shettleston. An hour and a half should be all we need here, eh Lexy?'

When Muir had left them he asked her, 'Have they still got a canteen here?'

She gave him a surprised look. 'Yes sir. Do you want me to go and get you a coffee or something?'

'No no. Let's just take a wee stroll down there. I fancy one of these iced gingerbread squares if they still do them.' He nodded up to the discreet camera that was mounted on the ceiling, she returning a knowing smile.

'So,' he said once they'd got settled down at a quiet table, 'this wee murder. Tell me all about it. Start to finish please, omitting no detail.'

She flicked over to the first page of her pristine ring-bound notebook, giving him the chance to admire, albeit upside down, her neat and precise handwriting. The product of a neat and precise mind, he hoped.

'Ok sir. So the crime took place almost exactly four years ago, at a semi-detached house on the Ardmore naval base on Loch More. It's one of these houses that are reserved for service personnel with families.

Lieutenant James McKay lived there with his wife Morag and their two-year old daughter Isabelle.'

'Poor wee thing' he said, knowing the girl's fate. 'A real tragedy right enough.'

'Yes sir, it is. So the Lieutenant was a weapons officer, who had served mainly on the nuclear submarine fleet. They're often at sea for months on end so I'm guessing it can be difficult for the families left behind. I mention that sir because I think it's very relevant to our case.'

'Noted. Carry on please.'

She furrowed her brow as she studied her notes. 'Yes, so he'd been at sea for about six or seven months on a training mission, I think I told you that on the phone, didn't I? Anyway, the submarine docked at about 6pm on the evening of the murder, and I suppose there was some stuff to do before the crew could leave the ship...'

Frank laughed. 'Aye, I guess they'd need to find a big enough parking space and then lock it up. It's an expensive bit of kit, a nuclear sub. And dangerous too, in the wrong hands. You wouldn't want some wee Glasgow neds nicking it for a joyride, would you?'

'Yes, something like that sir,' she grinned. 'But anyway, witnesses say it was near to a quarter to eight when he left the dockyard and started to make his way home. I've had a look on google maps and it's about a fifteen-minute walk, there or thereabouts.'

'So he would have arrived home at about eight o'clock then?' Frank said, thinking out loud.

'Yes sir, around then. And that's when, originally, it was alleged the murder was committed. The story was that he had gone home in some sort of a rage and more or less killed his wife and their child right away. The murder weapon was one of their own kitchen knives. Morag was killed by three stab wounds to her abdomen, and the wee girl had her throat cut.'

'God's sake. And he got caught at the scene, more or less red-handed. Is that right?'

Lexy nodded. 'That's precisely right sir. A neighbour or someone had apparently heard a disturbance and reported it to the police. A patrol vehicle with two uniforms rushed round there and then broke down the door when they got no answer. They found James McKay in the kitchen holding the knife with blood still on the handle and on his hands too.'

'So I suppose then the scene-of-crime guys would have turned up and this Professor Whiteside guy would have been dragged in to examine the bodies?'

'Yes, that's what the file says sir. The professor arrived at around midnight to establish the time and cause of death. Obviously he confirmed the causes of death were the knife attacks, and he put the time of both deaths at about four hours earlier.'

Frank gave a wry smile. 'That would have been handy for the investigating officer. Does it say in the file if and when DCI Pollock turned up?'

'Yes sir. He arrived at around ten o' clock and arrested Lieutenant McKay not long afterwards.'

Yes, the jammy bastard wouldn't have been able to believe his luck, and he definitely wouldn't have let anything as inconvenient as the facts get in the way of a nice easy collar. He could imagine how it played out, the pathologist turning up late, either pissed or hung over and pleading for a bit more time just to be sure, and Pollock overruling him and forcing the issue. It was shameful, no matter how you looked at it.

'But I'm guessing McKay denied everything?' Frank said. 'I mean, he's bound to have, given that we now know he didn't do it.'

'He did sir, you're right,' Lexy said. 'He said he'd found his wife and daughter already dead and had removed the knife from his wife's body because he thought he could save her. He said he gave both of them CPR and mouth-to-mouth but of course it didn't work.'

Frank sighed. 'Well it wouldn't, given they had both been dead for at least two or three hours. But that would account for why he was covered in her blood, the poor guy. And so that was it? That was the whole case against him?'

'No sir,' she said, flicking her notebook over to the next page, 'there was something else. In fact, I think it was *this* that mainly sealed the case against him.'

'Ok, so go on, tell me.'

'Right sir. Well in court, the prosecution produced email correspondence between the McKays going back about six months that suggested their marriage was in trouble.'

Frank gave her a puzzled look. 'But hang on a minute. Wasn't he on his sub all of that time? Don't tell me they can send and receive emails from two miles beneath the ocean.'

She smiled. 'Apparently they can sir. I don't think they're actually on line all the time though. They get a weekly update as I understand it. But I don't know how it works obviously.'

'No, me neither,' he grinned. But he knew someone who probably did, and he resolved to ask Eleanor on his return to London. 'But these emails, you say they were produced in court?'

'Right sir. Nearly a hundred of them. It started with his wife saying she was sick of her life as a naval wife and wanted a divorce. At first he told her he loved her and pleaded with her to change his mind.'

'Don't tell me. Then the threats began.'

'Yes sir. He told her he wouldn't let her take his daughter away from him and that he would kill them first. The threats were quite graphic, really horrific. They're all in the file sir, you can read them if you want.'

'I'll pass on that for now Lexy, thanks,' he said. But even as he said it, he knew the thing just didn't make any sense. A bitter husband, terrified at losing his marriage and his child, has a breakdown and commits a horrific murder after several months of threats, and is caught red-handed at the scene. It was little wonder the jury found him guilty, and he was reluctant to admit, little wonder that Pollock had him arrested and charged as swiftly as he did. But now they knew James McKay couldn't possibly have done it, meaning, obviously, someone else did, and did it at least two or three hours earlier. There was no question about it, the whole thing stunk to high heaven.

'So is there anything else in the file?' he asked. 'Anything else that suggested the investigating team had any doubts at the time?'

'No sir, I don't think so sir,' Lexy said, frowning. 'I'll have another look sir of course, to see if I've missed anything.'

'Aye do that,' he said distractedly. 'And what about his trial? Did they get anyone to speak on his behalf?'

'Only his sister sir. She denied that there were any major problems in the marriage, and she had been a friend of his wife too.'

'And what about the prosecution? Did they offer any other evidence of motive other than the emails?'

She nodded. 'In fact they did sir. They called a Commodore Macallan, who was the commander of the base and its fleet at the time. He said that Lieutenant McKay had been a competent officer but that he had reported sick on two occasions with mental health issues. I don't think that could have been very helpful for the defence sir.'

*Macallan*. The guy who had murdered his own son and then shot himself. Frank screwed up his face, trying to compute the chronology. *That* incident happened just six months ago, which was why Maggie and his brother were trying to sort out his will. But just because it happened more than three years after the McKay tragedy, that didn't stop him wondering if there was a connection. Lochmorehead and surroundings were hardly bigger than that giant superstore in his Isleworth manor, so what were the chances of two mysteries occurring in just the space of three or four years? He didn't do probability, so that would be another thing to ask wee Eleanor Campbell when he got back.

Contrary to what he'd told Sergeant Jim Muir, he wasn't heading back south after his parental visit to Shettleston. Tomorrow, he was going to be meeting with the staff of Bainbridge Associates in that nice wee hotel on the edge of Loch More. And PC Lexy McDonald was going too.

# Chapter 12

Back in his Battersea flat, it hadn't taken him long to figure out whose phone it was he'd nicked from Ardmore House. For wasn't he Geordie the polymath and frigging premier league cyber-genius? I mean, how hard could it be? A couple of false trails and then on the third one, bang, he'd cracked it. And what a windfall this was turning out to be. Those funeral pictures of the Macallan twins for a start, they were an absolute frigging gold mine. Elspeth pissed out of her tiny skull and Kirsty with her tongue down that guy's throat. No wonder the paper had been happy to pay thirty grand and no questions asked. The Audi had come to an unfortunate end, some teenage yobs cracking the code of the keyless ignition system and leaving it burnt out in Brixton after having their fun. At least, that was the story he'd made up for the insurance claim form. It was a shame in some ways, since he'd really loved that motor, but he knew the danger in hanging onto it after the Ardmore job. No matter how thorough the clean-up had been, there would still be all that forensic shit sloshing around. So it had been three hundred quid well spent, although the lads would probably have done it for nothing had he thought about it at the time, just for the fun of it. Nothing lost though, with the insurance pay-out already invested in a wicked Golf GTi hot-hatch with the twenty-one-inch alloys. A motor that was just as much fun to drive, but perhaps not quite as conspicuous. *Smart move.*

There was just one thing that continued to intrude on his sunny mood, and that was his bloody conscience. Who would have thought he of all people would have been afflicted by it, but there it was, nagging away like toothache. Well, of course it had seemed a really sweet idea at the time, leaking Commodore Macallan's big secret to his daughters. The feeling of power and revenge after the shit Macallan had dealt out to all these men and women under his command. And now he was dead. No great loss to the world of course, but he, Geordie, was partially responsible, not that anyone could ever connect anything back to him. Good riddance, that's what anyone who knew Macallan would say, so why wouldn't his conscience just leave him alone?

Well sod that, he'd just have to work through it, push these bothersome thoughts to the back of his mind. For now, he had to sit back and think through the next step in his plan. Now that he knew the ownership of that phone, and how much the owner wouldn't want the police to know they had been at Ardmore House on the night the Commodore had killed his son and shot himself, it was simply a matter of setting the price to be paid for his silence. Had he been an auctioneer, he would be starting the bids at a hundred grand minimum.

## Chapter 13

It had been Asvina's idea that they should fly up to Glasgow, declaring that her firm's fee for executing the provisions of the will had plenty of fat in it, more than an enough to cover the trivial cost of a couple of return flights on a budget airline. Maggie was quiet for most of the journey, immersed in silent contemplation of all things Macallan. As far as the Commodore's will was concerned, the meeting with Kirsty Macallan had pretty much knocked the final nail in the coffin with respect to getting the three parties in the affair to agree to a settlement. Alison Macallan had said no, Elspeth Macallan had said no, and now Rory Overton, Kirsty's husband, who had evidently taken it upon himself to be her spokesperson, had said no too. It was greed and stupidity in equal measure, and there was every chance that it would result in an outcome than none of them wanted. But the issue was, what the hell to do about it?

On that subject, she'd had a telephone call with Asvina the previous day to seek her friend's advice, but the best she could suggest was that they tried to get all three parties to go to binding arbitration. It seemed like a bit of a long shot, but she decided it wouldn't do any harm to run it past Jimmy and see what he made of it.

He was in the outside seat, his long legs extended into the aisle as he enjoyed a gentle snooze. From time to time, a couple of the female flight attendants had sidled by to take a look at him, giggling and exchanging lustful glances. In other words, just a normal day in the life of Captain James Stewart, formerly of the army bomb disposal squad. She gave him a not-so-gentle nudge in the ribs, causing him to wake with a start and then look quickly all around him as if trying to remember exactly where he was.

'You were snoring,' she lied, 'with your mouth wide open. Not a good look if you don't mind me saying.'

'What? Oh sorry Maggie, it was a bit of an early start this morning.' He stretched his arms above his head and gave a yawn.

She laughed. 'Is that what you used to say when you were in the army? Sorry sir, it's a bit early for me, do you mind if I have a wee lie-in?'

'Aye, I wish,' he said sardonically. 'I was an officer don't forget. It was me that had to get all the other buggers up.'

'You poor thing. But now you've had your refreshing snooze, is it ok if we get on to business?'

'Sure, of course,' he said, giving her a wary look. 'Just as long as you haven't changed your mind about who's going to meet with my father-in-law.'

'Nope, I'll do that, we've already agreed.'

Maggie smiled to herself. That was going to be a bit of an adventure, meeting with Dr Flora Stewart's father just a week or so after she had consulted with his daughter in the disguise of Mrs Magdalene Brooks, trainee hill-walker. That being the meeting that Jimmy knew absolutely nothing about, which only added to the complication.

'I'm so grateful boss,' he said, the relief in his voice obvious. 'The old man and me are not exactly best of mates given the circumstances. It would be a wee bit awkward, put it that way.'

She smiled, then remembered what she was calling her *Emma* project. 'No, I completely understand that. But you know, I thought you wanted to try and get back with Flora? Are you planning to see her when we're up in Lochmorehead?' It was a question she'd been meaning to ask him for the last few days, but somehow the right moment had failed to arise.

'I don't know. I might. It depends.' On what it depended, he either didn't want to share with her or didn't himself know. She suspected the latter.

'You might just bump into her,' Maggie said, smiling. 'It's a small place after all.'

'That's what I'm worried about,' he said, a look of concern spreading across his face. 'I've no idea what I'd say to her.'

She shrugged. 'Why not try hello Flora? Just start from there and see where it leads.'

He laughed. 'Yeah, you're probably right. But I'm planning to only go out at night and in full camouflage gear so I can't be spotted. But come on, enough about me. What's the plan when we're up there?'

She noted the change of subject and decided she wouldn't push it any further for now.

'Well, three things I think. So first off is a final attempt to see if we can broker a backstop agreement. I've been having a think about it and I've drawn up a proposal that gets Alison the gate-house and a small annual allowance, gives Kirsty and her caveman husband two-thirds of the house and the grounds, and Elspeth the unmarried twin gets a third of the house and the grounds but gets two-thirds of the cash and other assets.'

Jimmy shook his head. 'Sorry boss, but I think there's two-thirds of bugger-all chance that any of them will accept that. You must know that, given you've met two-thirds of them yourself.' He gave a quiet chuckle at his own joke.

'That's why it's called a backstop. I don't expect any of them to accept it now, but it's an insurance policy if the lawsuits start flying around and lawyers' fees threaten to devour the assets. Gives them something they can dust down if it all starts getting out of hand. They can then put it in front of the court and say they'll accept binding arbitration.'

'I love it when you do all that dirty legal talk,' Jimmy laughed, 'but it's not an *if* as far as the lawsuits are concerned, it's a when, surely?'

'Exactly. So I think we should start with Alison the ex-wife first, because she seems the most rational of the three of them, although that's not saying much.'

Two flight attendants were struggling down the aisle with the drinks and snacks trolley.

'Teas, coffees, snacks anyone? Contactless payment only please.' A heavily made up attendant of matronly appearance placed a hand on Jimmy's shoulder as they drew up alongside them. 'Can I get you anything sir? Tea, Coffee? Anything else?' Maggie laughed as a comic vision of what *anything else* might comprise of came to mind.

'Coffee for me please,' she said quickly. 'Same for you Jimmy?'

'Tea please.' The attendant smiled and leaned across to fold down their back-of-seat tables before setting down their drinks. 'Careful, they're hot,' she warned, although in Maggie's experience that rarely turned out to be true, and so it proved on this occasion. She made a face as she took the first sip.

'It's wet at least,' Jimmy said, returning the grimace. 'So, yes that's the first thing, this backstop agreement as you call it. And I assume we need that to be put in front of the twins too?'

'Exactly. I thought you could do that, particularly in the light of Elspeth taking a shine to you. Have you done anything about that by the way? Because something gives me the feeling you might be trying to put it off.'

He shrugged. 'Not exactly, but I can't say I'm very enthusiastic but I can see how it might help with the case.'

'Good boy,' Maggie said, laughing. 'Take one for the team. So the second thing we need to do up there is I think the most critical task of the whole investigation so far.'

'Which is why I'm really glad you're doing it,' he said, giving her a thumbs-up.

'It's a pleasure. Dr McLeod's been the Macallan's family doctor for more than thirty years, so if anyone knows anything about which of the twins was the first-born, then it'll be him.'

She said it confidently, but deep down she couldn't help harbouring doubts. Because surely if that was actually the case, one or other of the twins would have already called him in as a witness. But at the very least Dr McLeod would almost certainly know something about the events surrounding their birth, even a birth which had happened thousands of miles away and was far from routine. Maybe he would remember something, maybe he wouldn't, but they had to start somewhere. And of course he might have some titbit of information that might at least give them a clue where else to look. She hoped so, otherwise they were dead in the water. Which, when she thought about it was an apt phrase, given their impending proximity to beautiful Loch More..

\*\*\*

It had been a bit of a no-brainer to allocate the driving duties to PC Lexy McDonald, the first leg an easy twenty-five miles or so down to Helensburgh, the second the thirty-five-mile onward trip to Loch More. First of all, it would mean he could have a few beers at that dinner date he'd planned with Maggie Bainbridge and his brother, and secondly, he'd been left with no choice anyway because the civilian jobsworth who ran the police garage on Helen Street was adamant that pool cars could only be signed out to serving Police Scotland officers, due to some crap to do with insurance or something like it. They'd been allocated a big Volvo SUV for the day, one of the ones that were built to special order for the police forces of Europe and beyond, kitted out with four-wheel-drive and a high-performance turbo-charged petrol engine. Which suited him fine, until Lexy revealed to him that she'd only passed her driving test three weeks earlier, and that when she drove her dad's car, it was normally with the probationer plates still on. Frank, not exactly relishing the prospect of her piloting this beast up the twisty roads of Loch Lomondside and beyond, asked if they had anything smaller, to be answered with a curt, 'It's all we've got pal. Take it or leave it. And make sure it's back for twenty-three-hundred-hours sharp, it's going out again in the morning.'

As they cruised along the dual-carriageway that bordered the north shore of the Clyde estuary, she'd compensated for her nervousness by limiting their speed to about thirty-eight miles an hour. From time to time Frank glanced in the door mirror, cracking a smile as he caught a glimpse of the queue of nervous motorist that had tucked themselves in behind the patrol car, uncertain as to whether they should overtake or not. For a moment he thought about asking her to get a move on, but then had second thoughts, centred mainly around his personal safety.

'So who is it we're going to see again?' Frank asked.

She turned her head to answer him, just as a white van decided on an abrupt manoeuvre into their lane.

'Woah watch out!' he shouted, his heart suddenly crashing as a dose of emergency adrenalin kicked in.

'Sorry sir,' she said, flustered. 'Didn't see him.'

'Aye, I gathered that Lexy. So maybe just keep your eyes on the road ahead for a while?'

He wondered whether he should order her to go for the full siren and flashing lights treatment. And least then everybody would get out of their way.

She gave a sheepish grin. 'Yes sir. Sorry sir. But I'm getting used to the big car now sir I think.'

'Thank god for that,' he laughed. 'So getting back to my original question.'

'Yes sir. The woman we're seeing is Lieutenant McKay's older sister, a Mrs Jess Sinclair. She lives in Helensburgh with her two kids and her husband.'

'And where is she coming from as regards to the case? Then and now I mean.'

'I don't know sir. I looked through the file obviously, but I didn't see her being called as a character witness or anything. But I found a couple of media interviews she did at the time, where she said she couldn't believe her brother could do anything like that. Nothing else sir, not that I could find anyway. And nothing recently. But I guess she must be in shock with her brother dying the way he did. Taking his own life I mean.'

'Aye, it will have been a shock to her right enough. We'll just have to be very careful, you know, try and be sensitive to her feelings and all that. But obviously we still need to find out everything she knows. So when we're in there, let me lead, but feel free to jump in if you think of anything, ok?'

'Yes sir.' He could hear the excitement in her voice, and then he remembered this was probably the first proper interview she'd been on.

The Sinclair's house was an ex-council semi-detached villa located high above the town, what the local estate agents would describe as a charming seven-apartment in a desirable location, although as far as he could remember, he'd never seen a property's location advertised as being undesirable. The sat-nav had led them straight to the door, and already he was imagining the neighbouring curtains beginning to twitch as the garish police car drew up outside. A short concrete-slabbed path led to the front door, a door which was badly in need of a repaint. They wrapped on the faded brass knocker and waited. It took nearly a minute before slowly and uncertainly, the door opened inward.

Jess Sinclair looked around forty, rather overweight with greying unkempt hair that she had secured in a ponytail with a multicoloured elastic tie. She wore a shapeless bottle-green sweatshirt and dark leggings, adding to a general careworn appearance. But then that was hardly a surprise given what she had been through in the last few weeks.

'Mrs Sinclair? I'm Detective Inspector Stewart and this is PC McDonald.'

'It was me you spoke to yesterday,' Lexy said, giving a concerned smile. 'Can we come in please?'

'Of course,' she said listlessly. 'Come through.'

She led them through a scruffy hallway into her living-room, gesturing for them to take a seat on a worn velour settee. As he was about to sit down, Frank noticed it was generously covered with silvery dog hair. Bloody perfect that was, given he was wearing his best navy suit, but he supposed it couldn't be helped. Seemingly reading his mind she said,

'Sorry it's Dolly our Jack Russell. I should've hoovered it up for you coming. But I've let things go a bit I'm afraid.'

'No, don't worry about that,' Frank said. 'You'll have had other things on your mind, I know that.'

She nodded without saying anything.

'So Mrs Sinclair,' he began, 'if you don't mind, we want to ask you a few questions about your brother and of course the events around the tragic death of his wife and the wee lassie. And if it gets too painful, just say, because we don't want to upset you at all.'

'What's this all about?' she said guardedly. 'Are you opening up the case again or what?'

He shook his head. 'Not exactly. It's just that when something like this happens, I mean your brother taking his own life, then we just like to take another wee look at the case again, only out of respect if you like. It's just routine really. Standard procedure.'

He hated telling her that little white lie, but consoled himself with the thought that it was with the best of intentions. If they were going to make progress with this investigation, keeping everything nice and low-key was going to be absolutely vital. And top priority was making sure as few people as possible knew about the screw-up over the time of death of the victims, a screw-up that Frank hoped was causing Sir Brian Pollock to have sleepless nights. A screw-up that proved Jess Sinclair's brother couldn't possibly have done it.

'And I should have said of course, I'm really sorry for your loss. We both are.'

She looked at them impassively. They were just words, he knew it and she knew it, and she'd have heard it a hundred times in the last few weeks. But you still were duty-bound to say them, and although he didn't know her and hadn't known her brother either, the sentiment was genuine. He *was* bloody sorry that an innocent man had been convicted for something he hadn't done. And now he had to ask the question he really wasn't looking forward to asking.

He lowered his voice so that it was barely audible. 'Mrs Sinclair, have you any idea what drove James to take his life? I'm really sorry to ask, but it might help us.'

'I would have thought that was pretty obvious,' she said, not looking him in the eye. 'He adored that wee girl with all his heart, and without her... well, he just couldn't go on.'

'I know this will be very difficult,' Lexy said, 'but why did he choose to do it now? Four years after the event I mean?'

She gave her a sad look. 'I think the pain was unbearable for him and it just kept building up and building up. You might imagine it gets better over time but I can tell you it doesn't. The reason it happened now? He tried it just a few months after he was sent there, and so he's been on suicide watch ever since. But I think they were a bit short-staffed and weren't as careful as they should have been. And although it sounds a terrible thing to say, I'm glad in some ways. At least he'll be at peace now.'

Frank couldn't help but shake his head in disgust. An innocent man driven to despair and one day very soon his sister was going to find out the devastating truth, and all because of a piss-head pathologist and a short-cutting copper. It made him physically sick at the thought of it.

'I really hope he is at peace Mrs Sinclair, I really do,' he said. 'But you never ever believed he did it, did you? Why was that?' He was hoping she would give him more than a simple *because he was my brother*.

'He'd never have killed wee Isabelle. Not in a million years. No matter how angry he was with *her*.'

*No matter how angry he was with her.* He caught the nuance immediately.

'Was their marriage having problems then?' Frank asked in a sympathetic tone.

She looked uncomfortable. He guessed she was angry with herself for giving away more than she intended.

'I don't know, not really,' she said, staring at the carpet. 'I didn't think so at the time, but then you don't really know the truth about any relationship, do you? Not when you're looking in from outside.'

He assumed the question was rhetorical and let her continue.

'But they were very different, Morag and James.'

'How do you mean?' Frank asked.

'Well James was so quiet. When he was home he just like to potter about in the garden or play with Isabelle or just relax and watch the football. She was much more outgoing you see. I think she felt quite stifled by service life, and wanted more.' They way she said it, he could tell she didn't approve.

'Did you like Morag, Mrs Sinclair?'

'Like?' she said, then hesitating as if weighing up her response. 'Like? Well, we were friends I suppose, and yes I did like her in that regard. But I don't think she was always fair to my brother, looking back.'

'Why was that?'

'Well in my opinion, she just didn't appreciate what she had. My brother was a lovely person and his family meant everything to him, and it wasn't his fault if the job took him away for months on end. That's the reality of life in the navy and she should have thought about it before she married him.'

Frank smiled. 'You sound as if you're speaking from experience.'

'I am. My man was in it for eight years and I knew he'd be at sea for long periods. So you learn to cope. That's what you have to do if you're a navy wife.'

And Morag McKay couldn't cope and was therefore to be despised, that was the clear implication.

'But that was one of the main things the prosecution used during the trial wasn't it?' Lexy said, then looked at Frank. 'I'm talking about the state of their marriage. You don't mind if I ask about that sir?'

'No, go ahead,' he said.

'So there was a massive email trail between them, wasn't there Mrs Sinclair?' Lexy said, furrowing her brow. 'Whilst he was on his last mission. Mrs McKay said over and over again she was tired of her life in Ardmore and was going to move to the city with the little girl. At first your brother was pleading with her, telling her how much he loved her and wee Isabelle. But then his replies began to get more and more angry.'

'Until he threatened to kill them both,' Frank said. 'That's right, isn't it?'

'Yes sir,' Lexy said simply.

'That wasn't right.' Jess Sinclair shot out the words. 'It wasn't right.'

'What do you mean Mrs Sinclair,' Frank asked.

'I told you James was a quiet man, didn't I? Everyone was always teasing him about it, even his navy friends. You ask anyone and they would say the same thing. He's a man of few words your James, that's what they would say.'

'So what are you saying Mrs Sinclair?' he asked again.

'I don't know, I don't know what I'm saying.' She looked at him, her expression a mask of confusion. 'But James was such a quiet man. He wouldn't have said all these things.'

'But he did say them Mrs Sinclair, I'm afraid,' Frank said. 'It's all in our evidence file, in black and white. He did say them.'

\*\*\*

He kept his eyes firmly closed as Lexy, her driving having now morphed from over-cautious to over-confident, swung the big Volvo left and right down the twisty glen that led to the village of Lochmorehead.

Partially it was because he really didn't want to have to look where they were going, but it was mainly because it helped him think. Assuming he could stay awake that was, because the rocking motion was causing him to drift off.

Jess Sinclair hadn't been much help, other than confirming what they already knew. His marriage to Morag had been in difficulty and that presented a cast-iron motive for the killing. *If I can't have you, then no-one else will have you either.* They got about a dozen of these a year in the Met alone, so it was hardly unusual. So strong was the motive and the evidence, it was easy to forget that James McKay hadn't actually done it. He wondered too if there was anything in Jess's belief that he wouldn't have said all these things in his emails to his wife. But that was crazy, and he quickly dismissed it from his mind.

However, there was no doubting that whilst Pollock might be a sly bastard, he was no fool. He would have known at the time that the case against Lieutenant James McKay didn't quite stack up, and somewhere tucked away in that file there must be a fact or two that could prove it. The problem was that for them, it would be like looking for the proverbial needle in a haystack.

Then suddenly a modest smile of satisfaction spread across his features as, quite out of the blue, a rather brilliant idea came to him through his semi-meditative state. Because whilst he and Lexy might not know where to look in that bloody file, Chief Constable Sir Brian Pollock most definitely would. And what's more, Frank thought he now knew how to tease it out of him. For that, he would need to enrol the services of Maggie Bainbridge and her associate. And of course DCI Jill Smart had furnished him with plenty of budget in the kitty to cover it. *No bother.*

# Chapter 14

The flight from Heathrow to Glasgow Airport was a mere sixty minutes in duration and equipped only with overnight bags, it hadn't taken them long to de-plane, as the lead flight attendant had described it, and reach the concourse area, where the rental car booths were located. At which point the operation had gone somewhat belly-up, on account of Jimmy's driving licence having an out-of-date photo and Maggie having forgotten to bring hers with her at all.

'Look, you can see it's me,' Jimmy was arguing, holding up the licence and stabbing at the picture with his forefinger. 'It's supposed to be just for ID purposes, and anyone can see it's me. And we've got a booking. Look, here's the paperwork, I printed it out just in case.'

The desk clerk, wearing a badge that identified him as Calum, and clearly harassed from dealing with the early-morning rush, was determined to be unmoved. Maggie cursed their luck for finding this spotty youth on duty rather than one of the usual smartly-uniformed young women, upon whom Jimmy would have been able to cast his spell. She thought it likely the youth would be immune to *her* physical charms, that of a forty-two-year-old former barrister who never looked her best after an early start, but that didn't mean she couldn't dust down some of her old advocacy skills. Not that she'd been much good at that either.

'Calum,' she said, in what she hoped was a respectful tone, 'I know you're only doing your job, but this is really really important.' She dropped her voice to a whisper so Jimmy couldn't hear. 'And I'm sorry about my brother, but it's just that he's terribly upset. We're going to our mum's funeral you see. She died very suddenly and it's been a huge shock to us all as you can imagine.'

The youth gave her a suspicious look. 'I'll speak to my manager. Wait here,' he said, disappearing off into the little office behind the front desk. To the rear of them, a queue of customers who had been hoping for a swift and efficient transaction were starting to make their displeasure heard.

A couple of minutes later he re-emerged. 'My manager says we can retain a credit card as security on this occasion. And she says we'll have to charge you an extra insurance fee of a hundred and twenty pounds. She says it's refundable if you bring back the car on time and undamaged.' He didn't look or sound pleased about any of it.

'What did you say to him?' Jimmy asked, as they made their way to the multi-storey car park, keys in hand.

'I told him we were going to a funeral.' Maggie hoped he wouldn't ask for any more details.

'You lied,' he laughed.

'I'm a barrister, remember? That's what we do.'

They had three or four hours to spare before their early afternoon meeting with Alison Macallan in Lochmorehead, which Jimmy had decided would be used to show her some of the sights of his home city.

'Been to Glasgow before boss?'

'Nope, never,' she said. 'I don't think I'd even been to Scotland before my last trip to see Alison.' *That time when she'd sneaked a visit to Dr Flora Stewart.*

'Well you've got a wee treat in store,' he said, smiling. 'I'll take you up to the West End and show you the Uni and all my old haunts. It's beautiful at this time of year, with all the trees turning to gold in Kelvingrove. That's the park that sits alongside the river Kelvin. A really nice spot.'

They parked up on a long tree-lined avenue that seem to bisect the park, the University buildings set high on a hill to their left. On their right, a group of elderly men and women were playing bowls, their laughter audible above the gentle whistle of a cool wind.

'Sir George Gilbert Scott designed them,' Jimmy explained, pointing up at the buildings. 'The same guy that did St Pancras station in London. Gothic style, that's what they call it I think. Pretty fancy. Although he died before the Uni was actually built I believe. They ran out of money a couple of times and his sons had to finish it off.'

'Looks like Hogwarts to me,' she laughed, 'but it is beautiful.'

'We can take a walk up if you like, you get a nice view over the city from up there.'

'So this is where you did your law degree then?' she asked, as they wound their way up through a rhododendron-lined path, their verdant blooms now faded. But it was just an opener for the question she really wanted to ask.

'Yep, did my four years. I enjoyed it. Well, not so much the course, but I enjoyed Uni life a lot. I joined the OTC and that's what got me into the army.'

'The OTC?'

'Sorry, the Officers' Training Corps. It's a bit like the Boy Scouts but with real guns. It was fun, lots of outdoor stuff, you know, camping and hiking and the like. Right up my street.'

'And is this where you met Flora? At Uni I mean?' She tried to drop the question in as casually as she could.

He smiled. 'Aye, more or less right here in fact. Summer term. She was sitting on the grass having a picnic with some of her medic pals and we got talking. We just sort of hit it off right away.'

In other words, love at first sight. Maggie didn't find it difficult to understand how that would have happened, having seen Flora Stewart *nee* McLeod in the flesh, and she already knew all too well the effect her handsome colleague had on the opposite sex. They must have been a beautiful couple.

'Sorry, but I'm awful aren't I? So nosey.' She smiled at him, deciding not to push it any further. Unless of course he wanted to tell her more.

'No, that's all right. I've been an idiot and there's no excuse for it. But you make your bed and you have to lie in it.'

She hoped he might now go on to tell him how it had all started, that bizarre relationship he'd had with Astrid Sorenson the beautiful Swedish star of country music. The relationship that had blown his marriage apart. But it seemed he was now anxious to change the subject.

'See over there,' he said, pointing in the distance. 'That's the famous Finnieston Crane. They used it to lift big railway engines onto the ships when they were being exported, back in the old days. And that's the new BBC building just on the other side of the river.'

'Fascinating,' she laughed, her tone accidently ironic. 'No, honestly it is,' she added quickly, seeing the look he gave her. Knowing him, she didn't think he'd be permanently offended.

'How about we take a wee tour through the quadrangles and then wander down to Byers Road?' he said. 'And you can sample the culinary delights of the famous University Cafe. I don't think it's changed for about a hundred years and all the better for it. Although the coffee's fresh of course. And they do a nice sausage roll.'

That clinched it for her.

'Sounds delightful,' she said, and this time she meant it.

\*\*\*

North of Tarbet, the A82 main road alongside Loch Lomond changes in character, a sudden steep vertical rise in the terrain meaning the road builders had just about managed to carve out a winding course between the mountainside and the loch itself. It didn't pay to be in a hurry, your speed of progress being dictated by the giant tourist coaches and the articulated lorries supplying the supermarkets of Fort William and beyond. Maggie and Jimmy drove in comfortable silence, the sat-nav's estimated time of arrival at Lochmorehead still well in the black, allowing them to be content with the leisurely pace of travel. Earlier he had planned to stop off at Luss, a pretty little village on the edge of the loch that was popular with tourists, and a calling point for the cruise boats that plied their trade on the beautiful expanse of water. But it had started to rain, causing a hazy mist to descend from mighty Ben Lomond and hover just above the loch.

'No worries, we might be able to fit it in on the way back down tomorrow,' he had said, pointing to the junction that led down to the village.

Now they were finally clear of the lochside, the road straightening out as they crossed the boundary of the National Park and entered the Highlands proper.

'This scenery is amazing,' Maggie said, her nose almost pressed against the side window. 'I didn't really get the chance to look at it properly the last time because I was driving, and then it was pitch-black on my way back.'

'Aye, it is amazing,' Jimmy said, 'and if you carry on another thirty miles or so you're on Rannoch Moor, and that's *really* beautiful but really wild too. They chucked us out of a lorry up there in the middle of winter when we were doing our basic training and told us not to come back for five days. With no food, no water, no tents, nothing. And no phones, obviously.'

'But I'm assuming you survived,' she said, laughing, 'otherwise you wouldn't be here now.'

'Just about. Lost a bit of weight though,' he grinned. 'There's not much eating in a rabbit, especially when you're having to share it with five other guys. But anyway, this is our turn-off. B8214. Lochmorehead eleven miles.'

Twenty minutes later they arrived, Jimmy pulling the car into an empty space in the hotel car park, the same hotel which six months earlier had hosted the wake of

Commodore Roderick Macallan and his son Peter. *Births, marriages and deaths*. It was the only decent place for miles around and had seen plenty of all three. Glancing at his watch he said, 'Time for a quick lunch then?'

'Yes, I'm starving,' Maggie said, then remembering the sausage roll she had consumed earlier, 'although goodness knows why. But yes, we've got time and it's stopped raining too. It's just a fifteen-minute walk to Alison's from here and it'll be nice to stretch our legs after the journey.'

Lunch dispatched, they made their way along the beautiful lochside. An old Ford Focus, much in need of a good wash, had been parked at an oblique angle on the gravelled driveway, leaving the narrowest of gaps to squeeze through between it and the laurel hedge. They found Flossie the labrador lounging in the small porch that sheltered the front door, and after looking them over with mild suspicion, she struggled to her feet before padding over to greet them.

A few seconds later Alison Macallan opened the door and emerged.

'Hello again Alison,' Maggie said, smiling. 'I hope you're well. This is my associate Jimmy Stewart.'

'Hi,' she said. 'Come through, please. And sorry about my parking, I was in a bit of a rush.' Why that should have been so, she did not explain.

Maggie had been vague as to why she wanted to meet with her again, reasoning that complicated explanations about backstop agreements might not go down well. But she need not have concerned herself, because it seemed that Alison intended to take charge of the agenda, and she wasn't wasting time with any small-talk either.

'There's been a development,' she said. 'You see, I haven't been exactly truthful with everyone.'

'What do you mean?' Maggie asked, raising an eyebrow in Jimmy's direction.

'I know. I've always known of course. I just didn't want to cause any trouble between them, that's why I didn't say before.'

'So, are you telling us you know which of the twins is the elder one?' Jimmy said, sounding surprised. 'For definite?'

'Of course for definite. I was their step-mother. I *am* their step-mother,' she said, correcting herself. 'So *of course* I would know.'

Maggie nodded uncertainly. 'Well that would certainly clarify matters, no doubt about it. So which of them is it? Elspeth or Kirsty?'

Alison gave her a sharp look. 'I'd rather not say at the moment. Not until everything's tied up.'

'What do you mean by that?'

'Our lawyers say we should keep it confidential until everything's properly tied up. Until all the paperwork is completed and signed off.'

*Our lawyers.* Maggie shot Jimmy an ironic glance which he returned with a wry smile. She could tell he was thinking the same thing as her. Whenever there was money, there was always a lawyer. They could sniff the stuff out, in the same way a police dog could sniff out a drug stash.

'Who have you used, if you don't mind me asking?'

'McTaggart Ward,' she said, giving a suspicious look, 'they're a small Glasgow firm, but quite well known I'm told.'

'And are all three parties involved in this agreement or contract, or whatever you want to call it?' Jimmy asked in an innocent tone, causing Maggie to smile. She had been thinking exactly the same thing. *Cunning Alison Macallan has done a deal with one of the sisters, cutting the other one out.* The trouble is, it wouldn't work, and the only party to gain from it would be her new lawyers. They were evidently cunning bastards too, but then again, it came with the territory.

'I wanted to make sure my rights were protected,' Alison said, sounding defensive, 'so I have agreed a very acceptable settlement with the elder twin. It will all be neatly documented in a contract so that no-one can take it away from me, that's what our lawyers said.'

Maggie smiled. 'Well I don't blame you for trying to protect your position, but there is still a risk that a court will throw it out. I'm sure your lawyers will have explained that to you.' She was pretty sure they wouldn't have, which prompted her next question.

'So I'm guessing they're taking the case on a no-win-no-fee basis? That would be pretty standard for a matter like this.'

Alison hesitated. 'No. We've agreed what is a very acceptable fixed-price fee. And of course I only have to pay half of it. The other half will be paid by....by the elder twin. The whole thing is very satisfactory from my point of view.'

'Aye, but you'll still have to prove that the one you're *claiming* is the oldest one, really is the oldest,' Jimmy said, scratching his chin, 'if that makes sense. How's that going to work?'

'My lawyers say a court is almost certain to believe *me*,' she said, sounding more convinced than surely she must have felt. But Maggie knew there was a lot of sense in what Alison was saying. She'd married Roderick Macallan and taken on the twins when they were only four or five years old, and so had been in their life for more than twenty-five years. If she said she knew, definitely, and said it with sufficient conviction and authority, there was every chance that the judge or magistrate would be convinced too. Not a big enough chance though, she noted wryly, for her lawyers to go no-win-no-fee.

'Well, I guess that's to be seen,' Maggie said, shrugging, 'because I'm sure the other twin is likely to contest it. More fees for the lawyers I'm afraid.' Which was true, and of course the lawyer likely to be doing the contesting would be Asvina Rani of the prestigious London firm Addison Redburn. At twelve hundred pounds an hour, she could see this development, as Alison had described it, wouldn't be without its silver linings. And as for McTaggart Ward, the little Glasgow firm who were apparently quite well known, well pretty soon they would find they were way out of their league. But all of that was for some day in the future, and for now, that part of the agenda was closed.

'There was something else,' Maggie said, 'if you can spare another five minutes. Something Jimmy's been asked to look at.'

'Yes, I've got five minutes, sure,' she said, evidently relieved to be talking of something else, 'and sorry I've been so rude. Would you like a cup of tea or coffee or some water perhaps?'

'Tea would be great,' Jimmy said, Maggie giving a nod of confirmation.

'Ok, just be five minutes,' Alison said, disappearing into the kitchen.

He reached over and scratched Flossie under the chin, who gave a quiet woof of satisfaction.

'And I bet you'd love to stay here, wouldn't you my girl?' he whispered. 'See out the last of your days in the beautiful Highlands. That would be nice, wouldn't it?'

'Shush,' Maggie said, struggling to suppress a laugh. 'You'll upset the poor thing.'

'She doesn't look very upset to me,' Jimmy grinned. 'She's loving every minute of it.'

Alison had returned with a tray containing a china teapot, three matching cups and saucers, and a plate of chocolate biscuits.

'That's why I love coming back to Scotland,' Jimmy said, smiling up at her. 'You always get biscuits or a cake with your tea. Down south, you've got to bring your own.'

'Not in Yorkshire,' Maggie said, 'and if you're very lucky you'll get a slice of fruit cake with cheese on top. Delish.'

He gave her a mildly disbelieving look. 'Aye, if you say so. But Alison, if you don't mind, I wanted to ask you a couple of questions about the funeral. If that's not too painful for you of course.'

She shrugged. 'Fine by me. I only went because it seemed to be the right thing to do, and of course I wanted to pay my last respects to Peter. So yes, I'll help you if I can.'

'Well what it is, we've been asked by Elspeth to help her with a matter that she has brought to our attention. I don't know if she might have mentioned it to you at all?'

*Clever boy*, thought Maggie. This might help to tease out which of the twins she was in cahoots with.

'No,' Alison said, her expression impassive, 'no, Elspeth hasn't said anything to me about any matter.'

'Well, there were some photographs taken at the funeral that were a bit embarrassing for the twins. They found their way into a newspaper and then onto the net, and let's just say they didn't exactly show the girls in the best of lights. I wondered if you saw any of them?'

'They're always in the papers or on Instagram or whatever it is,' she said, her tone dismissive. 'It's what they do. I never look at any of it. It doesn't interest me in the slightest.'

'The thing is,' Jimmy continued, 'they were obviously taken by someone at the funeral, and I just wondered if you noticed anyone who was taking a lot of pictures.'

'Who takes pictures at a funeral?' she snapped.

'Someone did,' Jimmy said simply.

'Well I didn't notice,' she said, this time more conciliatory. 'I'm sorry, I don't think I can help you.'

Jimmy took a sheet of paper from his pocket, unfolded it and placed it on the table.

'I drew up a wee diagram. From photographs I found on the hotel's website, you know, of the wee function room where you held the wake.'

'So?' Alison said, disinterested.

'The person who took the pictures would have been about here,' he said, pointing to his diagram. 'Leaning against the bar I would have thought. Do you remember who was standing there that afternoon?'

'No, I don't,' she said, shaking her head. 'I just wanted the whole damn thing to be over with, so I wasn't paying attention to what was going on. I'm sorry.' To Maggie's ears, she didn't sound it. And now it seemed their short meeting was over.

'I think we're probably finished here,' Alison said, unsmiling, 'unless there's anything else?'

Maggie shook her head. 'No Alison, I think we understand where you're coming from. All I'd say is as a member of the legal profession, I've got a general duty of care in any of my dealings, and so I'd urge you to be cautious before taking this to court. And I mean that genuinely.' And it was true, she did mean it. Roderick Macallan's ex-wife was blinded by a dangerous mixture of revenge and avarice, unable to see the risks involved in the path she had chosen, and her little Glasgow law firm would be keen to skate over all of that. And there was one particular risk that she was anxious to make sure Alison understood.

'Naturally we'll be continuing our parallel investigations, which is our duty as executors of the will. That's where we're going next in fact, to see Dr McLeod. I guess he's your GP too, is he?' Without waiting for a response she said, 'It seems a reasonable assumption there might be something in the twins' medical records which might prove which is which, don't you think?'

'He won't tell you,' Alison said, suddenly sounding rattled. 'Isn't he bound by confidentiality or the Hippocratic oath or something like that?'

Jimmy smiled. 'He's not going to tell us anything with regard to their medical history, obviously, but we're not interested in that. And we don't even need him to actually *tell* us which is the oldest. All we need to know is if he *knows* which is which.'

'Yes, that's right,' Maggie said, cottoning on to where he was coming from. 'Then we can go through the official legal channels, so that it's all above board.' She wasn't quite sure what these official channels were or if indeed they existed at all. This was a potential problem she hadn't thought of before. What if there was no way to force Dr McLeod, or any other medical authority for that matter, disclosing what they knew? They'd just have to face that if and when it arose.

'Right Jimmy, time to go,' she said, smiling at her colleague. 'We probably won't meet again Alison, but I do hope everything works out for you.' Even although she was pretty sure it wouldn't.

'What do you think to that then boss?' Jimmy said as they strolled back along the lochside to the hotel. 'A right turn up for the books isn't it?'

'Yeah it is, and one of our twins will likely go ballistic when they find out what her sister has done. But come on, you've met them both. Which one do you think has made a deal with the wicked step-mother?'

He shrugged. 'I don't know. I thought maybe on balance Kirsty was the more reasonable of the two, but then again she's got her husband pulling the strings. So as I said, I don't know. Could be either of them.' He gave a grin as he realised what he had just said. 'Obviously.'

'But you could easily find out I think,' Maggie said, a hint of mischief in her voice, 'if you were to take up Elspeth's offer. The dinner date I mean. It would be strictly business of course.'

He gave her a sharp look. 'And do I have any choice?'

'No,' she said. 'No, you haven't.'

## Chapter 15

*Fuck off whoever you are.* That was the frankly *stupid* response he'd got from her after he made his opening gambit, requesting an entirely reasonable eighty-five grand to keep his mouth shut about everything he knew about the events up at Ardmore House that night. Well, she was going to find out sooner rather than later what a huge mistake that was. She was about to learn that screwing around with him never ended well, and her with so much to lose too, it was dumb beyond belief. Now his price was going up at the rate of ten grand a week, and you know what, he was so angry with her arrogance that he might just tell the authorities anyway. *Stupid cow.*

You see, every murder had to have a motive, and of course he knew hers. In fact, wasn't it him who had supplied it to her in the first place? And with access-all-areas to her Cloud back-up, it hadn't been difficult to find out where she lived, and now he was ready to leave his indelible mark on her pathetic life. The black and green aerosols he'd chosen would work very nicely on the whitewashed wall, and in a couple of days' time it would be all over the arts pages. *There's a new Geordie and it's one of his best*. That's what they'd say, and there would be silly speculation about how much his latest masterpiece had added to the value of the property. He'd enjoy reading them all, as long as they didn't come out with any of that *second-rate Banksy* crap again.

And maybe then *she* would realise that he was serious and that she'd better pay up or else. He'd give her seven days max.

In the meantime, that copper woman up in Manchester didn't seem to realise what serious shit she was in. He'd asked her twice for the money but still *nada*. Very well, if that was the way she wanted to play it, so be it. Soon she would find it didn't pay to mess with Geordie-boy.

# Chapter 16

It was three-thirty by the time they returned to the hotel, giving them ample opportunity to complete the check-in formalities before Maggie's four o'clock meeting with Dr Angus McLeod.

'Two *single* rooms was it?' the plump receptionist said, her emphasis on the word suggesting she would have been well-cast in a sixties *Carry-On* movie. 'As it happens we're quiet tonight so I've slipped madam into a very comfortable double overlooking the loch.' *Just in case you two should change your mind, nudge-nudge, wink-wink.* She didn't say any of that, but it was obvious from her lascivious expression what she was thinking. Maggie, in good spirits despite some trepidation about her upcoming encounter, decided to take it as a compliment. *Jimmy Stewart and Maggie Bainbridge, secret lovers.* That wasn't going to happen, not ever, but that didn't mean she didn't occasionally think about it.

The receptionist scribbled something illegible in the old-fashioned register then without looking up said, 'Hamish will take your bags up, and there's complimentary refreshments in the lounge just over there. Have a lovely stay.'

Maggie smiled. She didn't know there were people really called Hamish, but it was a nice name.

'That's great', she said, then turning to Jimmy asked, 'What are you going to do whilst I'm with Dr McLeod?'

'I'm going to a wee snooze, and then I'm going to get a wee cup of tea and have a wee read of the paper,' he said, dead-pan. 'It's been a stressful day and I feel the need to relax.'

She laughed. 'That sounds like a plan. So we'll meet up in the bar shall we, when I get back?'

'Now *that* sounds like a plan,' he grinned, 'and Frank should be here by then too.'

'Yes, it'll be nice to see him again.' It had only been about three days since they last met, but there was no getting away from the truth. She missed him. 'See you later.'

It took just a couple of minutes to reach Lochmorehead's little surgery, located in an attractive double-fronted house located within a neat garden surrounded by black-painted iron railings. As she had feared, the same receptionist as on her last visit was on duty, which was hardly surprising given the size of the practice. She doubted if Dr McLeod and Dr Stewart needed to employ more than one. Today Maggie was dressed in a sober grey business suit featuring trousers rather than a skirt, although the item had been purchased with the option of either, and wearing her hair down. On her last visit, it was tied up and concealed beneath that ridiculous hat, and of course she had been wearing her

Mount Everest-proof walking jacket. Nonetheless, the receptionist gave her a suspicious look when she announced herself at the desk. The trouble was, there was no disguising that Yorkshire accent.

'Dr McLeod is held up with his last patient,' she said, still wearing an expression that said *where have I seen you before*? 'Shouldn't be more than ten minutes. Just take a seat and I'll call you when he's free.'

*Ten minutes.* So what were the chances that Dr Flora Stewart would wander into her own reception area during that time and see her sitting there, bold as brass? Quite high, in all probability. But that didn't matter now, because Maggie had worked out exactly what she was going to say in the eventuality. It would require total honesty, the unleashing of the full Miss Emma Woodhouse. *He never stops talking about you Flora. Jimmy and I have worked together for nearly two years and I hear it day in day out, just how much you mean to him. He obviously still loves you very much. So when this matter took me to Loch More, then I just had to meet you. I hope you'll forgive me for the terrible subterfuge.* It sounded rather plausible, which given it was almost exactly the truth, was perhaps not so surprising. Leaving only one more thing to be decided, something that was rather a dilemma. If she was indeed to encounter Flora, should she let slip that Jimmy was in town too? She thought about what Austen's heroine would do in the same situation, which served to clarify it in her mind. Of course she would tell her.

In the event, the situation did not arise. An elderly woman with a stick tottered out from the door leading to the corridor and handed what Maggie assumed was a prescription to the receptionist.

'Dr McLeod told me to give you this Elaine,' the old lady said, smiling, 'and I've to book a follow-up appointment.'

'Thanks Mrs McPherson,' she said, then looked over to Maggie. 'Dr McLeod's free now Miss Bainbridge. *Or should I call you Mrs Brooks?*' So that was it then, the cat was well and truly out of the bag now. She shot Elaine a conspiratorial wink on the way past, which wasn't returned. Reaching his consulting room door, she gave a light knock before entering.

'Take a seat Miss Bainbridge,' he said. 'So what can we do for you today?' She guessed he repeated the words about fifty times a day such that it had become an automatic reflex. 'Not in a medical sense of course,' he chuckled, 'although feel free to bring anything up if you wish. No extra charge on this occasion.'

She laughed, grateful to him for putting her at ease. She knew pretty much exactly how old he was after Jimmy had told her about attending his sixtieth birthday party. Sixty-four or sixty-five and so she guessed he must be close to retirement, although she wasn't sure if doctors were allowed to carry on past that age even if they wanted to. He was of medium height but broad-chested, with cropped grey hair and the same piercing green eyes as his daughter. He was wearing a light blue shirt and slim purple tie, the sleeves rolled up above the elbows, straining under bulging biceps. For a man of his age, Dr Angus McLeod looked in good shape.

'I spoke to you briefly on the phone,' she said in way of introduction.

'Ah yes. About the Macallan twins. Elspeth and Kirsty.'

'That's right Dr McLeod. My firm is working for the executors of their father's will. There's this rather awkward provision that we're trying to straighten out.'

McLeod nodded. 'Yes, I think I remember Roderick telling me about it once. Some covenant that an old ancestor put in place, is that it?'

'Yes, that's right. So were you friends with the late Commodore then?'

He gave her a wry look. 'I wouldn't say friends exactly. We knew the family of course, given they own the estate and half of the village too, and they were all patients of ours. We played golf occasionally as well, although that could be rather frustrating.'

She laughed. 'I've never played, but my dad did when he was younger, and he usually came home swearing to himself. Or swearing *at* himself more accurately.'

'Yes it is a stupidly annoying game, but that's not what I meant. No, what I meant was that arithmetic was never Roderick's strong point.'

'You mean he cheated? Maggie asked, open-mouthed. 'I would have thought that's a capital offence up here.'

He shrugged. 'Everybody knew about it in the club. It's not a reputation that anyone would aspire to, but there you are.'

'Yes, well it was a terrible thing that happened, at Ardmore House.' She wasn't here to dig into the circumstances of the double tragedy, but she left the statement hanging in the air just in case Dr McLeod was prepared to venture an opinion as to what lay behind it all. But she wasn't surprised when he didn't.

'And now there's a will to be sorted out,' he said, his tone now businesslike. 'So what is it you want to ask me in that regard?'

She smiled. 'The will provides that the house and estate must pass intact to the eldest surviving offspring, but no-one seems to know if that was Elspeth or Kirsty, and the twins are each claiming it is them. So you can see my difficulty. Obviously, we wondered if there was anything in their medical records that would prove it one way or the other.'

'Yes, I see,' he said, stroking his chin. 'As it happens, I anticipated your question and so dug out the old paper records. We're all computerised now but we still have the old buff envelopes. But no, there doesn't seem to be anything in them which states which is first born. As you know, had they been born in Scotland it would have been a different matter, because here unlike Canada, the time of birth is entered in the register. Although to be fair, I don't think it is always recorded accurately. But that's irrelevant of course.'

'It must have been a terrible time for the family,' Maggie said.

'Yes it was, with Roderick stuck over in Canada with two newborn babies and his young son Peter. To be fair to the Navy, they arranged pretty rapidly for him to be posted back to Scotland. They found him a desk job here at the Ardmore base so that he could move back into the family home.'

'So who looked after the children then?'

McLeod smiled. 'Yes that was the priority of course. They managed to find a live-in nanny, who stayed with them for quite a few years. Until he married Alison in fact.'

'A nanny?' Maggie said, her eyes narrowing. 'And I assume you know who she was. Who she is, I should say?'

He nodded. 'Yes, of course. Susan McColl is her name, old Jim McColl's daughter. He was a local farmer, up at Ardrishaig. Long dead of course and the farm sold off.'

'But this Susan, I'm sure she must still be alive?'

'Susan? I'd imagine so. She was around forty then, so she wouldn't be that old now, perhaps in her early seventies I'd guess. But she moved away from the area, what, it must be twenty-five or more years ago.' He gave her a wry look. 'She married a sailor you see, as many ladies around here do. I seem to recall they moved down south when he was posted to another base. Portsmouth or Plymouth, I always get them mixed up. But I remember her married name. Susan Priest. He was a Petty Officer, worked in the ordnance stores as I recall. John or Jim, I think it was one of the two.'

'And *she* would know I guess, which twin was the elder?' Maggie asked, then thinking out loud, 'but goodness knows how we would track her down.'

McLeod nodded again. 'Yes, I expect she would.' Then out of the blue he said, 'But you could always ask my Flora of course.'

'Flora?' she said, feigning surprise. And hoping that her acting wasn't so bad as to arouse suspicion.

'My daughter. Dr Flora Stewart. She works here in the practice.' There was no disguising the pride in his voice. 'She was great friends with the twins when she was growing up, and they were always round our house.'

'Yes that would be great,' Maggie said, thinking that it would be exactly the opposite.

'She's not in today unfortunately,' McLeod said. 'She's up in Glasgow on a course. But she'll be back in tomorrow as usual. I'm sure Elaine could fit you in. And of course I'll ask my wife Elizabeth this evening. She would probably know too, now that I come to think of it.'

'Yes, well that would be great,' Maggie said, relieved, 'but we're actually heading back down south tomorrow so it will have to wait for another time. But thank you for your help Dr McLeod.'

He shrugged. 'I'm not sure I was much help but I hope you do get it sorted out. Now, is there anything else we can do for you today?'

She laughed as she got up to go. 'No, nothing I can think of thank you.'

She knew it was cowardly, but she wouldn't be bothering Elaine the receptionist with a request for an appointment, not right now at least. She planned to have a glass of wine or two back at the hotel and think through the next steps in her Jimmy-Flora reconciliation plan. Because now that Lochmorehead was so central to the

Macallan matter, it would be silly if he didn't arrange to meet her at some point.

*\*\*\**

It was only quarter to five when she got back to the hotel, finding Jimmy and Frank already propping up the bar with pints in hand, in the company of a uniformed WPC who was sitting on a bar-stool drinking a mug of tea.

'Hi Maggie,' Frank said, beaming a smile. 'Great to see you. This is WPC McDonald, Lexy to her friends. Lexy, meet Maggie Bainbridge. She's a lawyer beneath the innocent disguise so be careful what you say.'

Maggie laughed. 'Nice to meet you Lexy, and as Frank well knows, I'm actually a lapsed lawyer.'

'Once a lawyer, always a lawyer,' he said. 'Anyway, can Jimmy get you a drink? Usual chardonnay, is it?'

'That would be nice. I'm just going to give Ollie a call and then I'll join you.' She smiled then slipped out to the reception area.

It was one of the downsides of the job, having to leave her adored little boy back in Hampstead with their Polish nanny, but Marta was an absolute gem and she knew he was being well cared for, both physically and spiritually. She called her home landline number and it was answered by her son almost before the first ring.

'*Mummy mummy,*' he yelled, his voice crackling with excitement, '*I've been picked for the football team. I've to play in a flat back four.*'

'That's amazing darling,' she said. 'It's a very important position I'm sure.' After the call she would ask Jimmy or Frank to explain to her what it meant, not that she was likely to understand any of it, if past experience was anything to go by.

'*The first game's on Tuesday. Will you come to watch? Please mummy, please.*'

She laughed. 'Of course I will, and I'm sure you'll score lots of goals.'

'*Defenders stop goals mummy, they don't score them. Except from set pieces,*' he said importantly. That would be another thing she would have to ask the Stewart brothers about. *Jimmy and Frank Stewart.* She'd known them barely two years and in that time they had become the most precious people in her life after her little boy and her mum and dad.

'I'll be back home in time for tea tomorrow darling,' she said. 'I can't wait to see you again.'

She heard his sigh of disappointment, guessing correctly what had prompted it. '*Marta said we could go to McDonalds mummy.*'

She laughed. 'Well that sounds like a very good idea. I'll be there too if there's room for me. Now go and have some tea and be good for Marta. And don't stay up too late. I love you darling.'

*'And I love you too mummy.'*

It made her feel so much better to hear Ollie's sweet voice, and again she marvelled at his resilience after all they'd been through together. Recently he'd began to speak of his father again and she was fine with that, because the last thing she wanted to do was air-brush him from Ollie's life. Philip had been a complete pig to her but he'd been a good dad, and she owed him some respect for that at least.

'Everything ok?' Jimmy asked as she returned to the bar. 'Your wine's waiting for you, by the way. Large one, of course.'

'Naturally,' she smiled. 'Yep, everything's great. So Frank, how have you got on today? You were going to Helensburgh Jimmy said. Wherever that is.'

'Nice wee seaside town,' he replied, 'and we got on no bad, no bad at all. But look, I didn't tell you guys the last time we met, but the case we're working on is the Morag McKay murder. Morag Robertson as was. It was the husband's sister we went to see. Jess Sinclair.'

She could see Jimmy tense up. 'Jesus Frank, that was a horrible thing, with the wee toddler being murdered as well. So why has it landed on your lap then?'

'Long story. The short version is, her man didn't do it. There was a forensics screw-up over the time of death and he was still two miles under the Atlantic when it actually happened.'

'And you're trying to find out what *did* happen?' Maggie asked.

Frank nodded. 'Indirectly. Our job is to see if there's enough evidence to open the case up again, but it'll be the local prosecutors who'll make the final call. The prevailing view amongst the brass is that it should stay firmly closed. Too many skeletons buried in too many cupboards.'

'And how's it looking?' Jimmy asked.

'Well funny you should ask,' he said, winking at Lexy, 'because I think you two might very well be able to help us with that.'

Maggie shot him a suspicious look. 'So is this why you got Jill Smart to authorise some budget for us?'

'Well, yes and no,' he said defensively. *'Then*, I didn't have anything specific in mind. Now I do.'

'So come on, are you going to tell us what you want us to do?' she asked.

'No,' he said, 'not until I clear it with Jill. But let's just say that pretty soon, you're going to get the chance to speak with Police Scotland's esteemed Chief Constable Sir Brian Pollock. And in the flesh too. In London.'

## Chapter 17

They'd had a great night in the Lochmorehead Hotel, he had to admit that. The food had been wonderful, a traditional Scottish menu but served with an international flair, and the drink flowed freely, though not for his brother's designated driver WPC McDonald, who had nonetheless not let her sobriety dampen her spirits. There were plenty of laughs, and for Jimmy, it had been brilliant to be in the relaxed company of two of his best mates in the whole world, even if one of them was his boss and one of them was his big brother. That was the thing he missed most since coming out of the army, the camaraderie, the bonding that only came from facing danger together and suffering terrible loss, yet somehow managing to come through it unscathed. Physically unscathed that was, because no one ever came through it mentally undamaged, no matter how much of a hard man you pretended to be. He'd come to learn there was really no such thing as bravery. It was just that some guys had been better at disguising their fear than others, and he had been one of them. *Brave guy that Captain Jimmy Stewart.* He knew people used to say that, but the appearance of bravery came with the territory when you were a bomb disposal officer. You knew very well that every mission could be your last, with a Taliban booby-trap waiting to blow you to bits, but it didn't stop you from doing your duty. *Brave guy that Captain Jimmy Stewart.* What a joke that was.

Because if he was so bloody brave, why was he continuing to bottle the big question that might finally end the burden of sadness that he carried with him every day of his life? *Flora, will you take me back?* Maggie, bless her, had steered clear of the subject during their visit, but had raised it on the flight back, with a gentle diplomacy he was grateful for.

'You were glad Flora was away in Glasgow, weren't you?' she had said. 'I could tell, and I don't blame you for that. But you'll have to face up to it *sometime*, don't you think? You can't put it off forever.'

And of course she was right, but that sometime didn't have to be right now. *Kick the can down the road.* That was the expression opposition politicians liked to use when they accused the government of deliberately delaying an important decision, and that was exactly what he was doing now. But what was the big brave soldier so afraid of, the bomb-squad veteran with a five-year stint in the Helmand hell-hole under his belt? He knew of course what it was. If Flora said no, that was it. *The end. Finito.* So who could blame him for kicking that bloody tin can down the road as far as it would bloody well go? Now, two days later and back in their Fleet Street office, he tried to push it all to the back of his mind as he and Maggie planned their next moves, case-wise.

'So this nanny, Susan McColl,' she said. 'I guess tracking her down needs to be our priority, but I'm not sure where we would start. Any ideas?'

'That shouldn't be too hard you know,' he said, thinking on his feet. 'From what my father-in-law told you, her husband served for a number of years at the Ardmore base, so his records will be online on the government website. It's pretty good, I've used it to track down a few of my old mates since I left the army. And failing that, there's any number of associations for old service personnel. We'll find him, don't you worry about that.'

She smiled. 'Sounds like a job for you then.'

'Aye, no bother, I'm on it.'

'And then there's Elspeth and the dinner date,' she said, giving him a wry look.

Yes, the bloody dinner date. He'd thought about it quite a lot, and the more he thought about it, the less he liked the prospect. His brief and fatal affair with the Swedish country singer Astrid Sorenson had taught him of the dangers of being in the public eye, and it wasn't exactly going to help his mission with Flora if he was photographed at some fashionable restaurant with the beautiful influencer Elspeth Macallan.

'Well boss, I've been thinking about this,' he said, pursing his lips. 'I'm not so sure it's a great idea to be honest.'

'Well it's up to you,' she said, 'and I won't push it, but it might help us with the matter quite a bit. And it's not as if you would be deceiving her after all. A date is just a date, it doesn't mean you're looking for anything else. And you can tell her everything of course, about Flora I mean. She'll appreciate your honesty I'm sure.'

He laughed. 'What, you mean the same honest Elspeth that might be lying about being the first-born twin?'

But when he thought about it some more, he realised she was probably right. He hadn't been on many first dates but he vaguely remembered that there was always that *tell me about yourself* moment. So fine, he would go on the date, and if and when it came up, he would tell her everything and that would all be very straightforward.

'Alright, you know what,' he continued, frowning. 'I'll do it. Take one for the team. *Again*.'

'And what about Kirsty?' Maggie said.

He grimaced. 'I'm not asking *her* out too, forget that. Besides, I don't think her husband would be too pleased.'

'I wasn't thinking that. What I mean is, are we just going to use Elspeth to find out which one of the twins has done a deal with Alison?'

'Aye,' he nodded. 'If she denies it, and it's odds-on she will, then I'm hoping I'll be able to tell if she's lying.' Inside, he wasn't so sure, but he would worry about that later. 'So what are you going to be doing whilst I'm doing all the work?'

'Me?' she grinned. 'I'm going to bunk off early to watch my son playing in a flat back four behind a diamond midfield.'

'I've always preferred the wing-back system myself,' he said, pleased to have left her mystified.

***

It hadn't been quite as easy to track down ex-Petty Officer Priest as he'd hoped it would be. It turned out that to get onto the Government Gateway website you needed an obscure layer of passwords and permissions that he didn't possess, and most of the paraphernalia involved in registering a new account was, for security reasons, delivered by post, meaning it would be at least seven working days and perhaps more before he could gain entry. So he texted an old army pal who had a desk job in the central payroll department, and whom he guessed would have access to all the service pension records, and wouldn't worry too much about data protection either. He'd received a prompt reply - *see what I can do mate,* with a thumbs-up - but four hours later he hadn't heard anything and he didn't like to push it. But then finally it came through. *Petty Officer J R Priest. 12 St Alban's Road, Winchester, Hants.* Nothing else. No phone numbers, no email, but he wasn't really surprised. After all, names and addresses were in the public domain, you only had to check the Electoral Register so no data protection issues, but emails in particular were a different kettle of fish. A quick google and a browse of a couple of telephone directory sites didn't help. If he wanted to speak with the Priests, he was going to have to jump on a train.

He looked at his watch. *Five twenty-five.* He could be at Waterloo in twenty minutes and then it was about an hour and a half's journey and then no more than fifteen minutes' walk. All being well, he'd be on their doorstep at about half past seven, still pretty civilised for most people. Of course, they might not be in, but he could leave a note through their door asking him to contact him. It was a bit impulsive, he knew that, but wasn't that what private investigators were meant to do, dashing all over the place chasing up leads?

The rush-hour train was packed to the rafters, meaning that he and about two hundred other poor sods had to stand all the way, only the fact that he wasn't paying five grand a year for the privilege offering any consolation. The Priests semi-detached home was on a quiet estate, the architecture betraying its ex-council history, although the well-maintained appearance of both theirs and the neighbouring properties suggested they had long since passed into private ownership. He double-checked the address then jogged up the slabbed path to their door. He was just about to ring the bell when he noticed them, strung out along the inner window-sill of what he guessed was the living room. A row of greeting cards, maybe for someone's birthday or perhaps it was the Priests' wedding anniversary. But seared in his mind was a memory of an occasion back in his army days when he'd paid a sympathy visit to the parents of one of his men killed in action. The same row of cards, the same messages. *Deepest sympathies. Our thoughts are with you. We are so sorry for your loss.*

He rang the bell and a few seconds later the door opened. John Priest was short but powerfully-built, shaven-headed and wearing jeans and a black singlet that displayed the faded tattoos that decorated each arm from wrist to shoulder. To Jimmy, everything about him shouted ex-navy. An aging Popeye the Sailor-Man in the flesh, here in Winchester, more than fifty miles from the sea. He wondered if Susan Priest might look like Olive Oyl. But then the obvious struck him. All these cards, and John Priest standing here in front of him. It must have been Mrs Priest who had died. *This could be difficult.*

'Yeah, what do you want?' Priest said brusquely, a suspicious look on his face.

'Petty Officer Priest? I'm Captain Jimmy Stewart, ex-bomb squad.' There was a mutual respect between military personnel that survived long beyond their service days, and it was something worth using whenever you could. He saw Priest's expression soften into a mildly inquisitive look.

'I work for a firm of private investigators now...' Before he could say any more, the other man interrupted him.

'So how'd you find out about it?'

Jimmy gave a puzzled look. 'Sorry, I'm not with you.'

'My Susan's accident. The hit and run, at least that's what the police are calling it. How'd you find out?'

'Hit and run? I'm so sorry Mr Priest, I really didn't know anything about that.'

'So if you're not here to offer your services, what do you want then?' The brusque manner had returned, and he held on tightly to the door, as if uncertain whether he should let this stranger come in.

'I'd come to ask your wife about her time when she was nanny to the Macallan children,' Jimmy said, 'but look, I can see this probably isn't a good time...'

'Bloody hell, not you too.' Priest spat the words out. 'I'm bloody sick of hearing that name.'

'Look, I'm sorry,' Jimmy said again, 'but maybe if I could just come in for five minutes? I know how you must be feeling, and if it helps to talk about it, well you know...' He hoped Priest would recognise his genuine sincerity. Because he did know how it felt to lose someone. He'd known too many of them, good blokes and brave women, taken away much too early by a savage war they had no business being involved in, and every one of them leaving an indelible mark on his life.

Priest thought about it for a moment before acceding.

'Yeah all right.' He led Jimmy through to a neatly-furnished living room, one wall dominated by a long black leather sofa.

'Take a pew,' Priest said, picking up the remote and muting the television.

'You were at Ardmore base weren't you John?' Jimmy asked, making conversation.

'Yeah I was. Did a couple of years on the subs but then my ears went all up the creek with the air pressure and all that, so they gave me the stores job. That's when I met my Susan. Do you know the place yourself mate?'

Jimmy nodded. 'Aye, a bit. My ex-wife was brought up in Lochmorehead.' It hurt him just to say the words. *My ex-wife.* But then she wasn't his ex-wife, not yet. Not in his mind at least.

'So my Susan would have known her then?'

'Aye, I expect she would have. Flora McLeod she was then. She was friends with the twins when they were kids. But look, that's not important right now.' Lowering his voice he continued, 'Are you able to talk about what happened John? Only if it helps.'

Priest nodded, his expression bereft of emotion. 'It was just two weeks ago. There's a row of shops just round the corner and I'd sent her up there to get me some ciggies.'

Jimmy noted the casual misogyny, causing him to wonder what sort of life Susan Priest had had since leaving Scotland. Pretty shit was his assumption.

'Nobody really saw nothing, but that's what they're like round there, they ain't going to say nothing to no coppers. I've asked a few questions myself and all I know is it was one of them little hatchbacks, black or dark blue I think, like a Golf or a Focus or something. Came screaming round the corner and mounted the pavement in front of the shops. Killed instantly she was, and now I don't know what I'm going to do without her.'

'I'm so sorry for your loss,' Jimmy said, reflecting not for the first time how inadequate these six words were.

Priest shrugged. 'Yeah, well it's happened and we just have to get on with it don't we?' It sounded cold, but Jimmy recognised it for the coping mechanism it was. 'But you say you're a private eye? So can you help me find the toe-rags what done this?'

'It's not really our line of work John,' Jimmy said, shaking his head, 'but we do have some police contacts so I can ask if they could take a look if you like.' He wasn't sure if this one was too current to fall within the remit of Frank's cold-case-focussed Department 12B, but there would be no harm in asking.

'Yeah that would be good,' Priest replied. 'That would be good.'

They fell into a silence which for several seconds Jimmy didn't feel as if he should break. But finally he said, 'Would it be ok if we talked about the Macallans for a moment? You see, I'm working for the executors of their father's estate, that's why I'm here. Your late wife was the twins' nanny from just after they were born right up until they were four or five. Until Commodore Macallan re-married I believe?'

'Yeah, that's right. That's why she was being bothered by all this business, ain't it?'

'What do you mean, all this business?'

Priest gave a knowing smile. 'Well, it was all kicking off wasn't it? She'd read about that dispute between the twins in the paper, that's what I thinks. Tried to hide it from me of course, what she was doing and all that, but I found out. My Susan couldn't hide nothing from me, know what I mean?'

I know what you mean all right, Jimmy thought, recognising a bully when he saw one. And at that moment, he began to form a picture in his mind of what might have happened. Susan Priest's testimony could be crucial in establishing which of the twins was the elder, a testimony that could be worth millions for the parties involved. Maybe Mrs Priest saw her chance, to make a bit of money that would enable her escape from her sterile life and her controlling husband. And maybe someone didn't like the way that was going and decided she'd be better off dead.

'So was Susan approached by one of the Macallan twins do you think?' Jimmy asked.

'Nah', he shrugged. 'It was *her* approached one of them, that's what I think happened. After reading it in the paper, like I said. You see, my Susan obviously knew the truth, didn't she? She'd looked after them since they was babies, so she was bound to, wasn't she? And then of course the bloody stepmother turned up.'

'Alison Macallan came here?' Jimmy couldn't hide his surprise.

'Yeah she did. Bold as brass. Said she wanted to catch up on old times but I knew that was a load of bollocks. I mean, who drives six hundred miles just to do that, especially in a rackety old motor like hers? So after she left, I asked Susan what it was all about and she told me Alison wanted to know if Susan had spoke to anyone about the situation. And that's when it all came out that my bloody wife had been talking to one of them twins behind my back. That disappointed me, I don't mind telling you, the stupid cow.'

So it hadn't taken long for the mask to slip. *Never speak ill of the dead.* Obviously Priest had never heard the maxim before, or of he had, he had no time for it.

'So which one was she in contact with?' Jimmy asked. 'Elspeth or Kirsty?'

'Elspeth, Kirsty, how the hell should I know?' he sneered. 'They're twins, ain't they? And would you believe she wouldn't tell me, the selfish cow?'

No, she wouldn't, Jimmy thought. If a Macallan was prepared to pay handsomely to buy the support of the nanny who had cared for the twins since birth, and that providing that service would pay for her ticket out of her miserable existence, a despised husband would be the last person she would tell.

But now he surmised there wasn't much more he could accomplish here. Smiling, he got to his feet and said, 'It's been very helpful John, and once again, I'm sorry for your loss. As I said, I'll have a word with my contact in the Met and see if there's anything more can be done about the hit and run. And if you think of anything else, I'll leave you a card with my number.'

Suddenly Priest said, 'Well as a matter of fact, there *was* something else. Just before my Susan was killed, some scumbag called me out of the blue, and asked me if we knew anything about the will and who was the oldest girl and all that. Said he could make it worth my while. But then I asked him how much and he said that would depend on the quality of the information we had. I didn't like his tone, so I told him to sling his hook.'

'So who was this guy, did he say?' Jimmy asked, already suspecting the answer would be no.

'Nah. He just said he was ex-Navy like me, but a bit after my time. He'd been on the subs too, according to him.'

'But no name?'

Priest shrugged again. 'Nope, never said nothing. But there was one thing.'

'What?' Jimmy said, narrowing his eyes.

'The guy was a Geordie, no doubt about it. Accent as thick as a brick.'

***

The return journey gave Jimmy plenty of time to reflect on the interesting developments of the last half-hour. Independently, it seemed that at least two of the parties in the Macallan affair had realised the value of having Susan Priest on their side, and he wondered if she, displaying the canniness that was the hallmark of the Scottish stereotype, had played one off against the other, anxious to secure a life-changing financial settlement for herself. And what of the mysterious man from Newcastle who'd appeared from nowhere offering to do a deal? How did he fit in to the picture? And of course, there was the biggest question of all to be addressed. Was the hit and run death of Mrs Susan Priest really an accident?

Thank goodness tomorrow night was pub night, when there would be a chance to run it all past Frank to see what he made of it.

But for now it was clear they were going to have to put some awkward questions to all of the Macallan women. Maggie was scheduled to visit Kirsty and Rory Overton again, so that was covered, and she would also probably be willing to tackle Alison Macallan too. Which just left Elspeth, and one more compelling reason why he really needed to take up that dinner offer with her.

With some reluctance he slipped his phone from his pocket and dialled her number. From her voice, he could tell she was very pleased to hear from him.

# Chapter 18

He found three high stools alongside the narrow shelf that ran three-quarters of the way around the bar-room, not the most comfortable accommodation but all that was available. Normally the three of them liked to keep the conversation light on their Thursday evening get-togethers, but this evening there was a lot to catch up on case-wise, and for Frank, work had always come first. *All work and no play makes Frank a dull boy*. That old cliché could have been invented for him. It wasn't as if he was unhappy, although his life outside of work was, he had to face it, non-existent, if you didn't count the Friday night takeaway curry and on-demand movie that was the highlight of his weekend. But there was an emptiness that he was beginning to feel more and more, a feeling that was escalating pretty much in parallel with his stupid day-dreams of a life with Maggie Bainbridge. And here it was, another Thursday night. Or more accurately, another would-he-or-wouldn't-he-ask-her-out Thursday night.

As usual he'd got there first, at five-twenty on the dot which was ten minutes ahead of the scheduled start time, and as usual he'd equipped himself with a pint of Doom Bar, which as usual, he had more or less drained by the time Maggie and Jimmy arrived.

'Good to see you guys,' he boomed over the background hubbub of conversation. He shook his glass in Jimmy's direction.

'Aye I know, it's my round,' Jimmy said with a brief nod of the head. 'As usual.'

Maggie peeled off her coat and clambered up onto a stool.

'Good to see you again Frank. Been busy I guess?'

'Well you know,' he smiled. 'Lots going on but all early days.'

'Same with us. Except there's been some big news on the Macallan inheritance. Maybe I should let Jimmy tell you when he gets back.'

'And on that subject,' Frank said, lowering his voice, 'did he try and see Flora when he was up there? He's keeping it to himself if he did. He hasn't said a word to me.'

She shook her head. 'No, she was away, but to be honest I think he was glad. Between you and me, I think he would have bottled it if she *had* been around.'

Frank allowed himself a wry smile. He knew all about bottling it, but maybe, just maybe, tonight would be different. For a second it crossed his mind to ask her right now, whilst his brother was at the bar, but then thought better of it. Wait until he'd had another pint or two, ramp up the Dutch courage a notch and then go for it. That was the plan, if you could call it that.

Jimmy arrived back with the drinks and carefully laid them out on the shelf.

'Cheers guys,' he said, picking up his pint, 'and here's to success.'

'Aye, here's hoping,' Frank smiled. 'So this Macallan inheritance business. Tell me all.'

Jimmy nodded. 'Well let's just say it's all got a bit more serious. There's been another death, and there's every chance it's murder. That's just my opinion of course and right now it's not shared by the local cops.'

'What?' Frank said, sounding surprised. 'So who's been killed?'

'Susan Priest, the twins' old nanny. It was a hit and run and the Hampshire police seem to be treating it as a dangerous driving case, rather than a deliberate act. But get this. Before she died, Mrs Priest had been in touch with one of the twins. And not only that, the stepmother had paid her a visit too.'

'And now she's dead,' Frank said. 'That's quite a development.'

'Aye that's what we thought,' Jimmy said, 'so we wondered if you might be able to take a look at it?'

Frank furrowed his brow. 'Well, it's not really my jurisdiction, but maybe I can get Ronnie French to give the Hampshire boys a call, let them into a bit of the background.'

'That would be a great help,' Maggie said, smiling. 'The trouble is, I feel we've gone backwards with the case if anything. I'm going to have one last go at Kirsty and her caveman husband and see if they know anything. And obviously, I'm still trying to persuade them to accept a deal, although I don't hold out much hope. Then Jimmy's going to try and smooth-talk Elspeth Macallan into accepting a settlement too. Otherwise it will have to be sorted out in front of a magistrate.'

Frank laughed. 'Smooth-talk did you say? Well that's not going to work is it? Because I've never heard smooth-talking and my brother being mentioned in the same sentence before.'

Jimmy didn't seem unduly upset by the barb. 'Fair point bruv, but when you're working for a boss like mine, you do what you're told. It's worse than being in the army.'

'I can't see how it'll be that horrible,' Frank grinned. 'From what I've seen, Elspeth's a good-looking girl and she's probably rich enough to pick up the tab too.'

'Well why don't *you* do it then and I'll sort out your Ardmore murders. Fair swap?'

'Boys boys, stop your squabbling please,' Maggie said, laughing. 'I'm sure Jimmy will have a lovely time and his boyish good looks and charm will soon get to the truth.'

'Aye, that's right Maggie,' Jimmy said, nodding at his brother. 'It's just a pity it doesn't run in the family. But anyway, it's too late mate. I've already made a date, it's all arranged. I've to pick her up at her place on Saturday and then we're going to some fancy restaurant just up the road.'

Frank shrugged. 'Aye, well that's all good. But I should say, it's way over-rated, that boyish good looks and charm stuff, so it is. That's what I've found at least.'

But deep down, he wished nature had equipped him with at least a small dollop of either. Because one or the other might be useful for what he was planning later that evening. If he didn't bottle it, that was. He looked down at his glass and saw it was still three-quarters full. Ten seconds later, it wasn't.

'Another drink folks?' he said. Just as he was about to set off for the bar, Maggie said,

'Jimmy, what about that other thing? You know, the guy who called up the Priests offering to cut them in on some sort of deal.'

'Oh aye, the Geordie guy do you mean?'

And as he said it, there occurred what could only be described as a simultaneous light-bulb moment. Geordie. *Of course.*

'Bloody hell, you don't think they're connected do you?' Jimmy said, addressing his brother. 'Your hacker and this bloke who called the Priests?'

Frank gave a dismissive smile. 'What, with about half a million Newcastle lads to pick from and this one random guy happens to be *our* man? Doesn't seem likely, does it? But what you have done has given me another clue in the search for him. Because to be honest, and I'm embarrassed to say this, I hadn't considered that Geordie the hacker might be an actual Geordie, if you get my drift. Something to mention to wee Eleanor I think. So cheers for that. And on that note...'

He rolled off towards the bar without waiting for a reaction. For once, there wasn't a queue and his rolled-up twenty-pound note succeeded in catching the attention of a sullen-faced barmaid.

'Yes?' she said with a distinct absence of charm.

'Two Doom Bars, a large chardonnay and a wee triple whisky. That's three shots in a glass if you've not heard of it before, and Bells will do fine if you've got it.'

'We've got Teachers,' she said, turning her back on him. Listlessly she began to assemble his order, a process she evidently meant to string out as far as possible. It was getting on for five minutes when she eventually returned.

'Twenty-three thirty-five,' she said, fixing him with a mirthless stare.

'Christ, I should have taken out a mortgage,' he said, fumbling in his pocket for some coins.

The barmaid gave no response, he assuming it wasn't the first time she'd heard the jibe. He left the note and a pile of pound coins on the bar and told her to keep the change, which caused no improvement in her demeanour. Sneaking a furtive glance over his shoulder, he downed the whisky in one before heading back to the others with the drinks. Fortification for what lay ahead.

'Cheers brother,' Jimmy said, raising his glass. 'Nice one.'

'Yes, thank you Frank,' Maggie said, flashing him a smile, getting him thinking that maybe the good looks and charm were working after all. 'And what about your graffiti guy? I've not heard you mentioning how you were getting on with the search.'

He smiled. 'I'm just leaving all of that to wee Eleanor Campbell at the moment. She said she was getting close last time I spoke, but I've not heard anything since. But that reminds me. Did I tell you that our Geordie-boy did another one of his wee paintings about a week ago?

Some place down in Fulham, Clonmel Road I think it was called.'

'Hang on a minute,' Jimmy said, sounding surprised. 'That's where Kirsty Macallan lives with her husband. You don't know what the number was by any chance?'

'Not off the top of my head, but I can easily find out. But Christ, wouldn't it be interesting if the Macallans were the target? But no, it couldn't be, that would be mental.'

'I don't see why not,' Maggie said, 'because from what you told me, he targets people in the public eye. And both Kirsty and her husband qualify on that score.'

Frank gave her a doubtful look. 'Well I suppose so, but I don't really believe in coincidences. But maybe that's another one for my mate Ronnie French to check out. You never know.'

He saw Maggie glimpsing at her watch. Frank knew her routine off by heart now on these Thursday meet-ups. Two large glasses of chardonnay would take her through to quarter-to-seven, at which point she began to think about leaving, so that she would be back in Hampstead in good time to read her little boy his bedtime story. And quite naturally she was not going to allow herself to be late for that, meaning that the ask-her-out-window extended to no more than five or ten minutes, a window that he had thus far failed to take advantage of. But it was only twenty-to, so there was still plenty of time.

When he'd come in, he'd noticed the group of football fans clustered around a table in the corner, each attired in current-season replica shirts, shirts that would have cost them over eighty quid a pop from the club shop up at the Emirates. Arsenal were in Thursday-night Europa League action, a bit of a comedown for a club with such a solid Champions League heritage, but even this Mickey-Mouse competition made a good night out for the faithful. Without knowing why, he'd mentally kept tabs of their frequent trips to the bar, and now reckoned they were each five to six pints to the good. At that level of inebriation, there was every chance that some of them would be barred from entering the stadium, not that it bothered Frank. What did bother him was that with his policeman's nose for trouble, he could smell something brewing. Or more accurately, he could *hear* something brewing. Because when you heard a glass smash in a bar and nobody then said sorry and started asking for a brush and dustpan, you knew something was going to kick off. And this one, from what he had just picked up, had nothing to do with football.

'You been shagging my missus? Have you, you bastard?'

The man was about thirty, six-two in height and broad with it, with closely-cropped hair and a prominent tattoo on his neck that proclaimed his allegiance to his football club. He was holding the shattered glass with its jagged edge less than a centimetre from the face of another man, whose short and slim physique was no match for that of the complainant, even if he'd had the chance to put up a fight. Plainly terrified, he was protesting his innocence.

'No mate, that's bollocks. I swear it on my granddad's grave. Honest mate, I wouldn't do nothing like that. Honest I wouldn't.'

It didn't seem to have convinced his accuser. 'You're a fucking lying toe-rag Vince, and I'm going to rip your pretty face to shreds, see if I don't. And then we'll see how you get on with the ladies, won't we?'

Frank gave a deep sigh and fumbled in his pocket for his warrant card. It was just his bloody luck that it was happening this night of all nights, and that the antagonist was such a man-mountain of a guy. But duty was duty. *Worst luck.*

'Don't move you two,' he barked at Maggie and Jimmy. 'And call 999.' He strode purposefully towards the group of fans, thrusting his card out in front of him as he reached them.

'Ok, I'm the police,' he shouted, 'so boys, let's just calm it down a bit, shall we?'

The man with the glass spun his head around to face him, still with the jagged edge pushed into the other man's face.

'Sod off cop, I've got unfinished business here,' he snarled.

Frank gave him a sardonic look. 'Aye, well you just finish it off and you'll be looking at fifteen or twenty years. That's a lot of games you'll miss. Mind you, maybe that's no bad thing, given how crap you're playing at the moment.'

The man, still looking at Frank, pushed the glass forward and twisted it, this time drawing blood. He heard the other man give a gasp of pain as he raised a hand up towards the wound.

'Look, last warning pal,' Frank said, his voice remaining calm and steady. 'Put the glass down and we can just forget all about this. Because otherwise, you're in the deepest of deep shit. Last chance. Come on, put the glass down.'

'He's going to pay for what he's done, understand?' the man said, but this time there was an uncertainty in his voice.

'That sounds like a line from a bad movie,' Frank said, laughing. 'Come on pal, no woman's worth doing fifteen years for. And there's plenty more fish in the sea, you just need to look around this place. Lovely women as far as the eye can see.'

After he said it, he realised he could have chosen his words more carefully. But quite by accident it had the desired effect.

'What are you saying about my missus?' he screamed, now thrusting the glass in Frank's direction. The other man, seizing his opportunity, sprinted towards the door, dripping blood across the floor. 'She's a darling, she is.'

Not enough of a darling to stay faithful, was the first thought that sprang to mind, but this time he decided to keep his counsel. In any case, it was a bit hard to speak with a glass shoved against your throat.

'Look come on pal, this is your last chance,' Frank croaked. 'Put the glass down and I won't even take your name. And remember, my mates from Paddington Green nick will be swarming through that door in a minute, and they won't be so accommodating. So come on, put it down.'

Frank didn't see his brother approaching them from across the bar. All he was conscious of was something crashing into him, something that left him sprawled on his back on the floor and about four metres from where he had just stood. Dazed, he pushed himself up to see Jimmy face-to-face with the hooligan, his fists poised in front of him like an old-school Victorian prize boxer.

'Well come on pal, if you're hard enough,' he was saying, his tone menacing. 'Fancy it, do you? Well do you?'

***

*'If you're hard enough*?' Frank laughed. 'Did I actually hear you say that? Who do you think you are, Clint Eastwood or something?'

'Well cheers mate,' Jimmy said, giving him an indignant look. 'What about thanks for saving my life brother? I think that would be a bit more appropriate. And what about my rugby tackle? A beauty, wasn't it? Took you right out, clean as a whistle.'

'Yes it was and it did,' Frank conceded, 'and thanks.' He tried not to make it sound too grudging.

The uniforms had now turned up and were taking statements from the Arsenal contingent, who all claimed to have seen nothing and were complaining loudly that they would miss the kick-off if the police didn't get a move on. The wronged husband was in handcuffs and was facing a charge of assaulting a police officer, if Frank could be bothered to fill in the paperwork. And Maggie was pulling on her coat, anxious to get back to her little boy, now that it was clear that both friends had emerged unscathed from their encounters.

Frank swore under his breath, as he realised his plans were wrecked for another bloody week. In his pocket, he felt his phone vibrate. Slipping it out, he saw it was a text from Eleanor Campbell.

*Good news :-) finally worked out how to track down Geordie. Way cool. Bad news :-( it can't be done. Will (try to) explain when you're back in the office x*

He had no idea what she meant, but maybe the evening hadn't been such a disaster after all. And at least he was going to see Maggie Bainbridge again soon. In fact barely fifteen hours from now by his uncertain calculation.

## Chapter 19

They didn't normally frequent the Old King's Head in working hours, but Frank had arranged the meeting there so naturally they went along with it. This time, it wouldn't be just the three of them either, as today they were being joined by Yash Patel of the *Chronicle*. Maggie and Jimmy had bumped into him a few times on previous cases and shared the same opinion of him. Really nice guy, but in spite of the reverence for older generations that was such a credit to his culture, he would sell his own granny for a story. Probably already had, several times over, Jimmy had once commented. All they knew was that his presence had something to do with Frank's Brian Pollock affair, and that what he wanted them to do was slightly dodgy. On entering the familiar establishment, they were pleased to find that not only were Frank and Patel already there, but the drinks were already on the table, Maggie suspecting they would have been taken care of on a *Chronicle* expense account.

'Hi guys,' Frank said raising his glass. 'You know Yash, don't you? I assumed a large chardonnay and a Doom Bar by the way, hope that's ok.'

Maggie gave him a knowing smile in acknowledgement of the events of the previous evening then said, 'Great, and hi Yash, good to see you again.'

She noticed that Patel was carrying a large padded black bag which was slung over his shoulder on a robust strap. A bag that bore an instantly-recognisable logo. *Canon*. Curious that.

'Yeah, great to see you guys again too,' he said, bubbling with his customary enthusiasm. 'This is going to be an absolutely *top* story, don't you think? Wicked.'

Jimmy took a slurp of his pint and frowned. 'No idea mate. My brother's been a bit sparing with the info thus far.'

'Aye, well I'll bring you up to date now,' Frank said. 'Let's just say it's a wee undercover job for you two.'

'And it's dodgy,' Maggie said. 'You said that too.'

'Aye, a bit, but you'll not be in any danger or anything like that. Just a wee bit of subterfuge, that's all.'

'So come on then,' Jimmy said. 'Clue us in.'

'Aye, all right then,' Frank said. 'So I talked to Yash here about what's going on with the Ardmore murders and the screw-up with the forensics and everything. And obviously about Pollock's role in the whole thing.'

'This story's got absolutely everything,' Patel said, his eyes gleaming. 'The gory murders, the little girl victim, the wrong guy gets locked up then goes and kills himself, the screw-up by the senior investigating officer who now happens to be the Chief Constable. I mean, shit, my editor thinks he's died and gone to heaven, he really does.'

'And another wee award beckons for you Yash my boy?' Frank said.

'Yeah, I've already written the headline,' Patel laughed. '*How top cop crashed and burned - a Chronicle exclusive.* Sounds sweet, don't you think?'

Maggie gave Frank a sharp look. 'I'm sorry, but how do we fit into all of this?'

Patel reached into an inside pocket of his jacket and withdrew what looked like several pages torn from a magazine, then unfolded them and spread them out on the table.

'This is the puff piece,' he said, pointing to the headline printed above a large photograph of Sir Brian Pollock in his Chief Constable's uniform. '*The rise of a policing superstar.* Good, eh?'

'Puff piece?' Maggie said, looking puzzled. 'I've heard the expression but I'm not sure what it means.'

'Think of it as bait,' he said. 'When we request an interview, we send them this mock-up of what the final article might look like. It's all twaddle, puffing up their reputation and saying how wonderful they are. Hence the name. It's designed to hook them in, and it never fails, especially with someone with as high opinion of himself as Pollock.'

Maggie raised an eyebrow in Jimmy's direction and gave a discreet smile. She guessed he was thinking the same as her. *Takes one to know one.*

'And nobody ever looks at the small print,' Patel continued, 'which says we reserve the right to write anything we damn well like.'

'I get that I think,' Maggie said, 'but sorry to sound like a broken record. I still don't get what you want us to do.'

'You're going to interview him for the Chronicle,' Frank said, smirking. 'Yash has got it all arranged. Pollock will be down in London tomorrow for some Chief Constable's bash and you'll be seeing him at three o' clock. All you need to do is decide who's going to be the journalist and who's going to be the photographer.'

'Yeah, all arranged,' Patel nodded. 'I've squared it all away with my editor.' He fumbled in another pocket for a second or two. 'Here, we've got you a couple of fake press passes, and actually Maggie, you'll have to be the journo I'm afraid. You're going to be Caroline Watts, if you don't mind.'

'Who's she?' Maggie asked, 'or is she made up?'

'No she's real enough,' Patel said, 'but nobody's ever heard of her. She's a freelancer that we use occasionally. Nice girl, but not much of a writer.'

'Well that shouldn't be too difficult for me then,' Maggie said, smiling. She examined the pass he'd given her. 'No photograph on it?'

'Don't need it, not on the Chronicle's passes at least. Never have done. And Jimmy, you're going to be Robert Watts the photographer, no relation. And he's not very well known either.'

'Unlike you, Yash mate,' Frank laughed. 'Everybody's heard of you.'

'Yeah probably,' he said, making no attempt at modesty, 'and that's why we need you guys. I'm very well-known as a top investigative journalist you see, so if I turned up he would smell a rat. Whereas you two will just be a couple of freelance features guys with the Saturday magazine, doing a nice light piece for the weekend readers.'

Maggie allowed herself a wry smile. Clearly in the newspaper trade, the freelance features guy was bottom of the food chain.

'Well I suppose it shouldn't be that hard,' she said doubtfully, 'but I still don't get what we're supposed to say to him.'

'That's easy,' Frank said. 'You butter him up for ten minutes then you say that your editor would be looking for some balance in the article.'

'That's right,' Patel agreed. 'You ask him if he can think of an occasion in his career when things maybe didn't go quite so well.'

'Aye,' Frank said, 'and if he can't think of anything, and I would put money on the fact that he won't, then that's when you bring up the Ardmore murders. Drop it in nice and casual.'

'You mean light the blue touch-paper,' Maggie said.

'Exactly.'

Jimmy grinned. 'Well, the mission's clear enough to me and it looks like all I have to do is carry that camera bag. Easy. And then maybe I might be able to fit in a couple of wedding before I hand it back. There's real money in them.'

\*\*\*

The conference venue was the London Hilton on Park Lane, a location that Maggie and Jimmy knew quite well from a previous case. She found it a rather surprising choice, imagining that such a high-profile gathering would take place in a secure government building somewhere surrounded by armed guards. Instead the atmosphere was relaxed, the double-doored entrance to the conference suite guarded only by two smartly-dressed young women sitting at a desk who were ticking off delegates and their invited guests against a computer-printed list.

Maggie wandered up to one of them, wrinkling her nose as she tried to remember their pseudonyms.

'Caroline Watts from the Chronicle. I'm here to interview Chief Constable Pollock. And this is our photographer Robert Watts. And no relation, before you ask,' she added, smiling.

The young woman flicked over a couple of pages of her list until she found their names, giving a nod of recognition before scoring them through with a ruler and ballpoint.

'And do you have ID?' she asked.

Maggie handed over the press passes and watched as the woman gave them a cursory glance.

'They're fine. Sir Brian is in conference at the moment but if you'd like to go through to the exhibition area and wait I'm sure he'll be able to find you.'

It was a large room, brightly illuminated by the sunlight streaming through the picture windows that made up an entire wall. Along both sides were a series of small pop-up trade stands populated by smartly-dressed men and women of eager demeanour, most clutching glossy flyers which they were anxious to thrust into the hands of unsuspecting passers-by.

'Brochure sir?' An attractive brunette stepped in front of them, directing her attention solely at Jimmy.

'Aye ok,' he said pleasantly. 'What's it for?'

'It's roster planning software sir. We're Heartworks, I expect you've heard of us? Our software's installed in over forty forces around the country. We're the market leader in the UK.'

'Good to know,' he said, Maggie smiling as she recognised one of his brother's favourite phrases, 'but I'm just a photographer so I'll not be buying any software any time soon. Sorry.'

He handed back the brochure with an apologetic look. It did not seem to upset the brunette, who shot him a rather too familiar smile before retreating to her stand.

'When are we due to see Pollock?' Jimmy asked.

'Five minutes. I guess that must be when the next break is. Come on, let's go and grab a coffee before the rush,' she said, pointing to a table alongside another set of double doors that presumably led into the conference room proper.

A few minutes later the doors opened and the delegates surged into the exhibition room in search of refreshment. These were the brass, as Frank disparagingly called then, and today each one of them was dressed true to type, attired in their formal uniforms with the shiny buttons and epaulettes, although they looked more silvery than brassy in Maggie's eyes. He had told them that ACC Katherine Frost would be in attendance, she of the home-made porno movies, and that they should look out for her, just for their amusement if nothing else, which she thought was a bit cruel. Nonetheless she found herself scanning the room, and as coincidence would have it, found Frost standing in the refreshment queue talking to none other than Sir Brian Pollock. Maggie nudged Jimmy in the ribs and pointed her head in their direction.

'Wonder what they're talking about,' Jimmy said, grinning. 'Maybe she's offering him a part in her next film.'

'Come on,' she said, grabbing him by the arm, 'let's go and introduce ourselves.' Assuming she could remember who she was supposed to be, that was.

Brian Pollock was not a tall man, no more than five foot seven or eight, and not much older than herself she guessed, with greying hair and a neat goatee beard. She wondered when it was decided that brains rather than physical stature should become the main attribute for a career in the force. Frank had told her that he had been one of the first to come through Strathclyde Police's fast-track graduate scheme, and there was considerable prejudice against him in the rank and file as a result, although he had phrased it rather more colourfully. *It's because the guy's a complete wanker.* She remembered that Katherine Frost was also a fast-track entrant, wondering if everybody in the room had followed the same route to the top. Judging from their relative youth, she guessed they had.

'Chief Constable Pollock, I'm sorry to interrupt but I guess you're working to a tight schedule. I'm Caroline Watts with the Chronicle and this is my photographer Robert. You remember we've got an appointment.'

He turned and smiled to his companion. 'Yes sorry Katherine, but I've got a date with the national press. Let's catch up later shall we?'

'Actually Robert,' Maggie said, looking at Jimmy and furrowing her brow, 'an informal shot or two in this room might be quite good before we start. Perhaps one here with your colleague, would that be ok Sir Brian?'

He shrugged and gave a smile. 'Yes, I'm sure that would be fine. What do you think Katherine? Fancy getting your face in the papers?'

Maggie caught Jimmy's eye, assuming he was thinking the same thing. *Probably the last thing ACC Katherine Frost wants is to get her face or any other part of her anatomy in the papers.* But she seemed more than happy to go along with it.

'Yes, sure Brian, that's ok. Just let me fix my hair first.'

Maggie smiled. No-one would call Frost an attractive woman, with plain features and a bony frame that made her uniform look ill-fitting, but everyone wanted to look their best for a photograph. She whipped a small folding brush out of her bag and quickly dragged it through her cropped hair. It didn't seem to make much difference.

Maggie saw Jimmy had succeeded in removing the SLR camera from the bag and was now holding it against his chest, staring down at the large viewfinder.

*Just point and shoot*, she remembered Yash telling him, *and just don't forget to switch it on.* She wondered if she ought to remind him.

'Yeah, that's good,' he said, not looking up, 'and don't look at the camera folks please. We'll just get a couple of natural conversational shots. Yeah, that's good... hold it... yeah, got it. Thanks a lot.'

Maggie smiled at Frost. 'We'll just caption you as a colleague in the article, unless you want to be named of course?'

It seemed that she did.

'I'm Assistant Chief Constable Katherine Frost of Greater Manchester Police. Do you need to write that down?'

'No, I'll remember,' Maggie replied, catching Jimmy's eye.

'Right then, let's do this thing,' Pollock said pleasantly. 'I expect we can find a quiet spot in the conference room. The do's not due to restart until quarter-to.'

They went through to the adjacent room, empty except for a few stragglers, and arranged three of the chairs in a circle of about two metres in diameter.

*They're generally pretty relaxed for these kind of sessions*, Yash had advised. *They're expecting a pleasant half hour talking about how brilliant they are. Everybody likes that, don't they? That's the atmosphere you're looking to create.* She decided to take his advice.

'I obviously did quite a bit of research before I wrote my outline,' she gushed, 'and I must confess, I didn't realise you were so young. You must be one of the youngest Chief Constables in the country, aren't you? At forty-four.'

'Forty-three actually. And yes, I actually *am* the youngest I believe, and the youngest ever of any force in Scotland.'

'That's amazing,' she said, nodding enthusiastically. 'By the way, I hope you don't mind if we publish your age in the article? It's the first thing our readers look for. Everyone's interested in that, aren't they?'

'No, go ahead, of course,' he said, making no attempt to hide his self-satisfaction.

Rustling through her handbag, she withdrew the folded magazine pages that Yash had given her, expertly mocked up by the Chronicle's graphics department. *The puff piece.*

'You saw this I'm guessing? Did you like it?'

'I liked the headline,' he said, smiling, 'although I'm not sure all of my colleagues would necessarily agree.' By his tone, she guessed that wouldn't concern him one bit.

'*The rise of a policing superstar. New broom shakes up Scottish force.* That pretty much sums up what you're all about, doesn't it?'

'Well I'm not so sure about the superstar thing,' he said, 'but let's just say since I moved to headquarters I've tried to put my stamp on things. More diversity, softening the culture and making it more customer-friendly.'

She wasn't sure whether the customers he was referring to were the members of the public or the villains who found themselves forced to enjoy Police Scotland's in-cell hospitality. But there was no getting away from the results he seemed to have achieved. In the two years of Pollock's tenure, the crime figure had been heading the right way across all categories, that was, downwards. Something that she obviously had to mention.

'So how much do you think the encouraging crime statistics are down to you personally?'

'One doesn't like to take too much credit of course,' he said, 'but one likes to think one has had some influence, yes.'

'Tough on crime, tough on the causes of crime, is that what it is?' Jimmy asked, evidently forgetting that it was the journalists who were supposed to ask the questions.

He smiled. 'Well, if you like, although the police don't have much influence on the latter I'm afraid. That's down to the politicians, and they generally make a pig's ear out of that, don't they?'

'But it must be something you're immensely proud of,' Maggie said. 'After all, I guess that's what policing is all about, isn't it? Bringing down crime, and you've done that brilliantly.'

Was she overdoing it a bit? She wasn't sure, but it seemed to be having the right effect.

'Yes, well that's what I've been able to share with my colleagues today,' he said, relaxing back in his chair. 'Not every force is doing so well as we are in Scotland, and as a result there's great interest in my methods, as you can imagine.'

It was slipped into the sentence with no great emphasis but Maggie noticed it nonetheless. *My* methods, not *our* methods. No wonder the rank and file thought he was an arse. She wondered what the celebrations would be like after Frank had brought him down.

'And how would you sum up these methods Sir Brian?' she asked.

'As I said, it's as much about changing the culture of the force as anything. More diversity in our ranks and policing *for* the people not *against* the people if you like.'

'Yes, I can see that,' she said, not understanding a word of what he'd said. But the more she got to know this guy, the more she sided with Frank's opinion of him. Sure, the crime figures had come down but that was probably just because Pollock had got lucky. And now pretty soon his luck was going to run out.

She saw him glance at his watch. 'How're we doing? The conference will be starting up again in ten minutes.'

'No that's great,' Maggie said. 'I think I've got nearly everything I need, and to be honest the piece will come out pretty much in line with the sample we sent you. There's just one last thing if you don't mind. It'll take two minutes, no more than that.'

'Sure, go ahead.'

Now it was time to go for it. *Now or never*. Light the blue touch-paper and retire fast.

Taking a deep breath she said, 'It's just my editor always likes a bit of light and shade in his articles, so I was just wondering... I mean you've had such a stellar career but I guess there must have been *some* things that didn't go quite so well? Is there anything in particular you can think of? Something that might merit a paragraph or two, just so I can keep the editor happy?'

She saw his expression harden, although he was trying to disguise it with a forced smile.

'Well no-one's perfect of course, but nothing specific springs to mind, no.'

It was exactly the response she had expected. Either he wanted to keep his skeletons well-hidden or he honestly did believe he was without fault. With an ego his size, it was difficult to tell which.

'Forgive me for bringing this up,' Maggie said, 'and this might be nothing, but an agency journalist up in Glasgow mentioned to me a story she's working on at the moment. It concerns some naval officer who killed himself in prison a few weeks ago. Lieutenant James McKay I think his name was. The whole thing sounds like an awful tragedy, because apparently this guy was convicted of murdering his wife and daughter, and now there's a suggestion that it was a terrible miscarriage of justice. The reason I'm raising it is that the journalist knew I was meeting you and she says you were the senior investigating officer at the time.'

He continued with the forced smile but she could tell from his eyes that he wasn't smiling inside.

'I think your journalist friend is going to be sadly disappointed,' he said coldly. 'If any story should emerge, then I fear that the late Professor Whiteside will be the colleague who does not come out of it too well. As for the police, I believe we followed all due procedure at the time.'

Maggie nodded. 'I'm sure that's the case Sir Brian. It's just that she told me she's got some sort of mole on the inside, and apparently the file's pretty damning, and she also says there's an internal investigation going on at the moment, although it's all a bit hush-hush. Look, would it be ok if I just included a couple of sentences in my article that mentions it? A sort of cloud-on-the-horizon angle? My editor would love that you see. He calls it cross-pollination, you know, letting our readers know about another article that's coming soon. It helps to boost sales apparently.'

But she could see that Chief Constable Sir Brian Pollock wasn't listening to anything she was saying. All he would be thinking about was the little white lie she had dropped into the conversation. *The journalist's got a mole on the inside.* As soon as he got back to Scotland he was going to pull that file and go through it with a fine-toothed comb and then anything that showed the investigation in anything but a good light was going to magically disappear. But what he didn't know was that super-keen WPC Lexy McDonald had gone through that file with her own fine-toothed comb and now knew it like the back of her hand. If anything evaporated, she would know and then so would Frank. But Maggie didn't see any advantage in making an enemy of Pollock, not now at least.

'But you know, the more I think about it,' she said, furrowing her brow, 'I don't think this story, if it is a story at all, really fits in with my piece. I think what I'm going to do is just write a paragraph that says your rise hasn't all been plain sailing and there's been challenges on the way but your hard work and dedication has overcome them. Something like that, what do you think? Nothing specific.'

He lounged back in his seat once again, visibly relaxing. 'Yes, that would be fair, because of course there *have* been challenges on the way. But look, it's been excellent but I think we need to wind it up here if you don't mind.'

As they got up to leave, he shot a smile at Jimmy. 'Do you need any more pictures before we finish? Maybe with my dress hat on this time?'

\*\*\*

Less than an hour after they'd finished with Brian Pollock, Frank had relayed the news that WPC Lexy McDonald had been requested to hand the Ardmore files over to her sergeant, the order coming down directly from Police Scotland headquarters at Tulliallan. Maggie had frowned and asked if that meant they would never see the light of day again, but Frank had reassured her that that wasn't going to happen.

*'No no,'* he had said, *'you see they can't do that. Not when my wee investigation's in full swing. Because if that file doesn't re-appear, Jill Smart will be straight on the phone to Pollock and then what's he going to say? No,*

*we'll get them back again, mark my words. Suitably detoxified of course, or at least that's what they'll think. But we know better, don't we?'*

So that was it then. *Game on.*

# Chapter 20

Lexy McDonald had been surprised to find the tower of document boxes on her desk when she had come in that morning. No more than three days after she'd been instructed to check them back in, and against all expectations, here they were in front of her again. At first glance, they looked exactly as they did when she had passed them to Jim Muir. Fourteen boxes in all, stacked two-abreast and seven boxes high, each bearing a hand-scribbled label that approximated to what they contained. At least, what they *had* contained before they made the forty-mile trip to Tulliallan in Fife, where all the Police Scotland brass, including Chief Constable Sir Brian Pollock, hid themselves away.

Of course she'd asked her sarge why they wanted them, and he'd just shrugged and said it was a routine audit that they did from time to time with all the big cases, checking the contents against the index to make sure everything was present and accounted for, dull stuff like that. Which, as she learnt from DI Stewart, was the exact opposite of the reason why they had been rushed along the motorway by express courier.

She was just contemplating where to start when her phone rang. Not her desk phone or her work mobile, but her personal one, the one she was supposed to keep switched off during working hours. Without looking, she knew who it would be.

'Good morning sir, how are you?' she whispered, not that there was anyone in yet who might overhear her conversation.

'*Aye, not bad Lexy,*' Frank said. '*So if everything's gone to plan, you should at present be hiding behind a humongous pile of boxes. Am I right or am I right?*'

'You're right sir,' she said, smiling. 'The way they're arranged, it's like a brick wall. I could stay hidden behind them for days if I wanted to. But I was surprised to see them back so quickly sir, after what you had said might happen to them.'

'*Right, well I decided a wee bit of proactivity was required, if there's such a word. So I got my gaffer DCI Jill Smart to make a wee phone call to a woman called Marion Black. She goes under the impressive title of Police Investigations and Review Commissioner for Scotland, or so I'm told.*'

'I can't say I've heard of her,' Lexy said. 'Should I have?'

'*No don't worry, not many people have. But her job is to keep the cops on the straight and narrow and get them banged up if they stray from the path of righteousness. Chief Constables hate them as a breed, and our Ms. Black in particular seems to be a right wee terrier. Keen to make a name for herself is what I've heard.*'

'I see sir,' she said, although she wasn't sure that she did.

'You see the thing was, she didn't even know about these question-marks surrounding the Ardmore murders,' Frank said. 'The police are supposed to inform the commissioner about anything as significant as this, but somehow it seemed to have slipped their mind.'

'I wonder why,' Lexy said.

'Aye, exactly,' Frank said. 'But anyway, I'm sure she had a wee word in the right ears and we've got them back now. So I just want to make sure you're clear what the job is.'

'Yes sir. At least I think I am sir. I've to check the files and see if anything's gone missing since the last time I looked. That's it, isn't it?'

'That's it. Sounds simple, but believe me I'm not underestimating how hard this'll be, especially since the Tulliallan crew only had them back for two days. They would have pulled a lot of stuff I'll bet, just to be on the safe side. So it's going to be hard to see the wood from the trees I'm afraid. In fact, I wouldn't put it past them to have pulled some irrelevant stuff to deliberately make our job more difficult.'

'No I understand sir,' she said, absent-mindedly opening the cover of the uppermost file. 'I'll do my best sir.'

'I know you will. But the thing is, you've only got today to do it. It's really important that they still think I want *this to be a tick-in-the-box exercise as much as they do. So as soon as we're done, I'm going to call your Sergeant Muir and tell him that we're just giving it one day and then we're closing it down. So good luck, and give me a call if you think you've found something. But be discreet, ok*?'

\*\*\*

The question was, where to start? The box files were conveniently numbered one to fourteen, so that would probably be as good as any method to go at them. Glancing at the descriptions written on the spines, it looked like the first few covered the evidence that had formed the basis of the case against Lieutenant McKay, probably the stuff Pollock and his team had assembled for the Procurator Fiscal's office, the stuff that persuaded them there was a solid case against the accused. *Means, motive and opportunity.* She'd covered all of that during her basic training, where she'd learnt it was just as important to establish all three in real-life investigations as it was in crime fiction. In fact, she remembered there was a brief two-page summary in the file that laid out how McKay ticked every one of these boxes. The means and opportunity bits were complete no-brainers as far as the case was concerned. With regard to means, he'd stabbed his wife and slashed the throat of his wee girl with one of his own kitchen knives, and as for opportunity, he'd just walked up the road from the base and in through his own front door. It was all so neat and tidy, except for one thing, and she had to keep reminding herself of the fact. *He hadn't done it.*

Sifting through box one, she found the document still in place. She glanced down it to the section that covered *motive*.

*1. According to the base commander, the accused has a history of mental health problems and had sought help for these in recent months.* A circle had been drawn around 'base commander' and a few words scrawled underneath. *Commodore Macallan RN to testify.*

*2. The accused had been having marital problems as witnessed by the email exchanges whilst at sea, to be submitted in evidence. Accused has denied sending or receiving correspondence. Communications Officer Daniel Clarkson RN to testify.*

This last guy was presumably being called to the stand to refute the frankly crazy suggestion that somehow the email exchange between McKay and his wife was fake. The more Lexy thought about it, the more she became convinced that this more than any other factor would have sealed his conviction. She tried to put herself inside the head of a man who knew that he was innocent, but who also knew that the case against him was overwhelming. A man who had been caught red-handed at the scene, holding the blood-soaked murder weapon. Simply saying *it wasn't me* just wasn't going to cut it when all of that was against you. So obviously he'd decided on a different tack. *Challenging the motive.*

*I loved my wife and daughter more than anything in the world, why would I want to kill them?,* that's what he would have said. *Yes, but what about these emails?* the police would have said in response. *I didn't send them. I've never seen them before in my life.*

As a defence it was dumb beyond belief, and Lexy had no doubt that the navy's expert witness, this Daniel Clarkson guy whoever he was, would have had no trouble in demolishing his frankly ridiculous assertion. Poor McKay, and with that line of defence destroyed, his credibility would have been shattered too. It was no wonder that the jury returned a guilty verdict after being out for just sixty-five minutes.

*Except that he hadn't done it.*

Boxes eight to fourteen were labelled 'investigation notes', and she remembered they were a random collection of notes and observations, along with a regular photo snapshot of the investigation's whiteboard, inexpertly captured by the camera-phone of one of the team was her guess. There was about a dozen of them, and she remembered finding them interesting during her first review because they gave an insight into the thinking of the team as the investigation evolved. She presumed most of the content was just the random brainstorming of team members, scribbled on the board and generally appended with a question mark. Unanswered questions for the whole team to consider and hopefully answer. The problem was, she hadn't counted these whiteboard captures first time round, so there was no way of knowing for definite if any of them had been made to disappear.

She removed them all from the box and laid them out mosaic-style on her desk. They were dated, so she was able to sort them into more or less chronological order, which gave some insight into how the investigation had unfolded. They'd taken a snap-shot generally every two to three days, a good indicator as to how fast things were moving. Comparing one to the next, she saw that usually a couple of items had been erased and a couple more added. Gentle evolution but all moving in the right direction. But then she noticed it. *There was a gap.* Two and a half weeks into the investigation's timeline, there was a six-day gap between the last whiteboard image and the next. She could feel her heart begin to speed up as she realised the significance of what she had just deduced. *At least one of these routine captures had been removed, which meant there was something on them that Pollock didn't want them to see.* But what the hell was it? Was there something she remembered first time round, something that had caught her attention as especially significant? Like DI Stewart had said, it was like looking for a needle in a haystack. But there was nothing for it but to start looking, because today was the last chance they had before the pile of boxes was spirited away forever.

She realised she needed to look at it from the perspective of back then, when no-one was questioning the time of death and they were dealing with a suspect that had been caught at the scene of the crime. She'd come to like DI Stewart in the short time they had been working together, but she couldn't help but think he was being a bit harsh on her Chief Constable. Putting herself in his shoes, she was pretty sure she would have come to the same conclusion at the time. *Means, motive, opportunity.* It was all there, neat and tidy. Tidy enough to convince a jury, which it had.

And yet someone had scribbled something on that whiteboard, something that posed a question to the investigating team. *Are we sure about this?* Something that didn't quite square up, something that didn't quite fit with the facts. Something that Pollock now didn't want them to see.

Then quite out of the blue, it came to her. She was thinking of her visit with DI Stewart to Jess Sinclair and then the drive from Helensburgh to Lochmorehead, most of which he had spent with his eyes closed and his foot jammed down on an imaginary brake pedal. What was it, twenty-five or twenty-six miles at least, and she remembered that she hardly got above thirty miles an hour anywhere along the twisty route. *The same route the police had taken that night when they'd answered the anonymous call summoning them to the McKay house on Ardmore base.* The same call that saw them arriving at the house just in time to catch Lieutenant James McKay in the act of murder.

And now Lexy could see that the timing just didn't stack up. Someone, a neighbour or maybe a passer-by out walking their dog, hears a disturbance and dials 999. It takes at least five minutes for the operator to establish the facts and decide whether to take action. The call then goes out to Helensburgh police station and a patrol car is sent on its way. *Probably just a domestic* is the assessment, so there's no undue rush. An hour later the police arrive to find a man holding a knife, a knife that had been used in two murders. Two murders that had apparently taken place just a few minutes earlier. Of *course* it didn't stack up, and someone on Pollock's investigation team must have come to that conclusion too, causing them to scribble a bloody great question mark on that whiteboard.

So who *had* made that phone call, scheduling it to perfection such that the police arrived at the scene just a few minutes after Lieutenant McKay? There could only be one answer to that question.

*The murderer.* And a murderer who knew that at around eight that evening, Lieutenant James McKay would be walking up the hill from the berthing dock of HMS Azure.

## Chapter 21

It was the first time Frank had managed to make it back to Atlee House after his Scotland trip, what with one thing or another, and the second thing he was going to do after tracking down a coffee and a Twix bar was to track down the geeky forensic officer, to see if he could work out what the hell she had meant by that bloody emoji-festooned text she had sent him last night. He was hoping it signalled some progress on the Geordie affair, and it couldn't come at a better time too. Because earlier that day he'd been on the end of a bollocking from Jill Smart due to his failure thus far to find any trace of the hacker. This was out of character for his boss and he knew instantly what had prompted it. It was the news that a selection of ACC Katherine Frost's amateur porn videos had now surfaced on the web and as was to be expected, were gathering 'likes' by the ton. This guy had to be caught, and quick.

The fact that Eleanor had concluded the text with a kiss had been a surprise which, not being a normal feature of their communication, he assumed was either a reflex action or maybe an effort on her part to soften the blow of this unexpected failure. He found her at her adopted desk, which seemed to be now her permanent location, her visits to her official office over in Maida Vale labs now few and far between. Like himself, she preferred to work on her own, and by keeping out of sight in his Department 12B enclave, she could avoid the tedious schedule of weekly stand-ups and team meetings and communications briefs she hated so much. It also meant that, out of sight of her boss, she could spend more time on the phone to her on-off boyfriend Lloyd. Time when really she should have been working. But for the second time in a fortnight, Frank had failed to catch her out, which he reckoned might be some sort of a record.

'Hi Eleanor,' he asked brightly, pulling up a battered plastic chair alongside her desk, 'Lloyd ok?'

'Like *yeah*. Why do you ask?' she answered, giving him a suspicious look.

'No reason, it's just what people do. It's called exchanging pleasantries. You should try it some time.'

'Whatever.'

He smiled. 'Aye, whatever yourself. So wee Eleanor, are you going to explain that cryptic message you sent me last night? Because first you got me all excited then you broke my heart.'

'Yeah, soz,' she said, furrowing her brow. 'I thought I'd cracked it until I talked to Rosie.'

'Rosie?' he said, giving her a puzzled look. 'Who's Rosie?'

She shrugged. 'Rosie Winterton. She's like Director of IT or something. My mate Zak put me on to her.'

He smiled to himself. He'd learnt this was how Eleanor operated, informally drawing in a diverse range of expertise from across the law-enforcement landscape, her tentacles spreading beyond the Met into MI5 and MI6 and GCHQ and other more secretive groups that didn't even have the benefit of an acronym. And most of her contacts it seemed only had first names, this Rosie Winterton being the exception that proved the rule, he guessed on the basis of her obvious seniority in the organisation.

'Right, well you better tell me the whole grim tale,' he said. 'Go ahead please, leaving no stone unturned.'

'Do you want the good news or the bad news first?'

'I think I already know the bad news, which is that you.. sorry, I mean *we* can't actually do whatever it is needs to be done. So you'd better give me the good news then I suppose.'

She gave him an uncertain look, which was not at all like her, because generally speaking, self-doubt was not Eleanor Campbell's thing. 'I don't suppose it really is good news if we can't actually do it.'

'No no, I'm sure that's not the case,' he said encouragingly. 'Come on, let me be the judge.'

'Ok. So when you gave me the task, I needed to get all the data together on this Georgie guy...'

'Geordie.'

'... yeah, that's it. So I talked to Pete and he sent me a summary of the incidents that we had recorded in London.'

He didn't need to ask who Pete was, because he already knew. His good mate DI Pete Burnside, as obliging a bloke as had ever been issued with a warrant card.

'So there were like eight incidents in our area and I added the porno woman from Manchester to make nine in all.'

Frank laughed. 'Can I remind you that the porno woman as you call her is Assistant Chief Constable Katherine Frost, so please, show a little respect for the rank. And don't say *whatever* again, ok?'

'Whatever. So with that data set,' she continued, ignoring his sharp look, 'I realised we could do a cross-reference against the cell-phone databases and look for a match.'

'Explain please,' he said, interested.

'So we know where he was at particular points in time because of that weird graffiti he leaves behind? That means if we have the cell phone databases for each of those times and places, we could in theory do a giant cross-reference search and see if a particular phone number appeared in all the locations. Because it would be more than a coincidence if more than one number appeared in each of these places and at these specific times. Do you see?'

It was a lot of words to take in, but for once, he *did* see, a rare occurrence when he was on the end of one of her convoluted technical explanations.

'Christ that's bloody genius Eleanor, so it is.' But then he remembered the bad news. 'So why can't we do it then? This cross-matching thing.'

'I talked to Rosie,' she said, the disappointment obvious in her voice, 'and she said we would have to stand up a mountain of tin and then implement a bank of multi-threaded database servers. To do it, that is.'

'I'm sorry Eleanor, but I didn't understand a word of that. Can you simplify it for a technical cretin like me?'

She was happy to oblige. 'We'd need a really big computer. Rosie said it would cost three hundred grand and take about six months to set up. And we would need to get all the individual databases from about ten mobile phone companies and join them all together which would take a ton of project management because of all the data protection hoops we'd have to jump through.'

Frank sighed. 'Well it does sound like a hell of a job, and I don't think DCI Smart's going to sign off an three hundred grand budget. It's a pity, but you tried your best and I'm grateful for your efforts.'

'Sweet,' she said. 'It's just like a shame we don't work for MI5 or MI6.'

He looked at her sharply. 'What do you mean?'

She shrugged. 'They monitor every phone call in the universe. They've got the phone databases mounted twenty-four-by-seven, three-hundred-and-sixty-five days a year. Permanently online.'

Frank leapt to his feet, knocking over the flimsy chair in the process.

'Eleanor, come with me.'

\*\*\*

They found DC Ronnie French in his normal repose, leaning back in his swivel chair with his feet on the desk, phone jammed between his shoulder and cheek whilst he swigged from a beverage can. For a worrying moment Frank thought he was enjoying a sneaky beer, but on closer inspection he saw it was one of these caffeine-boost drinks, the kind that were supposed to give you wings. But never mind wings, it would have its work cut out just to get Frenchie off his fat arse.

He looked up and seeing Frank, shot him a nervous smile before judging it would be prudent to bring his call to a close.

'Yeah...yeah Harry, look mate, got to go. Thanks for that nugget mate, yeah nice one. See ya.'

'On to your bookie then Ronnie?' Frank said, conveniently forgetting that gambling had moved online ten years ago or more.

'That was Harry guv,' he said, unconcerned, 'one of me snouts. Given me a tip-off for a jewel job up the West End he has.'

Frank shook his head. 'You've been watching too many old episodes of the Sweeney mate, nobody nicks jewels these days. But what we're here for is to ask you about that pal of yours, Jason or something like that. The guy we used on the Aphrodite case, you remember?'

'Yeah, Jayden guv. The Jamaican lad with the dreadlocks.'

'That's him. Is he still at Thames House, with the MI5 crew?'

Frenchie gave an uncertain look. 'Yeah, I think so, although we've not touched base for a while. Got a job for him have you?'

'Aye we have. I'll leave you in the good hands of Eleanor here who'll tell you what we need him to do for us.'

'And what would be in it for him?' Frenchie asked. 'Because me and Jayden have always worked on a you-scratch-my-back-and-I'll-scratch-yours basis. He won't do nothing for nothing, Jayden won't.'

Frank gave a sardonic smile. 'Aye, really public-spirited then. But I seem to recall that your mate loves the ladies, am I right?'

'Yeah, he loves them all right guv,' Frenchie grinned. 'Mind you, they like him too. He's always getting himself into bother on that score. He's a bad lad.'

'Perfect,' Frank said, 'so you can tell him there'll be a hot date waiting for him up in Manchester when he's done. And tell him we'll supply the handcuffs.'

***

It was just six days later when Eleanor and Frenchie got back to him, considerably quicker than he'd expected given his admittedly vague understanding of the complexity of the matter. But then again, he assumed that the spooks had all of this stuff off to a fine art, with the phone records of every one of the UK's sixty-six million souls on tap, twenty-four-by-seven, three hundred and sixty-five days a year, as she had said. He thought it must be a giant pile of tedious routine, sixty-six million instances every day of *I'll be five minutes late* or *I've just got on the train* and suchlike, which made Frank wonder about the value of keeping it all. But in amongst it all, like the tiniest needle in a haystack the size of a galaxy, would be the stuff in which they were really interested. The coded messages arranging the terrorist outrage, the exchange of images between members of the paedophile ring, the malign activities of the hostile foreign power.

That was the good stuff, and all the other crap was the price the authorities had to pay to get their hands on it.

She'd booked one of the big conference rooms in Maida Vale labs, the one with the full-wall multi-media display panels, which he took as a good sign. There was a lot of online form-filling required to get your hands on one of them, and he knew she wouldn't have gone to all the bother if she hadn't some good news to report. The room was big enough to host fifty or sixty, but today only three others besides himself were in residence. Eleanor Campbell, Ronnie French and a tall rangy Rastafarian in a Hawaiian shirt who Frank assumed was Jayden the MI5 spook, or Intelligence Analyst, to give him his proper title.

'Morning all,' Frank said brightly, tossing his notepad down on the table and pulling out a chair. 'I guess you're Jayden.'

'Sure man,' the Rastafarian replied, 'that's me.'

'Well thanks for helping us out with this,' Frank said. 'It's much appreciated.'

Jayden raised a languid hand and lounged back in his chair. 'Pleasure man.'

Frank smiled to himself. That was the thing about stereotypes. They so very often turn out to be true, not that he was bothered, because Jayden seemed like a cool guy. The only think that was missing was his piña colada. Or, when he thought about it again, his joint.

Eleanor hammered a few commands into her wireless keyboard and the wall was filled with a giant map of the UK.

'So Jayden mounted the cell phone data records for the dates where we had the information on Georgie's activities.'

*'Geordie.'*

'Yeah Geordie, soz. Anyway, watch this.'

She punched in another few characters and a series of blue flashing dots appeared on the map.

'So these are the locations where he sprayed that weird graffiti and you can see on the label below the dot the date and times he was there.'

Frank stood up and peered at the screen through narrowed eyes.

'Aye, so it's mainly in the London area but there's that one up in Manchester I can see. I'm guessing that's ACC Frost's place?'

'I wouldn't mind getting an invite there myself some time,' Ronnie French said. 'Know what I mean?'

'Two things Frenchie,' Frank said, giving him a wry smile. 'First, Assistant Chief Constable Frost clearly prefers women. Secondly, even if she didn't, an old fat bastard like you would have no chance.'

'Doesn't bother me,' French said, shrugging. 'A man can dream, can't he?'

'Aye, well dream on mate. Anyway Eleanor, where were we before we interrupted you?'

'These are the locations where we know he was active,' she repeated, pointing at the flashing dots. 'So Jayden plugged the times and places into his cool software and ran a cross-reference sweep.'

'It's cool,' Jayden confirmed, his lilting Caribbean accent a perfect match for his laid-back demeanour, 'but I can't take the credit for it. It was developed by a bunch of hucksters over at GCHQ, really smart guys. I just run it.'

'Not just guys,' Eleanor said sharply.

'I think Jayden means guys in the non-gender-specific sense,' Frank said, jumping in. The last thing he wanted was the easily-offended forensic officer having a punch-up with the spook who was going to help him crack the case.

Jayden shrugged. 'Yeah, it's like Frank said. But we need to keep that kind of information secret, even the gender of the computer scientists. We don't want any of the bad guys getting to know too much. You'll appreciate that Eleanor of course.'

Frank doubted if she did, but their joint intervention seemed to have calmed the situation.

'Sweet,' she said, somewhat uncertainly. 'So can you demo it Jayden?'

'Sure,' he said, 'pass me the keyboard.'

She slid it along to him and without looking up, he punched in a few characters. On screen, a dense grid of numbers popped up to obscure the map, the rows scrolling downwards quicker than the eye could read.

'This is the cell-phone sweep,' he said. 'There's a heap of tin in their datacentre so it can process six million records a minute. It's awesome.'

'Tin,' Frank said, recalling Eleanor's earlier explanation. 'That's the computers, isn't it?'

'Yeah, we call it tin,' French said, nodding. 'Us IT geeks.'

Along the bottom of the display, a green progress bar was edging gradually towards one hundred percent.

'Should only take another minute or so,' Jayden said, nodding towards the screen. 'We've ran it before so it'll remember all the index records. Speeds it up by a factor of eight, sometimes ten.'

'Good to know,' Frank said, uncomprehending.

The sat in silence as the computer sped towards completion, announcing its victory with a pop-up dialogue-box that read *Match Successful*.

'See, that's it,' Jayden said, pointing again at the screen. 'There's the match.'

'There's *two* numbers in that wee box,' Frank said, squinting to read the small type. 'Am I reading that correctly?'

'Sure,' Jayden confirmed. 'We're assuming one's his normal phone and the other's one of the burners he uses for his iCloud hacking. Although both of them are unregistered pay-as-you-goes.'

'Shit,' Frank said, unable to hide his disappointment. 'So that means we can't track him down after all?'

Eleanor shot him a smug smile. 'Why don't you show him Jayden?'

'Sure,' Jayden said for the third time, prompting Frank to wink at Frenchie. This MI5 guy was nothing if not obliging.

'So once we can tie a number to an individual, it makes no difference whether they're on contract or not. We might not have their name and address, but we just dial in our hotspot clustering add-on. That nails them every time.'

Frank laughed. 'I've been doing pretty well to keep up so far, even if I say so myself, but this one's got me. Hotspot what?'

'Hotspot clustering,' Eleanor repeated in the teacher-to-five-year-old tone that she liked to use on him from time to time.

'We wouldn't expect the layman to understand,' Jayden interjected, his tone apologetic. 'What it does, is it looks for concentrations of cell registrations in particular geographical locations over a defined period of time.'

'Meaning?' Frank asked.

'It can show the locations that the suspect visits the most.'

'Got it. And now I hope you're going to show me?'

'Sure man.' He stretched over to grab the mouse from Eleanor then focussed the pointer on a scrolling menu at the top of the screen. 'The option's in here somewhere. Yeah, there it is.'

This time a series of flashing green dots appeared on the map, Frank noticing they were of varying intensity.

'What are we looking at?' he asked, although he thought he might already have figured it out.

'This is a twelve-month visualisation,' Jayden explained. 'It looks back over that timeframe and shows the places he's visited most often in that period, or at least where his phones have been. We can extend it back five years if we want, although that takes an age to process. But yeah, the bigger and brighter the dot, the more times he's been there. And just to be clear again, it tracks where his *phone* has been. Doesn't mean he was with the phone at the time.'

'But it's pretty likely he was.'

'Sure,' he conceded.

'But I do get it, what it's telling us,' Frank said, nodding at the screen. 'It's all the places he likes to visit.' Suddenly, he had a thought.

'Jayden mate, can you scroll it up to the right a bit? Aye, that's it. Just there.'

And there it was. *Confirmation*. Once again he kicked himself for not cottoning on to the bleeding obvious, and before the obvious connection was pointed out to him by his brother too.

'Look here Frenchie, seems like he's a Newcastle supporter. Season ticket holder I'd guess by the number of times he must have been up there.'

'Poor bastard,' French said, laughing. 'Poor Geordie bastard.'

So the guy was from Newcastle. It was good to know, but Frank wasn't sure how that would help them identify him. But at least they had a pretty good idea where he lived, given the location of the brightest dot on the display. *Right here in London*.

Frank wandered up to the screen and pointed. 'And this one here, I'm guessing this is where we hit the jackpot?'

'That's right,' Jayden nodded. 'That would be where he lives, most likely.' He flicked the scroll-wheel on the mouse to zoom in. 'Vicarage Crescent, SW1.' The screen filled with the image of a modern purpose-built apartment block, the sort that were snapped up for stupid money by young professionals. Young professionals like the over-confident Geordie, whose goose was now going to be well and truly cooked.

'Well well well,' Frank said, smiling. 'This is a result, isn't it? Very well done you three, very well done.' He doubted if Ronnie French had had much to do with any of it, but then again, it was Frenchie that had procured the services of Jayden Henry of MI5, so maybe he was being a bit harsh. He was just about to sit down again when he spotted something out of the corner of his eye. Another green dot, fainter this time, but it was the location that interested him. *Very much.*

'Jayden mate, see that one there? Can you zoom in on it please? Aye, that one.'

*Bloody hell. Bloody hell.*

'Can we get a date Jayden, when he was there?'

'Sure.' He clicked again on the menu, and a table of dates and times popped up.

'There it is. About six months ago. He was there from about eleven at night until two in the morning, there or thereabouts.'

*Bloody hell.* Frank didn't need to check the date because he'd long ago committed it to memory. It was the night up in Ardmore House when Commodore Macallan had murdered his son then turned the gun on himself. And if Jayden Henry's cool software was to be believed, their boy Geordie had been there too.

Now *that* was something that was going to take some explaining.

## Chapter 22

Maggie wasn't really sure why she was feeling so bad about the Macallan case. No-one could deny they they'd tried their best, and after all it wasn't really their fault if the potential beneficiaries were refusing to play ball. But when she thought about it a bit more, she began to realise what it was that was bugging her. Simply put, she just didn't like to let Asvina down after the faith her best friend had continued to show in her little detective agency. It wasn't a matter of money, and in fact Ms Rani was likely to do very well out of the matter if the whole horrible mess ended up in court, as seemed increasingly likely. It was more a matter of reputation. As executors, Asvina and her firm had a duty to discharge the provisions of the will in as economical manner as possible. If it got round that they had raked in tens of thousands of pounds in fees in the process, people might start to ask how hard they had really tried, and that was something that might very well lose them business in the future. That above all was the reason why Maggie wasn't going to give up on the matter without one final attempt to reach a settlement.

The problem was Kirsty Macallan and her husband had now imposed a strict radio silence, refusing to respond to any of her phone calls, emails or messages. So there was nothing for it but to turn up on their doorstep and hope they were in, which explained why she was driving around Fulham, semi-lost, early on this Saturday evening.

And with her son Ollie in the back of the old Golf, this being the day their nanny had off. He'd thrown a minor strop because she'd insisted on taking the car rather than the tube, but now, glancing in the mirror, she could see that peace had been restored. It was just that Ollie loved trains and it would have been a rare treat for him, but it had been raining and it was a ten-minute walk from their home to the nearest station.

Suddenly he shouted, 'I saw the sign mummy. Clonmel Road. You missed it.'

'Thank you darling,' she said, smiling into the mirror. Now, unfortunately, she was going to have to do a three-point-turn in this narrow suburban street and three-point-turns weren't exactly her speciality. She'd punched the address into Google maps on her phone but following its directions wasn't her speciality either. It was lying on the passenger seat and seemed to be giving her the option of carrying straight on, which was a whole lot better. That was if she'd read the arrow symbol correctly. So maybe she could just go round the block again and this time she wouldn't miss the turn-off. Both suppositions turned out to be true, and a few minutes later she was squeezing into a parking space alongside the Overton's mid-terrace home. She noted the sign that warned it was residents parking only, but what she needed to say was only going to take five minutes. They jumped out of the car and made their way up the short path. And there it was, just to the left of the door, painted on the wall in defiance of Frank Stewart's law of coincidences. *The latest Geordie mural.*

The scene depicted an old house by a lake, surrounded by tall pine trees and with a setting sun reflecting off the surface. And beneath the painting, the ornate signature of the artist. She was no expert, but the image was captivating and all the more so because it had been executed in monochrome, and evidently with just a few sweeps of an aerosol can.

'It's really nice isn't it?' she said to her son, then remembering she was a lawyer added, 'He must be a very clever man although we shouldn't really approve of painting on the walls of people's houses.'

'S'all right I suppose,' Ollie shrugged. She knew he wouldn't be impressed, since the subject matter was neither a fast car nor a footballer.

The door was answered by Rory Overton, as in her previous visit holding his daughter in his arms. By his expression, she gathered he wasn't pleased to see them.

'What do you want? I thought we made it plain we don't want anything to do with you.'

She nodded towards the painting. 'It's rather good isn't it? Reminds me a bit of Loch More when I come to think about it.' For a moment, she wondered if the work had actually been commissioned by the Overtons themselves, another marketing exercise to further boost the reach of Kirsty's social media channels. But apparently not.

'It's nothing but mindless vandalism,' he said, 'and we're sick of everyone coming round to gawp at it. I've got some people coming to wash it off tomorrow thank god. Anyway, what do you want?'

She smiled, remembering the phrase employed by Alison Macallan. 'There's been a development. Can we come in? It'll only take five minutes, no more than that.'

'All right then,' he said grudgingly. 'But you'd better be quick. We're going out to dinner in a minute.'

Maggie heard Kirsty's shout from down the hallway. 'Is that the sitter darling? We need to watch our time.'

'No, it's that lawyer woman,' he shouted back. 'She says there's been developments. God knows what that means.'

It had been a while since she'd been a lawyer in the practising sense, but she let it pass. Overton led them through to the kitchen, where Kirsty was removing the cling-film from a tray of sandwiches, presumably for the still-to-arrive babysitter. She was wearing a tight-fitting black knitted dress and silvery stiletto sandals, with a string of expensive white pearls adding to the effect of quiet sophistication.

'Hello again,' she said, her manner pleasant in stark contrast to her husband's. 'And this must be your little boy.'

'Yes this is Ollie,' she said, patting him on the head. 'He's eight and growing by the minute. But I must say you look lovely Kirsty, and that dress is absolutely beautiful. And the pearls too, they match so well.'

She smiled. 'Thank you. Rory's arranged for us to meet some friends for drinks and then we're having a late dinner. It's all been a lovely surprise, and I've still no idea where we're going. You won't tell me, will you darling? The dress is by Dior by the way. Rory wanted me to wear it tonight. It's his favourite.'

Why wasn't she surprised that this woman selected what she should wear based on what her husband liked, rather than her own preference? And it seemed he had decided where they should go for a drink and where they should have dinner too. She'd only met Rory Overton once before, but she already decided she didn't like him one bit. There was something controlling about the man, and that was something she hated, having suffered it in her own ill-fated marriage to Philip. But then she remembered that this was the Macallan twin who had made the shameless pass at Jimmy at Dr Angus McLeod's sixtieth birthday party. Perhaps Rory Overton had grounds to believe his wife needed controlling, although it still didn't excuse it.

He handed the child to his wife then gave Maggie a sharp look. 'You can see we're in a rush. So just say what you came to say, and then you can leave.'

'Ok, I will. I wanted to talk to you about Susan Priest. You know she's dead I assume?'

The Overtons looked at one another as if silently deciding how to react. Finally Kirsty said,

'Yes, of course we heard. It was such a tragedy. We were very upset, weren't we darling?'

Her husband nodded, although if he was upset he was doing a good job of disguising the fact.

'You'd been in touch with her not long before that hadn't you?' Maggie said. 'Why was that?'

Kirsty looked as if she was about to answer when her husband cut in.

'Who says we have? And what business of yours is it anyway?' His tone was nakedly aggressive and Maggie didn't much like it.

'Look, I'm just trying to doing my job,' she said, standing her ground. 'Which as you know is to try and sort out the mess of your late father-in-law's will. Because if we can't reach a settlement with all parties, then the only people who are going to benefit from that mess are the lawyers. But that's what you were trying to do too, wasn't it? Come to some arrangement with Susan so that she supported your version of the story?'

'I don't know how many times I've told you,' he growled. 'Kirsty is the elder twin and we are in a position to prove it should we be asked, and we didn't need a deal with Susan Priest or anyone else to do that. So you're wasting your time here I'm afraid.'

Maggie gave him a puzzled look. 'Forgive me if I'm missing something, but I don't see how you can prove it.'

'Let's just say we've done some research in Canada since your last visit and leave it at that. Now as I said, Kirsty and I are going out in a few minutes so if you don't mind we need to wrap this up now.' He pointed towards the hall, wearing a forced smile. 'I'm sure you can find your own way out, and please, don't come back again.'

As Maggie squeezed Ollie's hand and turned to go, she smiled at Kirsty, who was wearing an expression that wasn't difficult to decipher. *Incomprehension.* If Rory Overton had been conducting research in the twins' birthplace, then he certainly hadn't told his wife about it. And there was something else. When she had brought up the subject of Susan Priest, she had noticed a wave of alarm sweep across Kirsty's face.

But she hadn't just come to talk about the dead nanny. She'd promised Asvina she would do everything in her power to broker a settlement and she owed it to her friend to give it one last attempt. And there was still the matter of Alison Macallan's little deal to be examined. Which twin had she made it with, Kirsty or Elspeth?

'Look Kirsty, I really need you to think about a negotiated settlement, because if you don't, then it will simply come down to whom a judge finds to be the most credible witness on the day. Is that going to be Alison your stepmother, your sister Elspeth, or yourself. On that decision your whole future depends I'm afraid.'

'Is she right Rory?' Kirsty Macallan said, suddenly sounding alarmed. 'Shouldn't we at least consider this agreement, to see what it is she's proposing?'

But Rory Overton didn't seem in the least concerned. 'Miss Bainbridge, I'm perfectly happy with our situation as I told you before. I'll say it again, Kirsty is the elder and we can prove it. So if you don't mind, this conversation is over.'

It was naturally Ollie who had pointed it out to her as they returned to their car, the flashy Golf GTi, parked just in front of them. With the registration number KIR 5T.

\*\*\*

Elspeth Macallan had arranged that he should pick her up at her flat at seven-thirty, which struck him as a bit early for an eight-thirty dinner date at a restaurant that was no more than a fifteen-minute walk away, especially when it was common knowledge, divulged through their social media, that the Macallan twins rarely walked anywhere. Fearful of what her plans for him pre-dinner might be, he'd decided he would turn up fashionably late, which caused him a frankly absurd amount of mental stress, as he discovered how difficult it was to over-ride a lifetime of punctuality.

'Sorry I'm late,' he lied, as she opened the door to his first ring. 'My Uber didn't turn up and I had to re-book. But here I am now.'

'Don't worry Jimmy,' she said, stretching up to kiss him on the cheek. 'We've got plenty of time. You look very nice by the way.'

'Thanks, I thought I should make an effort.' In truth, it hadn't taken much of an effort, but the crisp white shirt and navy jacket worn with his ever-present black jeans just nudged the look into something you could call stylish. 'And you look lovely too of course.'

She was wearing the same dress as she had been in their last meeting.

'It's Dior isn't it? I remember you telling me about it. It's French as I recall.'

She laughed. 'Gosh, fancy you remembering, you *are* a clever boy. But actually it's not the same one. That other one was one they lent me for promotional purposes on my channels, but it sold so incredibly well that they sent me two others to keep. This black one and a lighter grey one too. You won't understand being a man, but I've already had both of them on three times each this afternoon. I just couldn't decide between them. But you can't go wrong with black, can you?'

He smiled. 'Aye, I had the same problem myself with this shirt. Blue or white, I couldn't make up my mind.'

She led him through to the stylish kitchen, dominated by a large island topped in expensive granite. At one end lay a silver tray with two champagne glasses and a bottle on ice. Without asking, she filled both without spilling a drop then passed one to him, her fingers lingering on his hands as he took it from her.

'You've done that before, I can tell,' he said, slightly disconcerted, 'and thanks, I don't mind if I do.' And then he noticed that the bottle was already half-empty. Or still half-full, depending on which way you looked at it.

She raised her glass. 'Here's to a lovely evening.' And then she drained it in one.

'I'm sorry, but I'm going to have some more. I hope you don't mind?' She was smiling but he thought he detected a nervousness in her voice. He couldn't imagine it was him that was causing it.

'Go ahead,' he said, then raised his own glass, 'and yes, here's to a lovely evening.' He watched as she poured herself a refill, taking care to fill it right to the brim.

'Don't worry, there's another bottle in the fridge,' she said, squeezing his arm. 'Let's go through to the lounge and you can start to tell me all about yourself. Or maybe you could just kiss me. Whatever you want.'

He thought it an extraordinary thing for her to say, and then he remembered her sister's behaviour at his father-in-law's birthday party. Maybe it ran in the family or maybe the Macallan twins were just so used to getting what they wanted.

'Well I don't much like talking about myself,' he said, 'but I suppose I could give you the five-minute potted history if you insist.'

She gave a coy smile. 'Well as long as it's only five minutes. Because to be honest, I'd rather you kissed me.'

He shrugged. This was taking one for the team, big time, and he was going to make bloody sure that Maggie Bainbridge never forgot his sacrifice. But then again, as his brother Frank had pointed out, how horrible could it really be?

\*\*\*

At least there hadn't been a scrum of paparazzi waiting outside *La Garrigue* when the Uber pulled up outside. She'd promised a quiet dinner in a nice little French restaurant, but Elspeth and Kirsty Macallan lived their lives in the public eye and he worried their idea of quiet would be quite different from his. He knew exactly where his apprehension came from though. It was that crazy five months he'd spent with Astrid Sorenson, the Swedish country singer who had ruined both his life and his marriage. Except it hadn't been her fault at all, because he'd ruined it perfectly well all by himself. It was true that he'd fallen for her when he was at the absolutely lowest point in his life, but that was a poor excuse. *Post Traumatic Stress Disorder.* Now it had become a whole bloody industry, with a thousand charities jumping on the bandwagon. Help for Heroes, Veterans in the Community, the Invictus Games to name but a few. All well-meaning of course, and he wished none of them ill, but unless you had *been there*, seen half a dozen of your best mates blown to pieces in front of your eyes, then you didn't have a bloody clue what it was all about. When something like that happens and you're three and a half thousand miles from home, then a man just can't bloody think straight. So when the Swedish princess had turned up at that Helmand concert like some bloody modern-day Vera Lynn, well what was he supposed to do? It was she who had made the first move, but he didn't have to say yes. Sure, she was beautiful and alluring, but then so was Flora. Looking back, he knew exactly why he had said yes. It was simply because she was there and he'd needed something that night. Tonight was different. Elspeth Macallan too was beautiful and alluring and had already made it plain she was available. But that just wasn't going to happen. He was with her for one reason and one reason only. To find out what she knew.

On arrival, the *maître d'* had taken Elspeth's jacket and passed it to a colleague, then led them to a quiet corner table where he handed each a leather-bound menu. He allowed them to settle for a few seconds then asked, 'Sir will be choosing the wine this evening?'

'Aye, I suppose sir will be,' Jimmy said, taking the menu from him. The only problem was that before they'd left her home, Elspeth had finished the bottle of fizz, out-drinking him in a ratio of three to one, and he wasn't sure how wise it would be to allow her some more. And then he checked himself. *Allow her some more.* What was that all about and who did he think he was exactly? If she wanted to get herself pissed, that was entirely up to her. And in any case, it seemed she had her own ideas on the subject.

'Of course he will,' she said, suddenly looking serious, 'and whilst he's doing that, bring us some champagne please.'

'Certainly madam. And I'll give you a few minutes sir, shall I?' the waiter said before gliding away.

'Are you ok?' he said, sensing her change of mood.

'Yes, I'm fine,' she said. 'Honestly. I suppose it's just everything that's going on. I can't seem to put it out of my mind.'

'Aye, understandable,' he said, not quite sure if he believed her. It had been more than three months since she'd discovered the perverse terms of her father's will, and over six months since the tragic incident at Ardmore House. And she'd been fine back at her place, when she'd been knocking back the champagne and running her hands all over him. So whatever the reason for her mood change, he felt it had somehow been prompted by their arrival at the restaurant.

As he skimmed through the wine menu and finding not unexpectedly that it comprised exclusively of French vintages, he saw her take her phone from her bag and place it on the table. *Screen down.* Maybe she just didn't want to be distracted during a lovely romantic meal, or maybe she didn't want him to be able to see the ID of any callers or texters. He wondered which of those it was. Perhaps both.

'Any preference?' Jimmy asked, wearing a perplexed look, 'because I'm more of a new world man myself. Shiraz if it's red and Sauvignon if it's white. And I usually choose the one that's a pound dearer than the cheapest on the menu. Although I read somewhere that's what they want you to do. It's usually the crappiest wine and the one they make the most profit on.'

She shrugged. 'Let's get the waiter to choose after we've ordered our food, shall we? They'll probably recognise me eventually so they'll want to make a good impression. They may even decide it's on the house, that happens a lot. Kirsty and me can make or break a restaurant you know.' It was said with an absence of conceit. He guessed for her, she was simply stating a fact. And by mentioning her sister, it left an opening for a question he wanted to ask.

'How are relations with Kirsty if you don't mind me asking?' he said, dropping his voice so as to dial down any potential offence. 'I know it must be difficult for you.'

'It's shit, since you ask. We were so close until our father died and now this stupid will's screwed everything up. I just don't know what's got into her, I really don't. Because she *knows* I'm the elder twin, of course she does. But it's Rory who's behind all of this of course. He's a hateful man and so money-grabbing. And he's got Kirsty twisted around his little finger. She can't even go for a piss without asking his permission. It's pathetic.'

Just in time, Jimmy remembered. *Rory Overton and Elspeth Macallan had history*. So it wouldn't be a surprise to find that her opinion of her sister's husband was coloured by that relationship.

'It's a terrible shame though,' Jimmy said. 'I mean, me and my brother Frank aren't always best mates but I'd hate if anything came between us.'

'It is a shame,' she said, 'but look, here's the waiter coming to take our order and I don't really want to spoil our evening talking about all that boring stuff.'

So she wanted to change the subject. The only problem was, he *did* want to talk about all that boring stuff. That was the mission, to find out what she knew and have one final attempt at getting a deal, but he could see it would have to be delayed for the time being. Smiling he said, 'I'll second that Elspeth. But there's just something I wanted to ask you, it's about your old nanny Susan Priest. I assume you know she was killed recently? In a hit and run accident?'

She shrugged. 'An old nanny? God, that must have been twenty-five years ago at least. No, I didn't know. Why should I? I've never given her a day's thought in all of that time.'

He remembered what John Priest had said to him. *Elspeth, Kirsty, how the hell should I know*. Maybe she was telling the truth, and whatever the case he doubted if she was likely to admit it if it had been her who had been in touch with Mrs Priest. For a moment he thought about pursuing the matter, but then decided to keep his powder dry. Instead he said,

'Aye, it was a tragedy right enough, a terrible thing altogether. But you asked about me, well, there's not much to say really. I'm thirty-two years of age, six-foot two, weigh one hundred and eighty pounds, born and brought up in Glasgow, did law at Glasgow Uni, joined the army, went to Afghanistan, came out, got a job with Maggie Bainbridge Associates. That's my life in one sentence.'

'Is that all you're going to give me?' she said, her tone subdued. 'Because I can't help noticing you didn't mention your marriage to Flora McLeod.'

He gave her a grim look. 'That's because it hurts, if I'm being brutally honest with myself. It was my biggest screw-up and make no mistake.'

'But she's lovely your Flora, isn't she? Beautiful and clever too. The beautiful and clever Dr Flora Stewart with the handsome-hero husband.'

And now he noticed it, as clear as a blue sky in summer. *Jealousy*. He remembered at the same time what Rory Overton had said. *She's still jealous babe. That's what it is. Jealous of me and jealous of Esme.*

'You knew Flora of course. When you were kids I mean.'

'Yes I did. We were at the primary school together, in Lochmorehead. That girl who was murdered by her husband was there too, I don't know if you knew that?'

'Yes I did. Morag, wasn't it?'

'That's right. Morag Robertson. But she was more friends with Kirsty and Flora. They were so bloody popular, all of them.'

There it was again, a bitterness that seemed to be undiminished after more than twenty years.

'They had their own stupid language. Kirsty, Flora and Morag, making up silly words for everything, and they wouldn't tell me what they were. It was pathetic.'

'And you weren't part of this?' He knew he was treading on dangerous ground so checked himself just as he was about to ask the question beloved of TV interviewers the world over. *How did that make you feel?*

But she answered it without being asked. 'It didn't bother me. I had plenty of other friends at the school although sometimes that was quite hard because we were away quite a lot. You know, when my father had another posting. Although we always came back when we could.'

'Because of Ardmore House and the estate I suppose?'

'Yes, it's in the Macallan blood. We didn't like to stay away from the place for too long. No, more than that, we *couldn't* stay away. That's why my father always tried to get a posting to the Ardmore base. He felt exactly the same.' And it explained too why gaining ownership of the place was such a big deal for each of the twins. Maybe it was time to bring up the subject again? But then a waiter appeared alongside their table, a plate in each hand.

'Fish for you madam I believe, and the bourguignon for you sir?'

'That's right,' they said simultaneously, causing each to smile.

The main course passed pleasantly enough, with Elspeth doing most of the talking, much of which, being focussed on her world as a social-media influencer, Jimmy neither understood nor was much interested in. From time to time the waiter would come to refill their glasses, and each time it seemed hers was quite empty. And with each glass marking a milestone, there was a perceptible drop in her mood. Something wasn't right, he could tell that.

'Are you sure you're ok Elspeth?' Jimmy asked again, as gently as he could.

'Yes, why do you keep *asking*?' She spat out the words, her voice loud enough to cause a number of the other diners to steal a glance in their direction.

'Sorry, I'm just concerned for you that's all. After all, you've been through a lot.'

'No, look I'm sorry too Jimmy,' she said, this time quieter and with a smile that was obviously forced, 'I shouldn't let my troubles spoil our evening.'

He heard her phone vibrate, and for a moment she froze, as if deciding how to react. And then finally she said, 'I'm sorry, I'm being a hopeless date, and I've had a little too much to drink as well. I'm just going to pop to the ladies' room and freshen myself up, and then I'll be fine.'

She picked up her clutch bag from beside her chair, popped her phone into it then stood up.

'Won't be long,' she said.

A man at an opposite table caught Jimmy with a look that spoke of solidarity. *Women, they're such high-maintenance aren't they?* The waiter appeared again and attempted to top up Jimmy's glass, he placing his hand over the top to decline. He was already beginning to feel drowsy, the combined effect of the rich food and rather more wine than he was used to. But when she came back, he would have to raise the subject immediately, irrespective of her mood. *Have you done a deal with your step-mother?* This was work after all, and that was the question he needed answered. He couldn't duck it any longer.

The only problem was that after nearly ten minutes, she still hadn't returned. *Odd.* He began to wonder if the alcohol had overcome her and she had passed out in the ladies. He got up and approached the nearest waitress, a fresh-faced teenager wearing an eager smile.

'Excuse me.'

'Hi sir, can I help?'

'Aye, it's my date,' he said, his voice apologetic. 'She went to the ladies quite a while ago and she's not come back yet. I'm a bit worried about her.'

'No worries sir, I'll go and look. What's her name?'

'Elspeth.'

He followed the girl through an archway and into a narrow passageway, at the end of which were two doors marked *Hommes* and *Femmes*. The waitress pushed open the right-hand door and went in.

'Elspeth? Hi Elspeth, are you ok?' He could hear her call out again, this time her voice muffled as the door closed behind her on its spring.

A few moments later she emerged wearing a perplexed expression.

'There's no-one in there sir.'

'What?'

'No sir, no-one. Perhaps she's popped outside for some fresh air or a cigarette?'

'She doesn't smoke, but thanks, I'll take a look.'

He pushed open the door and stepped out onto the pavement. The restaurant was tucked away on a quiet side-street just off the Fulham Road, and at just past nine o'clock it was deserted. He looked up and down but there was no sign of her. And then he had a thought. *An embarrassing thought.*

He turned on his heel and went back inside. The young waitress was standing just inside the doorway, apparently awaiting his return. He smiled at her and said, 'Just one thing before I let you get back to work. Can I ask you, where do they put the coats?'

'There's a couple of hangers beside our little bar sir. I'll show you.'

'Ok, thanks.'

He wasn't exactly sure if he could remember what Elspeth's jacket looked like. Short-ish, perhaps light grey in colour and silky in texture, that was the best he could come up with. But as he carefully sorted through the dozen or so garments that hung on the pair of coat-stands, the problem resolved itself. There was nothing that remotely resembled hers, which meant his worst suspicions had now been confirmed.

His date had done a runner. And already he was dreading having to reveal the mortifying outcome to Maggie and Frank.

Worse than that, now he was going to be landed with the bloody bill.

## Chapter 23

For Frank, it had been a more or less satisfactory day. Satisfactory, insomuch as the ratio between progress and set-back had looked like settling at around two to one in favour of the latter, and after twenty years on the force he recognised that was generally as good as it got. *One step forward and two steps back.* That was the metronome that guided the rhythm of routine police-work. Day in and day out, you just had to chip away at the tedious minutia of an investigation and then eventually everything would click into place.

Spirits had been raised when he'd got the sensational call from wee Lexy McDonald telling him that she'd only gone and found it, hadn't she? That she'd found that absolutely *priceless* piece of information that had every prospect of nailing Brian Pollock to the wall *and* wiping that smug bloody smile off his face forever. The 999 call that had sent Police Scotland scuttling from Helensburgh round to Ardmore must have been made either by the murderer or an accomplice, that was now becoming clear. And now the key to working out exactly what had happened on that terrible evening was to track down who had made it. He knew that the initial call would have come into a British Telecom call centre, these being the guys who asked *which service do you require?* Then it would have been passed along to the Police Scotland call-handling centre in Govan. And at both stages, it was pretty odds-on they would have kept records. Who called, from which number, and when. That was all they had to find out to settle Pollock's fate, and he was looking forward to getting stuck into that task later that day.

Then not more than an hour later, he received another call, this time from Ronnie French, who apparently the previous day had enjoyed a sneaky day out in Winchester. When Frank had asked him to take a look at the Susan Priest hit and run case, he'd envisaged a couple of phone calls with the local force, but fair play to the lazy shirker, he'd seemed to have come up with the goods. A casual conversation with some youths who habitually hung around the shops where the incident took place revealed that on the day in question, they had noticed an unfamiliar Ford Focus parked up fifty yards or so down the street. An old mark one, on a two-thousand-and-five plate. It was the kind of motor they liked to nick for a swift half-hour's joyride, on account of its hopeless security and tidy handling, but by the time they'd thought about it, their attention had been diverted by the excitement of the hit and run. No, they couldn't say if it was that motor that had done it, and no, they didn't catch sight of the driver, but it was a useful lead nonetheless. Focuses of that vintage were becoming rarer by the day and there was every chance that one of the local ANPR cameras would have picked it up. By any measure, that was progress.

But then came the less encouraging news that tracking down the precise location of Geordie wasn't going to be the work of five minutes as he'd initially hoped. The problem was, the building where he lived was an eighteen-storey tower-block with sixteen flats on each floor. Which flat was his was thus impossible to say, and there was no way they could do a door-to-door, because as soon as Geordie-boy saw a squad of coppers swarming all over the place then evidence would be quietly destroyed and they'd be left without a leg to stand on. No, this had to be approached with stealth if they were going to get anywhere. Luckily, Jayden Henry's clever location software had established his current place of work, an international bank in Canary Wharf, but initial enquiries revealed they employed over two thousand staff at the site, and with data protection laws what they were, you couldn't just ask them to hand over a list of employees, and in any case, he might just be a contractor or something and so not actually on the payroll. The same went for the records of the names of the residents of Geordie's block. The leaseholder would have that data, obviously, but it would need warrants and associated paperwork to get them released. But with any luck it wouldn't take more than a week, ten days at the most, and then they would have a name.

So not brilliant, but by the standard of things, a more or less satisfactory day. That was, until he'd got a third call, this time from his mate DI Pete Burnside over at Paddington Green. After which, things took a decided downward spiral.

*'I don't expect you've heard pal, but our big friend DCS Barker's got your brother banged up in an interview room over here. Some woman he was having dinner with last night was found up an alley in Fulham, dead as a doorknob. Some of the SOCOs have just got back and they're telling me it's a right mess, three stab wounds to the lower abdomen and blood everywhere, and her clothes ripped too. There's signs of sexual assault too apparently. Her knickers were removed and there's scratches on the inside of her thighs. They're just getting the body down to the morgue for the formal ID but a couple of the young coppers on the squad recognised her right away. Anyway, he's got that Maggie solicitor lady with him and they're questioning him right now. You best get over here sharpish mate.'*

It was fortunate that Frank knew most of the guys at Paddington Green and fortunate that all of them despised DCS Colin Barker as much as he did, so he was able to waltz unchallenged past the front desk and down the maze of corridors that lead to Interview Room 6. A uniformed constable whom he vaguely recognised was standing at the closed door.

'I think the tape's running sir,' the constable said apologetically. 'They're in a formal interview session.'

'Good to know,' Frank said, then pushed open the door.

'So what's going on here?' he said, surveying the scene. On one side of a small table sat Jimmy and Maggie, on the other his nemesis Detective Chief Superintendent Barker with a guy he didn't recognised but whom he assumed was a DI or DS assigned to the case.

'Bloody hell, stop the tape Jones, will you?' Barker said in an exasperated tone. 'So it's DI Stewart. I might have known that you would turn up like a bad penny as soon as you heard about this.'

Frank smiled. 'Sorry sir, but I heard the victim was a Macallan and I thought there might be a connection to a line of enquiry we're pursuing.' It wasn't quite true, but it wasn't exactly a lie either. 'So is my wee brother under arrest or what?'

'Jimmy's just helping DCS Barker with his enquiries,' Maggie said pleasantly. 'As far as I can see the police have no evidence against him, so we'll be wrapping this up and leaving in a few minutes.'

'That's for me to decide,' Barker said, adopting his customary pompous tone.

'With respect, it isn't,' Maggie said, raising an eyebrow. 'It's the law. So unless you plan to arrest my client, we're out of here.'

Frank smiled. 'She's got you there sir, I think.'

'If I needed advice on the law, you're the last person I would ask,' Barker said sharply. 'And it might interest you to know that we have a number of witnesses who heard your brother arguing with the victim just a few minutes before she left the restaurant. So it's perfectly reasonable we should identify this man as a possible suspect.'

Jimmy leaned back in his seat and looked at the ceiling. 'How many times do I need to tell you we weren't arguing? She just got annoyed with me for asking how she was, that was all.' His defence was spirited but Frank could tell he was worried.

'So Jimmy,' he said, 'have you told DCS Barker everything you know?'

'Yes,' he replied, 'I told him we had a couple of drinks at her flat, then got a cab to the restaurant. And I told him she was a bit distracted during the meal and then she just took off. To be honest, I thought I'd just been dumped.'

'And that was everything?'

'Aye. I got a wee waitress to look in the ladies' loo in case she'd passed out or something, and then when I saw that her jacket was gone, I assumed she had legged it. So I settled the bill and went home, a bit pissed off to tell the truth. I sent her a sarcastic text, you know, thanks for a lovely evening or something like that, then went to bed and forgot all about it. And then thirty-six hours later the bloody police turn up at my door saying she's been murdered.'

'So I'm assuming you didn't actually kill this woman then?' Frank said, smiling.

'No, of course I bloody didn't.' Jimmy shot out the words, evidently in no mood for a joke. 'Why would I do that?'

'Well that's fine then,' he said, smiling at Barker. 'Just wanted to make sure you weren't planning to make a confession or anything like that. So like Miss Bainbridge said sir, I think we're done here.'

'Now just wait a minute,' Barker said, spluttering. 'I'm not finished with him yet. There's a lot more background we need to find out.'

'That's fine,' Maggie said, giving a dry smile, 'and of course my client will be delighted to help you with that in any way he can. But we're not doing it here. Make an appointment and you can pop round to our Fleet Street offices at your convenience. Come on Jimmy, let's go.'

\*\*\*

'We'll nip down to the canteen and grab a coffee and you can tell me all about it,' Frank said. 'And I'll tell you about my developments. I think you'll find them more than interesting.'

It was about the only attraction of Paddington Green nick when he came to think about it. They had much better coffee than the vending machine stuff at Atlee House, properly expensive barista stuff with a rich nutty aroma that you could detect from a mile away, served from machines that went woosh as they emitted steam from every pore. They settled down at one of the long wood-laminated tables, leaving a few empty chairs between them and a group of uniforms who he assumed had just come off an early shift.

Frank spoke through a mouthful of blueberry muffin. 'So Jimmy boy, what's the story?'

'Not much to tell,' Jimmy said, giving him a rueful look. 'Around nine-ish Elspeth said she was going to the loo to freshen up and she never came back.'

'And that's it? Nothing else?'

'Well there's one thing that I've just thought of. You see, she got a text or a WhatsApp or something, a minute or two before she went. But she didn't look at it, and I remember thinking at the time that it was a bit odd. You know, as if she was expecting it and already knew what it was all about.'

'What, you mean it was pre-arranged or something?' Maggie asked, evidently amused. 'That's going to a lot of trouble just to be able to walk out on a date, getting a friend to text you.'

'Aye, very funny,' Jimmy said. 'I mean, maybe it was nothing but it would be good to look at her phone records.'

'Well hopefully Barker's boys will have thought of that already,' Frank said, looking doubtful, 'but I'll chase that DI Jones up and remind him, just in case.'

The thing was, he'd been in and around DCS Colin Barker's investigations often enough to know that nothing could be taken for granted, not even the absolute basics. For years, it had puzzled him how the useless lump of lard had held onto his job. That was, until that clever wee Eleanor Campbell had got him access to his iCloud account. It was surprising how far you could go in the police with the right handshake.

'I tried to tell Barker about the will of course,' Maggie said, 'but he wasn't listening. Because with Elspeth dead, it doesn't half simplify things.'

'Aye, and it's a cracking motive for her sister and her husband, isn't it?' Jimmy said.

Maggie nodded. 'Yes, and for her step-mother too, don't forget. If she's come to some arrangement with Rory Overton and Kirsty, then it's all suddenly looking very neat and tidy.'

'Or it might just have been an opportunist sexual assault,' Frank shrugged. 'A beautiful girl like that walking alone along a quiet side street at that time of night. Every bit as likely in my opinion. But listen, I'm sure Barker will get on top of this soon enough and the first thing he'll want to do is check out the alibis of all the Macallans. I wouldn't have thought that would be too difficult, even for that fat arse.'

'Kirsty and her husband were going out that night,' Maggie said. 'They told me they were meeting some friends for a drink and then going on somewhere to dinner. It was some sort of surprise and Rory hadn't told his wife where they were going. It did occur to me at the time that they might turn up at the same restaurant as Elspeth and Jimmy. It would be worth checking if that was their intention, don't you think?'

Frank smiled. 'I'll add it to my list, or at least the list I'm going to pass on to Barker. And maybe you could ask them too? Because I assume there's now going to be a lot to be tidied up with respect to the will.'

'Well that's true enough,' she said. 'But I'm not exactly top of their Christmas card list at the moment. They're not taking my calls or answering my messages.'

'Ah well,' Frank shrugged, 'it'll just have to be a police matter then. I might just get my mate Ronnie French to pay them a visit, unofficial-like.'

Which caused him to smile inwardly, since he knew it would piss off Barker big-time to have his wee Department 12B clumping all over his murder investigation. That in fact was what would make it all the sweeter. But he couldn't hide the fact that he was worried about his brother becoming unwittingly involved in this brutal murder. The unscrupulous Barker had a track-record of playing fast and loose with trivial little things like actual evidence, and it wouldn't be hard to imagine how he could easily spin a half-credible case against Jimmy. The non-existent argument in the restaurant would be amplified into something it wasn't, and then they'd find out about the nervous breakdown his brother had suffered after witnessing the murder of that young female soldier in Belfast. *The damaged bomb-squad officer loses it in a fit of rage after having his sexual advances rejected, and lashes out.* All lies of course, but the motive would have to be disproved, since nowadays the concept of innocent until proven guilty seemed to be out of fashion in the prosecution system. No, he was going to have to keep a bloody careful eye on the case and be ready to step in if he didn't like the way it was going.

But now he was just going to give them a wee update on progress on the Morag and Isabelle McKay murders before heading back to Atlee to see how they were getting on with the Geordie warrants. In a moment of madness, he'd delegated responsibility for that task to Ronnie French, a task so outside the lazy turd's zone of competence as to be on another planet. Dismayed, he realised he'd best get on to Google as soon as he was back at his desk.

To check for the signs of early-onset dementia.

## Chapter 24

It was no surprise to Maggie that Kirsty Macallan had swiftly taken to her social media channels in the days after her sister's brutal killing. In every appearance, it was evident her stylist had been to work, expertly-applied make-up revealing the tracks of her tears and her hair carefully dishevelled for maximum effect, but there was no concealing the dark crescents under her eyes and the genuine heartache in her voice. Although as Jimmy had pointed out with ill-disguised bitterness, the Macallan twins had been media-trained to within an inch of their lives and it could just as easily be faked. Whatever the truth, Kirsty was now regularly pleading for anyone with any information that could help the police in their quest for her sister's killer to come forward. Interspersed with these direct appeals were a series of heart-wrenching vignettes addressed to her dead sister, telling her how much she had loved her and how her life could never be the same again. It was Jimmy who had pointed out that indeed, her life would not be the same. Sure, she had lost her twin, no more than six months after losing her father and brother, and all in the most terrible of circumstances. But she had gained a beautiful country house and a six-thousand-acre estate.

What had been a surprise was that the press had somehow discovered that Maggie Bainbridge Associates had been tasked with sorting out the mess surrounding the late Commodore's will. That gave them the excuse to re-run a sort of greatest hits compilation of her and Jimmy's past life difficulties, reminding their readers and viewers that she had been at one time dubbed the most hated woman in Britain, on account of engineering the acquittal of the teenage terrorist Dena Alzahrani, and that he had been the Hampstead Hero, saving the life of a six-year old child in Alzahrani's follow-up outrage with no regard to his own safety. And not only that, Jimmy Stewart had been the last person to see Elspeth Macallan alive, and was therefore seen as a possible suspect for this baffling crime. The murder and everything connected to it was now dominating every media outlet, but nobody seemed to be asking the most obvious question of all. Was Kirsty Macallan in any way responsible for the death of her sister?

This was the question Maggie was asking Frank as they waited for Jimmy to return from the barista's counter with their order. They were once again in residence at their favourite Starbucks on Fleet Street, conveniently located a stone's throw from the salubrious offices of Maggie Bainbridge Associates. The fact that it was an inconvenient two-tube ride from Frank's Atlee House base seldom seemed to discourage him from attending their frequent and informal case conferences, and Maggie was glad of that. She liked Frank and she liked to see as much of him as possible.

'Aye, well the motive is clear enough,' he said, 'but talking to that DI Jones who's working the case, their alibi's rock-solid.'

'Yes, I saw them earlier on the night in question if you remember,' Maggie said, 'and they told me they were having drinks with friends and then going on to a restaurant.'

Frank nodded. 'And that checked out. They left the pub at about quarter to nine in an Uber and arrived at the restaurant at about ten-past nine. Some place in Chelsea it was. Anyway, DI Jones' lads have apparently chased up the driver and it all seems to stack up. Although to be fair, the guy didn't speak much English so they're not sure if he understood what they were asking. They've asked Uber for the cab's GPS records, so we'll see what they bring. But it looks solid as I said.'

'So what is the thinking now?' Maggie asked.

He nodded toward his brother who was returning with their coffees. 'Jimmy-boy's the only suspect they've got, and before you say anything, no-one's taking that seriously, don't worry. It's just the way these things work. The brass go mental if there's not at least one name in the frame. So, to get back to your question, the thinking is now opportunist sex attack. Someone sees Elspeth coming out of the restaurant onto that quiet street, and with that handy wee alley-way next door thinks, hello, here's my chance. He drags her into the alley and tries it on, hence the ripped knickers, but then she fights back and he panics, pulls out the knife and stabs her. Then scarpers, obviously.'

'And is that what you think happened?' she asked.

'Aye, I suppose so,' Frank said.

Maggie detected the uncertainty in his voice.

'But?'

'But she was stabbed. Which means the assailant came prepared. I'm not saying it means anything, but I've mentioned it to the murder team.'

'But it's been what, nearly three weeks now?' Maggie said. 'And no leads?'

Frank shrugged. 'Aye, it's another DCS Barker masterclass. But I'm probably being unfair to him.' To Maggie, he didn't sound the least bit concerned if he was. 'The thing is, the forensic boys haven't found anything worthwhile. I know it's a bit unsavoury to say it, but normally in these attempted rape cases the perpetrator's got his dick out and well...well, often they find traces of semen. But nothing in this case.'

'So that's why they've been able to release the body to the family for the funeral?' Maggie asked. 'Because the forensics have drawn a blank?'

'Aye, I suppose so,' Frank said again. 'Not so much drawn a blank, but rather they've got everything they need. And they know that funerals are sad, but they do help in the grieving process. So they don't like to hang onto the body any longer than they have to.'

'And there were definitely no witnesses?' Jimmy asked.

'Nothing,' Frank said, shaking his head. 'No-one's come forward and there's no CCTV on that quiet wee side road. The fact is, if you were looking for somewhere in London to get away with murder, it's well-nigh perfect.'

'And what about that text or WhatsApp or whatever it was?' Jimmy asked. 'You know, the one she got just before she ran off.'

'Well that's a funny thing,' Frank said, screwing up his nose, 'because when they looked at her phone records, there was nothing. Are you sure you didn't imagine it mate?'

'Definitely not,' Jimmy said. 'Like I told you, it was as if she'd been expecting it. That's why I remember it so clearly.'

'Well there was definitely nothing in the call records. Maybe it was some notification or alert or something.'

At that moment, Jimmy's phone rang. Or at least, it blasted out one of the many musical ringtones he liked to attach to his regular callers. What he had chosen for her, she couldn't say, although it had to be a good fifty-fifty bet it was his namesake Rod Stewart's *Maggie May*. Frank's was the strident opening riff of Nirvana's *Smells Like Teen Spirit*. This one was altogether gentler and instantly recognisable. *Let It Go, Let It Go, The Cold Never Bothered Me Anyway.* That bloody song from *Frozen*, an ear-worm if there ever was one.

He gave a coy smile. 'It's Elsa, from the office.' *Of course.* Elsa Berger, native of the Czech Republic, the sweet and efficient administration manager of Riverside House. Elsa Berger, who was hopelessly in love with Jimmy Stewart.

He laughed as they shared some private joke and then she saw him raise an eyebrow in evident surprise.

'Really?' he said. 'Tell him not to go anywhere. We'll be there in five minutes.'

'Well?' Maggie asked impatiently, after Elsa had finally allowed him to hang up.

'We've got a visitor. It's Rory Overton, and he says he wants to do a deal.'

\*\*\*

Elsa had managed to secure one of the shared meeting rooms at short notice, and was now bustling around clearing up the empty coffee-cups and mineral water bottles that the last occupants had thoughtlessly left behind.

'You want drinks?' she enquired, without interrupting her labours. 'Coffee, tea, water?'

'Mr Overton?' Maggie asked. 'Would you like a drink?'

He shook his head. 'I'd just like to get on with it if you don't mind.' The tone was smoother than usual, which made her suspicious. *He must want something.*

'I'm so terribly sorry for your loss,' she said. 'We both are, especially poor Jimmy, given how close he was to the terrible events. And I can't even begin to imagine how your wife must be feeling right now. To lose a close family member is just so awful, but to lose your identical twin is simply unimaginable.'

'Thank you,' he said, giving her a sad look. 'She's coping, that's the best we can say. Just taking every day at a time. I know it's a cliché, but that's exactly how it is.'

'Aye, it must be incredibly tough for her,' Jimmy added, 'especially the way poor Elspeth died. I didn't get to know her very well, but she was a lovely girl.'

'Yes she was,' Overton said. 'It's been a terrible loss to everyone. Which I suppose is why I'm here. There's been quite enough suffering you see, and I don't want Kirsty to face any more of it.'

Maggie gave him a quizzical look. 'Everyone would agree with that sentiment, but I'm not sure how we can help.'

'You can help, I think,' he said. 'It's Alison you see. We want to do right by her. And a court battle won't help anyone. Not now. There's been enough bad feeling and we don't want any more on top of what's happened.'

She nodded. 'So would you like us to try and draw up an arrangement that would be agreeable to both parties? Is that what you want us to do?'

'Yes, in a nutshell. That's it. And we want it wrapped up as soon as you can. In days, if that's possible.'

Maggie furrowed her brow as she tried to work out what this meant. They knew one of the twins had already done a deal with their stepmother that basically said *you tell the court under oath that I'm the elder and we'll see you are all right*. So did this mean that it must have been the late Elspeth who had come to that arrangement with Alison Macallan? Whatever the case, surely it didn't matter now that there could be no dispute as to who would inherit Ardmore House and the estate? And yet here he was, in their offices, anxious to do a deal.

'Yes, well I'm sure we can come up with something,' she said, smiling. 'So do you have anything in mind? A starting point for the negotiations?'

'We'll leave the details to you,' Overton said, 'but you can go up to a million.'

'A million quid?' Jimmy said, unable to hide his surprise. 'That's a hell of a lot of money.'

Maggie caught the faintly pitying look that flashed across Overton's face. *Not to us it isn't. Not now that we've inherited a country estate.*

'There's just one condition,' Overton said, 'and just so you're absolutely clear, it's a deal-breaker.'

'What's that?' Maggie said.

'She can't live on the estate. She'll need to give up the lodge house and find somewhere else to live. I know she likes Edinburgh. I'm sure she could find a very comfortable place there with that sort of money.'

She gave him an uncertain look. 'Well, yes, but Alison really loves Ardmore, I know that from when I spoke to her at the start of all this. And it's been her home for twenty-five years at least.'

'So?' Overton said. 'There's nothing to keep her there now, and a new start is probably exactly what she needs. I mean, who would want to live somewhere where there's so many unhappy memories?'

Well *you* would for a start, Maggie thought, or so it seemed. But then she already knew his desire to be lord of the Ardmore estate trumped any other considerations in his life. She wondered if Kirsty Macallan shared the same desire. Somehow she doubted it, but it was Rory Overton who called the shots in that marriage and Kirsty would have little option but to go along with it.

'Very well,' she said, 'I'll see what we can do. But it might not be as easy as you think.'

He smiled. 'I'm sure you can work something out, both of you. I have every faith. And as for your fee, how about five grand plus expenses?'

'We charge by the hour,' Jimmy said. 'Two hundred pounds plus expenses. But yes, five grand might just about cover it.'

'Fine, whatever,' Overton said dismissively. 'So we're good to go then?'

'Agreed,' Maggie said. 'I'll speak to Alison as soon as I can, and see where we end up.'

He stood up and edged towards the door. 'That's all good then. Oh, and there's one more thing before I go. It's about the funeral. We want it to be a quiet gathering with just family and close friends. So I'm afraid you won't be able to come, either of you. I hope you don't mind, but I'm sure you understand.'

***

Of course, afterwards when Maggie and Jimmy reflected on the outcome of the meeting, they could see very well what was going on. The Overtons, or the Overton-Macallans as they had recently restyled themselves, were forging ahead with a brand new future in Scotland and they wanted as far as possible to sever connections with the past, to somehow wipe it away as if it had never existed. But that didn't really explain why an innocuous private investigator and her assistant, whom they had met on only three previous occasions, should be barred from Elspeth Macallan's funeral. Unless they had something to hide, that was, which made Maggie all the more determined that they should be represented.

The problem was, she could think of only one way that could legitimately come about, and she feared that Jimmy Stewart was not going to like her proposal. And when, after no little trepidation, she told him what she had in mind, her fears were realised.

# Chapter 25

Frank was feeling pleased with himself. It was the day of the planned raid on the home of Geordie, the egocentric hacker and street-artist, and for once, and contrary to expectations, he'd managed to get all his ducks in a row from a paperwork perspective. When you were planning one of these raids, especially an armed raid, there was a mountain of forms to be filled in and a barrage of brass-level signatures to be obtained. But because of this, these operations often had the propensity to go tits-up schedule-wise, due to the availability, or more accurately the lack of availability, of the latter. The brass set their own timetables and in particular liked to get out and about, glad-handing with politicians, community leaders and businessmen, and no ACC was going to give up a round of golf just to be in the office to sign a poxy Department 12B chit. But today, by some miracle, he had all the papers on his desk, all neat and tidy in a blue transparent plastic folder with every *i* dotted and *t* crossed. The raiding squad would be all ready to go later this evening when, if Geordie followed his normal routine, he would be arriving home from his latest assignment as a cyber-security consultant at an international bank over at Canary Wharf. Naive bastards, they clearly had no idea what sort of guy they were employing.

It had been Ronnie French's idea to postpone the raid until eight o'clock in the evening rather than the six-thirty it had originally been planned for, on the basis that they were more likely to find the Geordie guy on-line and thus have the opportunity to catch him mid-hack, if that was the right way to describe it. Frenchie's reasoning was that most people prepared something to eat and relaxed for a while immediately after returning from work, a reasoning that was hard to argue with, so Frank didn't try. It had also been Frenchie's idea to go in hard with the armed response squad. That particular proposal hadn't surprised Frank, since he knew from previous experience that nothing excited Ronnie more than to pile into a raid with all guns blazing. In fact, nothing excited the somnambulant Ronnie French *except* the prospect of an armed skirmish, or so it seemed. However, what had really annoyed Frank was that his boss DCI Jill Smart agreed. She had, as was her way, performed a risk assessment of the upcoming operation which concluded that since there was a material chance that the suspect could be armed, then the police should be armed too. Frank for the life of himself couldn't see why some terminally vain computer geek should be more likely to be armed than any other low-life but saw no point in arguing, especially since Jill had undertaken to take care of all the tedious paperwork involved herself. And so it was that at seven-fifty precisely they were assembled at the entrance door of Geordie's block of flats, they being Frank, Ronnie French and two taciturn armed officers in full riot gear, one of whom was equipped with a sturdy battering ram.

'Are we going to smash the front door in too boss?' French asked, pointing at the semi-glazed entrance. 'I think it's safety glass so we should be ok.'

Frank gave him an indulgent smile. 'I know you're desperate for a big rumpus mate, but let's just wait a couple of minutes shall we? There's always a bit of to-ing and fro-ing in these places.'

They didn't have to wait much more than half a minute when a stern-faced middle-aged woman appeared on the pavement alongside them. She shot Frank a disapproving look.

'What's going on here?' she said sharply.

'Nothing to worry about madam,' he said, beaming her a reassuring smile. 'Just a routine police matter, that's all. Tell me, do you live in these flats?'

She nodded. 'Of course I do.'

'And what floor are you on?'

'I'm on the second. Flat twenty-two.'

'Aye ok then. So we'll just come through with you if that's all right. We're heading up to the fourteenth in a minute so we'll be taking the lift. Now off you go and have a nice evening.'

She looked at him uncertainly before complying.

'Right boys, we're in,' Frank said. 'And remember Frenchie, let me knock first before you give the boys the nod to batter his bloody door down. Because the Met has to pay for any damage.'

'Ah come on guv, where's the fun in that?' Ronnie said.

'Don't worry, I'm sure there'll be plenty of fun once we're in.'

Frank had done a fair amount of groundwork in preparation for the raid, and in particular had managed to suss out the physical layout of the place, courtesy of a short conversation with the leaseholder of the building. It turned out the suspect occupied a river-facing flat, one of eight on that floor, his front door immediately opposite the entrance to the lift with the safety stairwell alongside, which was perfect for securing the op scene. All they had to do was station one of the armed boys in front of the lift doors and there would be no means of escape even if he did manage to burst past them. And as to the name of the suspect, the Canary Wharf bank and the leaseholder of the building had finally come up trumps, although it had taken them a fortnight to do so, and then it took just five minutes to cross-reference the two lists. There he was, standing out resplendently in both. *Daniel Clarkson.* It was early days, but now they had a name, it wouldn't take long to put together a profile of the guy. The request had already gone into the bank's procurement department to release whatever personal details they held on their cyber-contractor, and they expected to get a lot of useful information from that. Disappointingly, he didn't seem to have a criminal record, but of course that was about to change. *Big time.*

'Right lads, you know what to do,' Frank said as the lift doors slid open. 'I knock the door, we give him twenty seconds, and then in we go. And please, no shooting.' It was meant as a joke, but neither of the armed guys responded with a smile.

He rapped on the door three times. *'Daniel Clarkson. This is the police. Open up.'* They stood silently, awaiting a response.

'Daniel Clarkson. Police. Open up.'

'We need to go in,' French said impatiently. 'He might be destroying evidence. Guv, come on, let's get in there.'

Frank raised an eyebrow in mock disgust. 'Aye all right then. Ok, in we go now boys.'

The officer with the battering ram took a wide backswing and then let rip, smashing open the flimsy door with his first attempt.

'Daniel Clarkson,' Frank shouted as they streamed in, 'this is the police. Stay exactly where you are and don't move.' Behind him, he saw one of the officers had drawn his pistol. 'No bloody guns I said, for god's sake. He's a hacker not a bloody terrorist.'

It seemed as if the suspect had been relaxing on his sofa before their unexpected arrival. On the wall, a huge wide-screen television was showing a Premier League football match but with the sound muted. A laptop sat on a small table, open on a Facebook page. *Geordie, Street Artist*. So now there was no doubting they'd got the right guy.

'Right, grab that laptop Frenchie and then let's see where he's hiding.' He pushed open a half-closed door and found himself in a kitchen, feeling the breeze on his face from the wide-open window.

'Not here,' Frank called. 'He can't be far away. There's just two bedrooms and a bathroom.'

'We've already looked,' shouted one of the officers. 'No sign of him.'

'Well we're on the fourteenth floor so he's not jumped out of the bloody window, has he?' At least, he hoped he hadn't. 'Have you looked under the beds and in the wardrobes.'

'Yeah, all clear,' came the reply. Which just left that door in the hallway, the cloakroom or broom cupboard or whatever you wanted to call it.

Silently, Frank took hold of the handle then nodded to the officer with the Glock 17, who dropped down on one knee, pistol pointed at the door. With a deft movement, he yanked it open.

'Bloody hell.'

Slumped against a bundle of coats was the body of a man, mouth and eyes open in a grotesque expression, frozen in place by rigor mortis. Beneath him, a pool of congealed blood had spread almost to the door of the little cupboard, evidence to this being the location where the murder had been perpetrated. Six to eight hours probably since he'd been killed Frank reckoned, but they'd let the forensic guys work that out exactly. What was certain was that Daniel Clarkson wasn't going to be answering any of their questions now.

\*\*\*

Next day, down at Paddington Green, Frank and Ronnie French were with DCI Jill Smart and DI Pete Burnside for an informal briefing on the Clarkson murder. The critical question they were addressing was if there was any concrete evidence linking it to the Elspeth Macallan case, and therefore should it be handed over to Detective Superintendent Colin Barker to become a joint investigation. The truth was, Frank couldn't say one way or the other.

'What are the forensics saying?' Jill asked. 'About the cause of death I mean.'

'Stabbing ma'am,' Frank said. 'Two or three times in the abdomen. They're doing the formal autopsy later today and then we'll know for sure.'

'Poor guy,' Jill said.

'Sounds like he got what he deserved,' Burnside said with characteristic lack of sympathy.

'So ma'am,' Frank explained to Smart, 'one interesting thing is the phone records put him at the scene of that tragedy up in Scotland where Elspeth's father killed her brother Peter and then shot himself. We don't know why Clarkson was there and whether he saw anything, so we don't know if there's a connection. To be fair, we don't know too much about the guy at the moment, but we should be able to fill in most of the blanks with a bit of digging.'

'I'll be on to that as soon as we're done here ma'am,' French said helpfully. 'Now that we've got his name and address and where he works it shouldn't be too hard.'

Frank nodded. 'And as to his murder, it seems likely that someone took exception to being blackmailed and this was done to shut him up. So that's going to be our first line of enquiry.'

'Yes, I'd go along with that,' Smart said, nodding. 'Find out who else he was blackmailing.'

*Who else.* Because there was no avoiding that bloody great elephant in the room. That they already knew the name of the person who had the greatest motive to shut Geordie up for good. Or to exact revenge, as was more likely.

'I suppose we'll have to question her ma'am?' Frank asked. 'ACC Frost I mean?'

Jill gave a despairing shake of the head. 'We need to go easy on that. We can't question her unless we have grounds that she was involved. Evidence-led, that's how it's supposed to be, remember? Even if she is the prime suspect.'

'Understood ma'am,' Frank said. He saw the look of disappointment on Ronnie French's face. 'But I'm sure we'll find something.'

'Good,' she said, giving French a stern look. 'So there's probably no need to hand the investigation over to our friend Barker right now I would say. And if you're ok with it Pete, I'd like to keep it with Frank in Department 12B for a day or two just to tidy it up, and then we'll pass it to your Serious Crimes team.'

'Sure ma'am,' Burnside shrugged. 'Fine by me. I don't need the work, believe me.'

Jill smiled at Frank. 'I assume you've still got that slightly questionable relationship with that forensic officer?'

He returned her smile. 'Eleanor Campbell you mean? I do, and it's strictly professional before you ask. But yes, I'm sure somewhere in Clarkson's cyber history is the key to his murder and she'll help us find it, no question.

We've got his laptop remember? We'll get onto it right away.'

So now once again, progress in a case was in the hands of the temperamental prima donna of Maida Vale Labs. But then again he thought, it could be worse.

He might have had to rely on Ronnie French alone.

## Chapter 26

WPC Lexy McDonald had woken with a mixture of trepidation and excitement that morning, as she contemplated the importance of the day that lay ahead. A day, that if it went to plan, which might very well unlock the key to who had carried out the terrible killings of Morag and Isabelle McKay. And by doing so, start to put right the horrendous miscarriage of justice caused by the sloppy police work that was fast becoming the shameful hallmark of the case. That's what DI Stewart had told her at least, and she was determined not to let him down.

The key was of course to find out who had made that anonymous call reporting that a murder was in progress. She had discovered through her initial enquiries that BT only routinely kept records of incoming emergency calls for six months, although occasionally they would hold some older ones if they were monitoring calls for training purposes during the period in question. But unfortunately they didn't have these extra ones for the time they were interested in, meaning that they would have to ask the police emergency call response centre in Govan, which had every prospect of being rather more problematic. Because she would need to tell them *why* she wanted them, and that would mean breaking cover. And they had already discovered that when that happened, things had a habit of going missing.

'Aye, well don't worry about that,' DI Stewart had said when she had asked his advice. 'Just tell your sarge what

I've asked you to do, all tidy and above board. I'm sure it'll cause ructions behind the scenes, but that in itself will tell a wee story, don't you think?'

So she had taken his advice, going so far as asking Sergeant Muir if he would come along with her to the call centre on the basis that they might get more joy if it was an experienced officer who was asking the questions. But not unexpectedly he declined, and furthermore decreed that her visit would have to wait a day or two, due to him having a higher-priority task for her. There had been a spate of burglaries in the nearby Castlemilk housing scheme, and the police were having a crackdown, flooding the area with uniformed officers as a show of strength and conducting intensive door-to-door enquiries. All hands to the pump, that was the clear message being handed down by the brass, and all other matters would have to wait in the queue until the two-day exercise was complete. Two days in which anything embarrassing at that call-centre could be quietly tidied away.

Still, she had actually enjoyed the diversion, relishing the chance to get out and about in the real world, although it had to be said that the drug-invested real world of Castlemilk seemed rather less than pleased to see them. With fifty-five percent unemployment and the same percentage of single-parent households, it was a microcosm of the social problems that still afflicted the great city, despite years of gentrification, a gentrification that had taken a wide swerve to avoid this bleak outpost. But she'd met plenty of folks who had been brought up in places just like it, yet had gone on to do very well for themselves. There was always hope, even if you had to look hard to find it.

On the map, it had looked an easy walk from New Gorbals to the call-handling centre, but it turned out to be a good forty-five minutes at a brisk pace, and she'd worked up quite a sweat by the time she got there. The centre occupied a discreet low-rise office block with minimal signage identifying its purpose. Lexy wasn't quite sure how these places worked, but had a vague understanding that the staff were mainly civilians but under police management. A few years ago they'd gone on strike, she remembered that, over plans to consolidate locations and slash pay and conditions, or at least that's how the unions had portrayed it, but that all seemed to have settled down now as far as she knew.

The double front doors opened into a tiny reception area. A female receptionist sat at a desk, protected behind a vertical glass panel that reached all the way to the ceiling.

'Hi, WPC Lexy McDonald from New Gorbals,' she said, flashing her warrant card. 'I think I'm seeing a Jane Scott.'

'Yes that's right,' the receptionist said pleasantly. 'We have you on our list for Jane. Could you sign the register please?' She slid a visitors' book and a ball point pen through the slot. Lexy was expecting something altogether more hi-tech, and then she caught sight of the CCTV camera that was pointing straight at her and beaming her face onto a wall-mounted TV monitor. As she scribbled her name, the facial-recognition technology would be quietly working away in the background, cross-checking her identity to make sure everything stacked up. A few moments later, a door opened and a smartly-dressed woman in her mid-thirties stepped through to greet her, carrying a buff folder in one hand.

'Hi, I'm Jane Scott, morning-shift supervisor,' she said, extending the other hand. 'Follow me, I've booked a wee room for us.'

The door opened up into a vast open-plan office peopled by a small army of head-set equipped call-handlers housed in tiny cubicles, presumably to screen the sound of their voices from their near-neighbour, although she wondered if even with that protection they could hear anything, such was the volume of chatter filling the room.

'This is where it all happens,' Scott said. 'We get over a thousand calls a day. Twenty-four-by-seven. It's non-stop, as you can see.'

'I can imagine,' Lexy said, feigning interest. They got a lot of calls. They answered them. *Big deal.* She could see where they were heading, towards a glass-walled meeting room tucked in the corner of the office, and she could see they were to be joined by a third party, already installed at the head of a small table. And as she got close, she could make out the badges on his epaulette. A crown and one pip. *A Chief Superintendent.*

'WPC McDonald, is it? Welcome to our Govan facility. Sit down, please.' His manner made it clear who was going to be in charge of this meeting, if she hadn't already guessed.

'This is Chief Superintendent Watson,' Jane Scott said. 'He's in overall charge of our facility here.'

'So how can we help you McDonald?' he said, wearing a condescending smile. Surely this was a rhetorical question because she'd told Scott exactly what she wanted when she'd called to make the arrangements a couple of days ago. But he waited patiently for her to answer.

*Young, keen, dumb, naive.* That was the way to play it, not that it would be too difficult for her to pull *that* trick off. And in any case, WPCs just a week or two out of probation would be inconsequential pond-life to a guy like Watson.

'The DI I'm assigned to wanted me to get some incoming call records for that date I told Jane about sir.' She gave him what she hoped was a nervous smile. 'I'm afraid I don't really know why sir. He didn't really explain it very clearly sir. I'm sorry, I suppose I should have asked sir. Before I came, I mean sir.'

He smiled at her, this time with some warmth. 'Well that's all right WPC McDonald, I'm sure we can help you. And please, go easy on the sirs if you don't mind.'

Turning to Scott he asked, 'Well Jane, how did we get on with her request? Find anything?'

'Yes Chief Superintendent, I pulled the records for the period in question. We were looking for calls between around four-thirty and six-thirty. It was a fairly quiet evening by our normal standards. There were fifty-four calls so it wasn't too difficult to find the one that PC McDonald was interested in.'

Watson clasped his hands in front of him and nodded. 'Good news then.'

There was something in Scott's manner that made Lexy suspect it wasn't.

'Well yes sir, I suppose it is. Look, here it is.' She took a sheet of paper from her folder, laid it on the table facing them and pointed to a row in the list. 'It came in at seventeen forty-eight. Reported disturbance at Ardmore village, number fourteen Loch Road. That's the one, isn't it?'

'Yes, that's it,' Lexy said, wearing a perplexed expression, 'but that column there, incoming number?...'

'Yes, I'm afraid so,' Jane Scott said, giving a rueful smile. 'Number withheld.'

***

Of course he had bloody well known, she could tell that from his smug expression. Because otherwise he wouldn't have gone through the whole elaborate charade, to pretend that his outfit was being *so* helpful when it was being anything but. She had little doubt that if there had been an incoming number on the records, then it would have conveniently disappeared, just like that white-board capture had. And now she would have to call DI Stewart and tell him the bad news, and she didn't expect him to be exactly over the moon, not that he would blame her of course. But that didn't take away from the fact that this was a setback, and a setback on her watch too. It was disappointing, and she didn't like to disappoint him.

And then, out of the blue, she remembered the story he had been regaling everyone with on that excellent evening up in the Lochmorehead Hotel. About a clever forensic officer called Eleanor Campbell and an even cleverer intelligence analyst from MI5 called Jayden Henry. And how they had instant access to every phone call in the whole wide world. Suddenly she felt a whole lot better.

As she picked up her phone to call DI Stewart, some part of her was annoyed with herself for not having thought of it earlier, saving herself having to be the subject of Watson's self-satisfaction. But then when she considered it again, she changed her mind. Yes, the visit had been a waste of time as far as the primary objective was concerned, but on the other hand it provided further confirmation of their suspicions. Now there could be no doubt there was a conspiracy, orchestrated from the highest levels in the force, to conceal the truth about the McKay murders.

And so it was that five minutes after she had spoken to Frank, he had called Ronnie French, who, five minutes after that, had called his mate Jayden at MI5, requesting a special favour. And five minutes after that, they had discovered the 999 call had come from the landline of Ardmore House, the sumptuous lochside home of Commodore Roderick Macallan.

*The home of the murderer, Commodore Roderick Macallan.*

# Chapter 27

Maggie knew it would be the hardest thing she had ever asked Jimmy to do in the two years they had worked together, a task way outside what was reasonable for any boss to ask of an employee. Not that boss-employee was an accurate description of their working relationship, because although it might be her name on the business cards, she and Jimmy were partners in every sense. Without him, she knew there could be no Maggie Bainbridge Associates, and more than that, without him, hers would only be half a life. And floating along in the recesses of her mind was the thought she did not dare bring to the surface. Without Jimmy, there would have been no Frank. Soon, they would be back in Scotland, with a promise that this time they would find time to stop off on the bonnie banks of Loch Lomond and share another of these lovely dinners. And maybe, finally, this time, that little spark of *something* that existed between them might catch alight at last.

But in the end, and not without considerable reservations, she had asked him to do it. *Speak to Flora and ask if you can accompany her to Elspeth Macallan's funeral.* From the outside looking in, it wasn't such an unreasonable request, and after all, estranged couples often found themselves thrown together, albeit reluctantly, for family events. Weddings, bar mitzvahs, school plays and such like. Now Maggie stood in the little church yard in Lochmorehead, watching them as they waited to enter the church, Flora elegant in a full-length black wool coat, her flame-red hair tied back in an elaborate double French plait, Jimmy in a dark grey suit, white shirt and black tie, the universal uniform of respect for the dead. And in the glinting autumn sunshine, they stood silently together, looking perfectly beautiful, their physical forms interlocking as if designed for one another. She had never seen him so quiet as he had been on the flight up and then during the onward drive, and she thought she knew what he would have been thinking the whole time. *This may be my last chance.*

She caught Alison Macallan laying a modest spray of flowers against the marble tombstone of her late husband, no more than a few metres from the open grave that would be the final resting place of poor Elspeth.

'Hello Alison,' she said, smiling and glancing up at the cloudless sky. 'At least we've got a nice day for it.'

'Yes, but I'm really sick of funerals. There's been too many. It's as if this place is cursed.'

Maggie nodded, remembering that Jimmy had expressed exactly the same emotion.

'Your family has suffered so much. I really do hope there are better times ahead for all of you.'

'Well, you've helped enormously with that Maggie,' she said, giving a soft smile. 'I really can't thank you enough.'

'It's the least I could do.' *We'll leave the details to you but you can go up to a million.* That was the instruction Rory Overton had given her and she always followed her clients' instructions to the letter. Except, feeling sorry for Alison Macallan, she'd gone straight in with the offer the full sum. 'Have you made any plans?'

'Yes, I've seen a nice little flat just off Charlotte Square. I've friends nearby and it will be lovely. A new city and a new start, that's what it is, isn't it? And I won't miss this place. I thought I could never leave but I was wrong.'

'And you could always come back and visit,' Maggie said uncertainly.

'No,' Alison said, quite firmly. 'I've done a lot of thinking in the last few days, and after everything Roderick put me through over all these years, I realised that most of the memories are bad ones. The loch is beautiful of course but there's hundreds of beautiful lochs in Scotland. I don't need to see this one ever again.'

Maggie wasn't sure if this was the appropriate time or place, but she decided to ask anyway.

'I knew you and your husband were separated towards the end, but I didn't know you'd had problems before that. But forgive me, it's probably something you don't want to talk about.'

She shrugged. 'I didn't know it when I married him, but then we never do, do we? It was the power you see, and it went to his head. He was the commander of the base with over two thousand men at his command and the pastoral responsibility for the families too. There were so many of them over the years. Promises of cushy postings, the right word in the right ear when it came to the promotion boards, all that sort of thing. And all in return for little favours, if you know what I mean. He nearly got kicked out ten years ago when he got an officer's wife pregnant, but it was all hushed up in the end. And it never stopped him, he just kept on doing it. So yes, you could say we had problems. But really, I don't want to talk about it ever again.'

And yet here she was at his graveside laying flowers. She knew it only too well from her own disastrous marriage. You could love someone and hate them at the same time. And then Maggie remembered what Jimmy had told her about Susan Priest and her controlling husband.

'I think poor Susan Priest may have suffered in the same way. Her husband didn't seem to be a very nice man.'

Alison gave her a perplexed look as if struggling to recall the name, then said. 'Susan Priest? Yes of course, Susan McColl, the twins' old nanny. I heard what happened to her. It's all around the village as you can imagine. It was so awful.'

It wasn't the reaction that Maggie was expecting. 'But...' she started, then bit her lip. And then she thought about what Frank had told her, about Ronnie French's visit to Winchester, about the old Ford Focus seen lurking just along the road from where the terrible incident took place. She remembered her last visit to Alison's lochside home, where the path to the porch was blocked by the old car parked on the tiny gravel drive. It seemed impossible to believe, but surely there could only be one reason why Alison Macallan had failed to mention her visit to the Priests not more than three weeks earlier?

Now it was important to act perfectly normally, for Maggie not to betray her suspicions until she could pass them onto the police. She smiled at her,

'Yes, these teenage joy-riders are a plague, aren't they? They get high on drugs and then cause so much devastation to the lives of their innocent victims. I expect the police will catch the perpetrator sooner or later. But anyway, maybe we can get five minutes in the hotel after the wake, get your agreement signed and draw a line under all of this?'

'That would be great,' Alison said. 'But here, it looks like the service might be about to start. I'd better go in, though I'm not looking forward to it. Will you sit with me Maggie?'

'I'm not invited I'm afraid. Friends and close family only.'

Maggie turned to look at the door of the old church, just in time to catch Jimmy and Flora entering.

They were holding hands.

*** 

He supposed you could call it a team meeting, although generally speaking Frank didn't do teams nor meetings either. But now he could sense they were within a whisper of solving the convoluted tangle of linked murders, and he couldn't slot in these final pieces of the jigsaw without the assistance of wee Eleanor Campbell and the annoyingly laid-back Ronnie French. Now it seemed almost certain that it had been Commodore Roderick Macallan who had murdered Morag and Isabelle McKay, but the motive was still a mystery, and was there a connection to Daniel Clarkson? The brief he had given Eleanor was as wide-ranging as it was in fact brief. *Find out everything that Daniel Clarkson was up to*. She had, as he had expected, initially bridled at the task, because that's what she always did, but eventually, and only after he had threatened to ask another of her Maida Vale colleagues instead, she complied.

In parallel, French had been tasked with piecing together Clarkson's life story, and Frank had to admit, albeit reluctantly, that the lazy slug had done a decent job. *Thirty-one years old, raised in Gateshead, joined the navy at eighteen, trained as a communications specialist, served on the nuclear submarines, based out of Ardmore, joined civvy street after ten years' service, set himself up as an IT contractor specialising in cyber security.* That made Frank laugh. Talk about poacher turning gamekeeper. But it was the discovery that Clarkson had been at Ardmore base at the exact same time as Lieutenant James McKay, both under the overall command of Commodore Roderick Macallan, that had excited him most. Because there was no way that was just some sort of bizarre coincidence. *No way.*

And now, a few days later, they were huddled round Eleanor Campbell's desk, waiting for the great diva to deliver her wisdom, and hoping what she had discovered would cause everything to drop neatly into place.

'So how have you got on?' Frank said, trying not to betray the anxiety he felt. If none of this delivered, he feared the investigation might crash and burn before it really got started.

'You said find everything,' she said sourly, 'that's like *a lot*.'

He winked at French. 'Exactly. That's why we picked you. So, how have you got on?'

She gave him a glum look. 'He was using 128-bit encryption. So, *not good*.'

'Does that mean we're like buggered then?' Frank said.

She either didn't notice his gently mockery or chose to ignore it. 'No-one can hack 128-bit encryption. Not even Jayden. But I did manage to get *some* stuff.'

That was the thing about Eleanor, he thought. She liked to tease you with wee snippets of information, forcing you to drag it out of her so that she felt appreciated. So he tried to sound appreciative.

'That's amazing, well done,' Frank said, hoping his insincerity wasn't betrayed by his tone. 'Tell us more, do.'

'So he'd left some things unencrypted on his hard drive,' she began earnestly, 'and also I got into his bank account. He was quite rich. Nearly a hundred and eighty grand in his current account.'

'You hacked his bank account?' Frank said, impressed.

'Not hacked, *accessed*,' she corrected. 'Jayden lent me an app.'

'Good old Jayden. And do we have any ideas how our boy Geordie came by this pile of dosh?'

'Like, *yeah*,' she said, giving him a disparaging look. 'That Commodore dude paid him a hundred and twenty thousand.'

'*What*?' Frank spat out the response.

'Yeah, like four and a half years ago. Maybe an investment in his cyber business or something?'

'Nah,' French said. 'He only started that a couple of years' back when he came out the navy. Four years ago he was serving on HMS Azure, according to what I found out.'

'And are you sure Eleanor?' Frank said, still struggling to process the information. 'It was definitely Roderick Macallan who paid it?'

'Like, *yeah*,' she repeated, clearly offended that her statement should be challenged. 'Defo.'

'Interesting,' Frank said, his mind racing as he tried to work out what it meant. 'So why would he do that?'

'Services rendered guv,' French said simply. 'That's what it always is, ain't it?'

Frank nodded. 'Aye, you're probably right but it must have been something bloody big for that sort of money to be handed over.'

'Or dangerous,' French mused. 'I mean, risky-dangerous.'

'Well maybe,' Frank said. 'But isn't it more likely that this is keep your mouth shut money?'

The question wasn't meant to be rhetorical, but that's how it turned out. Because as soon as he said it, he knew he was right. Roderick Macallan had killed Morag and Isabelle McKay, he was sure of that, but this one hundred and twenty grand said that Clarkson was involved too in some way. And then he remembered. Clarkson had been called as an expert witness in the trial of Lieutenant James McKay, where he had testified that it was impossible for the communications between McKay and his wife to have been tampered with. Which meant almost certainly, although Frank didn't know how, that they *had* been. Now *that* sounded more like a hundred and twenty grand's worth of work.

Out of the blue he said, 'Eleanor, have you any idea how they communicate with submarines when they're underwater?'

'Packet-encrypted technology,' she answered with an air of nonchalance, as if everyone in the world should know it, 'but you wouldn't understand it.'

She was right, he didn't understand it, but that didn't matter, because he knew what it meant. Somehow, Daniel Clarkson had interfered with the email conversations between Lieutenant McKay and his wife, and in doing so had incriminated an innocent man. He could feel the anger growing inside him when he reflected on that breathtaking miscarriage of justice. An innocent man comes home from seven months at sea to a scene of unimaginable tragedy, and then, wrongfully imprisoned and unable to cope with the unbearable loss of his family, takes his own life. A terrible injustice that would have been avoided if the senior investigating officer had done his bloody job properly.

He was so consumed by his thoughts that he failed to notice that Eleanor was still speaking to him, talking about something else she'd found whilst rooting around Clarkson's hard drive.

It was a document he had evidently hacked from Roderick Macallan's computer. A document titled *The Last Will and Testament of Roderick Archibald Macallan.* A document dated just four months before Macallan shot his son and killed himself in the unknowing presence of Daniel Clarkson.

And now Frank could see how it all fitted together, sweet as a nut. *Everything.*

\*\*\*

The sombre sound of the organ drifted out into the churchyard, harmonising perfectly with the soft whistle of the wind blowing in from Loch More. *The Lord is My Shepherd, I'll Not Want.* Maggie didn't think the Macallan twins were religious in any way, so assumed the comforting hymns had been the choice of the minister. Whatever the case, they were succeeding in bringing back memories of her own Yorkshire childhood, of the Sunday morning routine of Sunday School then snaking into the old church to join the grown-ups for the last ten minutes of the service, then home for a proper roast beef lunch. Sweet memories they were, but in fact what was occupying her mind more than any brief bursts of nostalgia was Elspeth's brutal murder, not her sad funeral. The fact was, Maggie just didn't buy the opportunist sex-attack motive, not one bit, and now she had learnt from Frank that due to some mysterious development that he was not yet ready to share with her, he didn't buy it either. The first problem was that text or WhatsApp Elspeth had received just before she left Jimmy in the lurch in the restaurant, a text that seemed to have summoned her to her death, and yet, according to the police telecoms gurus, didn't exist. You didn't need to be Sherlock Holmes to know that something didn't add up with that. And something else that Frank had said was spinning around and around in her mind. *The fact is, if you were looking for somewhere in London to get away with murder, it's well-nigh perfect.* So, a text that didn't actually exist lured the beautiful young influencer out into the quiet street, where she was dragged up an alleyway and killed with no-one seeing a thing. *Something didn't add up.*

She became aware of the music becoming louder, and as she looked round, she saw the old oak doors had been opened and the procession was beginning to emerge. She took a step back so that she was part-concealed by the old yew tree, wishing to be respectful of the family's wishes but from where she could still observe Jimmy and Flora. Rory Overton was the lead pallbearer, one of six in all, and she wondered what was going through his head at the moment. For he had been in a relationship with Elspeth Macallan before switching allegiances to her sister Kirsty, a relationship that led to marriage and a child and a perfect picture-postcard life in West London. And now, conveniently, Elspeth was dead, leaving the inheritance of the Ardmore estate undisputed. Was that what Overton was thinking, an arrogant satisfaction as he considered how well everything had turned out for him?

*In the name of god, the merciful Father, we commit the body of Elspeth Anne Macallan to the peace of the grave.* The minister gave a silent nod and watched as they lowered the coffin into the grave, surrounded by the clutch of mourners standing with heads bowed in quiet contemplation, Jimmy and Flora shoulder-to-shoulder and still holding hands. Above the soft wind she could hear the sad sobs of Kirsty and she wondered once again how it must feel to lose a twin. Maggie was an only child and had spent much of her earlier childhood wishing for a brother or a sister, but now she was strangely grateful that she would never experience that pain herself.

Rory and Kirsty had now returned to the stone entrance vestibule, ready to accept the formal condolences of the mourners. She saw Jimmy touch his wife on the elbow then trudge over towards the yew tree.

'Well done,' Maggie whispered to him, 'and I hope everything was ok.'

He shrugged but didn't answer directly.

'I thought I'd best leave this bit to friends and family. And I always find these things a wee bit awkward, don't you?'

She nodded and gave a half-smile. The mourners had formed a line and were shuffling past the bereaved couple, some smiling, some sombre, exchanging a word or two, most looking as if they wished the ordeal to be over as soon as possible. As Jimmy had said, it was always an awkward moment. They watched as it became Flora's turn. Her face wore a sympathetic smile, and as she approached, she clasped Kirsty's hands in hers, leaning forward to whisper something in her ear. Then momentarily there was a change in Flora Stewart's expression, a mixture of apology and puzzlement, as if, unknowing, she had said the wrong thing. In a moment the smile had returned, empathetic and concerned as was mandated on these occasions. But Jimmy had noticed it too and gave Maggie a questioning look.

There was to be a modest wake at the Lochmorehead Hotel, a finger buffet with tea and coffee, scheduled to be done and dusted by one o'clock, although with the bar open for business it was expected there would be a few stragglers. Jimmy said he would put in a brief appearance, taking the opportunity to make some peace with his father-in-law and mother-in-law after three years of estrangement. With a full schedule of afternoon appointments, Dr Flora Stewart was heading back to her surgery, and Maggie somehow suspected that Jimmy would be relieved at that. Originally the schedule had including dropping off the inheritance agreement at Alison Macallan's lodge, and it had been agreed with Frank that they should continue with that whilst the

Hampshire police were tidying up the evidence on the Susan Priest hit and run. A walk had been planned, Jimmy keen on a near ten-mile expedition that would see her bag her first Munro, a label awarded to every Scottish mountain over three thousand feet in height, of which there were apparently two hundred and eighty-two. He had over one hundred to his name, his brother Frank precisely nil, which made her smile, because it was impossible to imagine the elder Stewart brother in a cagoule and walking boots. Rather like herself in fact, which is why, as diplomatically as possible, she had declined the offer. Instead they agreed on an all together gentler lochside stroll, taking in the eastern side to the point where it joined the sea. An easy five-miler there and back, but still allowing plenty of time for her to ask him once again the million-dollar question, but only if she dared. *How was it with you and Flora?*

'We should have hired a boat,' Maggie said. They stood on the rickety jetty that was the property of the hotel, looking down the loch towards the Atlantic Ocean. 'See how the sun shimmers on the surface, reflecting the mountains. It's so beautiful, isn't it?'

'Aye it is,' Jimmy conceded, 'but it's also bloody treacherous too. Have you not heard of the Loch More tidal race? It comes in and goes out at about thirty knots, and it's perfectly designed to capsize wee boats. It's absolutely lethal so novices like us are going nowhere near it. We'll stick to the shore, thank you very much.'

She laughed. 'Roger that Captain Stewart. So just a little stroll is it?'

'That's it. The path takes us up to the headland where we'll get a magnificent view right over to the islands, according to my map anyway. Ninety minutes there and ninety minutes back. We should be back in plenty of time for tea at my in-laws.'

'What?' She looked at him with astonishment.

'Sorry, didn't I tell you?' he said, smiling. 'Angus and Elizabeth have asked us to tea. It's a Scottish thing. Tuna sandwiches, shortbread biscuits and fruit scones. Five-thirty sharp.'

Maggie raised an eyebrow. 'So does that mean that relations are thawing then?'

He shrugged. 'They said it was nice to see me again. So perhaps.'

And now she could ask the question.

'And what about Flora? Is there a thaw there also?'

He shook his head. 'I don't know. Maybe you can give me some womanly insight when you see her later.'

She laughed. 'I don't think I'd get many votes as a relationship guru, given my track record. But I'll try my best.'

A few hundred yards down the path stood a pretty wooden boat-house, almost directly opposite the gatehouse which Alison Macallan was soon to vacate. Maggie had passed her suspicions on to Frank and now the Hampshire police were looking again at the Susan Priest hit and run, re-interviewing eye-witnesses and re-examining CCTV footage. It was only a matter of time before they came knocking on this door, exchanging Alison's dreams of a better life for twenty-five years in Cragton Valley prison.

Through the part-open door they could see a small rowing-boat, bobbing up and down on the ebbing tide. Painted on the stern was a name that must have seemed amusing at the time the owners conceived it. *Tinytanic*.

'Don't even think about it,' Jimmy said, catching her eye.

'Wasn't,' she lied, smiling back at him. 'And I remember what happened to the real Titanic.'

'Aye, although luckily there's no icebergs in Loch More as far as I know.'

They spent the rest of the afternoon in pleasant companionship, talking of this and that, or enjoying periods of comfortable silence. The scenery was breathtaking and she wondered what it must have been like to have grown up in such a paradise, immersed in nature's abundance. *Flora, Morag, Kirsty, Elspeth*. And now two of them were dead, brutally murdered, the idyllic childhood no protection against the bitter twists of unpredictable fate.

*\*\**

Angus and Elizabeth McLeod were warm and welcoming, their beautiful Victorian home decorated in rich hues that melted in seamlessly with the varnished wood panelling that was a feature of every room. The room they were in was dominated by an imposing stone fireplace featuring an elaborate cast-iron grate, which by the look of it had not been pressed into service for some months, even as the autumn shadows were lengthening. On a varnished oak sideboard, a sumptuous buffet had been laid out, as yet untouched as they awaited the return of Dr Stewart from her afternoon surgery.

'This has always been called the morning room,' Elizabeth was explaining, 'from long before our time here, although goodness knows why, because it actually catches the afternoon sun.'

'It's a lovely room,' Maggie said, 'and with such a beautiful view over the lake. Sorry, loch, I keep forgetting. And sorry again, I know it sounds like lock the way I say it.' By mentally adding around thirty years to Flora's thirty-two, she worked out that Elizabeth McLeod must be well into her sixties, but she certainly didn't look it, and the same went for Dr McLeod too. They were a good-looking couple and these superb genes had been combined then passed down to their beautiful daughter intact.

'Aye, you Sassenachs,' Angus McLeod said, in a kindly tone, 'but I hear from your accent you're a Yorkshire lass, so that's an honorary Scot in my book.'

'I'm indeed honoured,' she said, laughing. 'But I've spent the last two years working with Jimmy and his brother, so I feel as if I'm half-Scottish now anyway.'

'Yes, well they're from Glasgow, so the least said about that the better,' Angus teased. It seemed to Maggie that Jimmy's assessment was correct. Relations were thawing in the McLeod family. And then she saw him glance at his watch.

'Flora's a bit late, isn't she? Her last appointment was at half-past four so she should be here by now.'

'Paperwork dear I expect.' Maggie caught the glance between husband and wife, wondering if this soirée had been engineered by the McLeods in the hope of effecting a reconciliation, with their daughter a reluctant participant.

'Aye, that'll be it,' Angus said. 'Let's all have a wee sherry whilst we're waiting, shall we?'

But when three quarters of an hour had passed and there was still no sign of Flora, the atmosphere began to change, and the concern, at first mild, became more elevated.

'She's not answering her phone,' Elizabeth said, 'and I've tried the surgery switchboard and I'm just getting the answerphone.'

'Ach, it'll be fine,' Angus said, but there was no disguising the concern in his voice. And as Maggie's mind drifted back to the murder and the funeral and everything to do with the death of Elspeth Macallan, suddenly the mist cleared and it was all falling into place. *Everything.* She thought about the text message, and she thought about the quiet location of the little Fulham restaurant and she thought about the look Flora had given Kirsty Macallan. And she thought about something that Elspeth had said to her. *They had their own stupid language. Kirsty, Flora and Morag, making up silly words for everything. It was pathetic.*

'Something's wrong,' she said, her voice clipped and urgent. 'Something's badly wrong. Where would she go Elizabeth? Where did they go when they were kids? Flora and Morag and the Macallans?'

But Jimmy was already on the move. 'The boathouse. Elizabeth, will you call the police and the coastguard, and Angus, can you go and get your wee boat ready, quick as you can.'

\*\*\*

He was conscious that Maggie was trailing way behind him, but there was no time to worry about that now. There was only one thing on his mind. He had to get to her before brooding Loch More worked its malevolent destiny, its merciless currents racing and swirling, intent on swallowing any defenceless craft that was stupid enough to venture out on its waters. It only took two minutes to reach the boathouse, where his darkest fear was confirmed. *Tinytanic was gone.*

'Shit.' He ran to the edge of the little cobbled beach, scanning the loch, his eyes squinting against the glare of the low sun. *Shit, shit.* It had to be out there somewhere, but where? For a moment, he studied the water lapping against the edge and in an instant he had made the computation. The tide was on the turn and soon anything caught in that race would be dragged out to the Atlantic at a rate of knots. He had five or ten minutes at the most to save her.

He became aware that Maggie had arrived at his side.

'The boat's gone, hasn't it?' she said, her voice anxious. 'Can you see anything?'

'No, but it's got to be out there somewhere.'

'There,' she said suddenly. 'Look, can you see it? It's hard to spot with the sun in our eyes. Straight ahead.'

And he could just about make it out, the tiny boat bobbing around like a cork, miraculously still afloat but low in the water. *Dangerously low.* He estimated it was around three to four hundred metres away and he remembered back to his army days and that survival training course they'd sent him on, and that chart they'd splashed up on the screen in the warm Glencoe classroom. *Survival times in cold water.* But these waters, warmed by the Gulf Stream, although bloody cold, rarely got below freezing, so he'd have fifteen minutes at least and probably more. Not that these technicalities were going to influence his decision one bit.

'I'm going in,' he said, tearing off his shoes. 'Keep me in your line of sight if you can, in case the coastguard turns up.'

'But what about the currents?' Maggie said anxiously. 'You said it wasn't safe.'

He knew it wasn't safe, of course he knew, but what else could he do? And he was a strong swimmer, his broad shoulders capable of powering him one hundred metres in close to a minute. In a warm swimming pool, that was. Out here, it would be quite different, lucky if he could do the same distance in under three. But he had no choice.

As he plunged in, the icy coldness took his breath away, but he was ready for that and soon he was into his stride, his arms and legs synchronised in perfect harmony, extracting the maximum thrust from every stroke as he carved through the water. And on this outward leg, he was getting some assistance from the current although he knew the prevailing vector would be pushing him seaward. Meaning that getting them both back to the shore was going to be pretty much impossible, but that was something to worry about later. All that mattered right now was getting to Flora before the tiny dinghy gave up its struggle.

As he got further away from the shore the waves grew higher, a constant spray of salty water stinging his eyes, causing him to struggle to see where he was going. It was difficult to maintain a straight path against the cross-current, and the effort needed to correct course was beginning to sap his strength. His upper arms burned with pain as he ploughed on, forcing out one stroke after another, his body begging for him to stop. It was like his army survival training, except today there was no brutal sergeant-major making damn sure it would be more unpleasant to give up than to keep going. But today, the stakes were immeasurably higher. Today, it was a matter of life and death.

As he got closer, he could see her, sprawled across the bottom of the dinghy, her body already partially submerged as the waves crashed over the side, so close to sinking the flimsy craft. With a final effort he reached it, grabbing hold of the stern, grateful to have a moment to regain his breath. Now he could see Flora was unconscious, a trail of half-dried blood running down her cheek from where she had been struck a disabling blow on her temple. *Bastards*. He remembered vividly what they had drummed into them back on that survival course. *Stay with the boat if you possibly can.* Aye, if it was still afloat that was, and he could tell just by looking that the wee dinghy was seconds away from being overwhelmed. One more decent-sized wave and that would be it. The fact was, he had no choice. He had to get her out right away, before it dragged them both to a watery grave.

He pulled himself round so that he was parallel with her shoulders, where this close, he could see her chest moving, if imperceptibly, but enough to know she was still alive. *Thank god*. He reached over the side, keeping himself afloat by balancing his chest on the rim of the boat, and placed his hands under her armpits. As gently as he dared, he drew her towards him, the buoyancy of the salt water thankfully taking some of her weight. Now he had to flip onto his back, the classic passive-rescue position he had been taught in the army but had never before put into practice. *Hook your arms under the armpits of the casualty. Support their head with your hands. Tread water to save energy. Do not attempt to swim to shore except when there is no hope of rescue.* All so easy to accomplish when you were reading it in a book. Not so easy when a ten-mile-an-hour tide was pushing you away and the cold was draining you of every ounce of energy you possessed. But he managed to get some leverage by pushing with his knees against the side of the dinghy, forcing it to tilt towards him, and then with a powerful leg-stroke, he propelled them free.

Now, all they could do was wait for the rescue party and hope that it came bloody soon. Because Flora hadn't stirred, and he began to fear the onset of hypothermia, remembering another of these damn slides from the survival course. *At a water temperature of zero to six degrees, death is likely to occur between thirty to ninety minutes.* Flora was strong and fit, but she'd been in the water at least thirty minutes, probably more, and he had no idea the extent of her injuries. *Shit.* He held her closer to him, knowing that it wouldn't make a damn bit of difference, but he wasn't going to let her die on him. *Stay with me darling, stay with me. Don't leave me.*

A few metres away Tinytanic, now totally submerged, had given up its heroic struggle and was about to embark on a one-way journey to the bottom of Loch More. So that was it, they were on their own. And then he heard it, the angry buzz cutting through the cold evening air. An outboard motor, coming from the direction of Lochmorehead. *Thank god.* Then the slap of the inflatable boat as it carved through the waves, its prow raised like a Viking long-ship. Jimmy raised an arm in the air and yelled at the top of his voice although he doubted he could be heard above the noise of the engine.

'Angus! Angus! Over here!'

He heard the engine note change as Dr McLeod eased off the throttle, allowing the prow to settle back in the water, tweaking the tiller to bring the inflatable alongside his daughter and her rescuer. Jimmy answered his father-in-law's question before it was asked.

'She's alive Angus, but she's in a bad way. We need to get her warm as soon as we can.'

'I've got blankets and towels, and it's only a few minutes back to the jetty,' Angus shouted. 'Let's get her into the boat.'

It was difficult, but somehow between them they managed to bundle her limp body over the side. As her father swaddled her in the warm blankets, Jimmy dragged himself up and flopped onto the bottom of the boat, spent with exhaustion.

'Get her home Angus, get her home.'

Dr McLeod gave a nod of acknowledgement and opened the throttle to its maximum setting.

'Hold on to her Jimmy, it's going to be a rough ride.'

And as Jimmy pulled her close to him, he knew he could never ever let her go again.

\*\*\*

It seemed as if half the village had been waiting for them at the jetty, together with the coastguard helicopter, which somehow had managed to land on the hotel's front lawn and was now waiting to fly Flora to hospital in Glasgow. She had regained consciousness, but was only able to give the vaguest description of what had happened to her. She remembered two hooded figures approaching her as she left the surgery, and then she remembered been struck on the head and then nothing. It was assumed her abductors had bundled her into a vehicle then made the short drive to the boathouse, laying her in the dinghy before setting it adrift to face the wrath of the dangerous tidal race. Attempted murder of course, the method and opportunity as crystal clear as the waters of Loch More, but what of the motive?

Maggie Bainbridge knew, ninety-nine percent certain, but she needed Flora's confirmation to be absolutely sure. So she had approached her just as the paramedics were about to slide the stretcher into the helicopter, its engines already roaring in preparation for take-off so that it was almost impossible to hear. But by placing her ear within a whisker of Flora's lips, Maggie could just about make out the answer to her question.

*'It wasn't Kirsty. She wasn't Kirsty.'*

'I know,' Maggie said. 'I know she wasn't.'

## Chapter 28

They were in the departure lounge at Heathrow waiting for their flight to Glasgow, and although it was just quarter-past-ten in the morning and he was technically on duty, Frank still felt justified in enjoying a pint. A *celebratory* pint, because after all, it wasn't every day you solved *seven* murders and an attempted one too, surely some sort of record for his wee rag-tag department. He glanced over at Jill, deep in conversation with Assistant Commissioner Margaret Walsh, whom he'd just worked out was her boss's boss's boss. Anybody else he would have accused of arse-licking, but not DCI Jill Smart. It just wasn't her style.

Truth be told, he was a bit peeved that he hadn't been invited to the big Sir Brian meeting, but he knew there was a well-established protocol about such things, and when you were going to launch a process that would well and truly shaft the career of one of the top brass, convention dictated the bad news had to be delivered by an officer of broadly equivalent rank, explaining why Jill was to be accompanied to Tulliallan by the Assistant Commissioner. Chief Constable Sir Brian Pollock was to be suspended on full pay pending the outcome of an internal enquiry into the handling of the original McKay murders, but in parallel, the Crown Office of the Procurator Fiscal was considering an allegation that evidence, specifically whiteboard records of the proceedings, had subsequently been tampered with, an allegation that would lead to a

Perverting the Course of Justice charge against the officer responsible. Yes, Brian Pollock was finished, and back in London, star journalist Yash Patel had pushed aside the journeywoman freelancer originally commissioned to do the puff piece, and was getting stuck in to composing the ex-Chief Constable's career obituary for the Chronicle. *The Rise and Fall of a Policing Superstar*. There was no doubting it had a nice ring to it.

Frank had just taken a slurp of his pint when he realised the AC was speaking to him.

'Jill's just been telling me more about the Macallan murders. This has been excellent work DI Stewart,' she said, 'and a real feather in the cap for Department 12B. I assume the suspects are being held in Glasgow somewhere?'

'That's right ma'am,' he spluttered. 'In my old nick in the Gorbals. We picked them up at the airport trying to board a flight to Spain.'

'And the evidence is good?'

'A work-in-progress ma'am. It's pretty solid on the Flora Stewart case, and we're hoping we'll get some forensics on the others. But aye, it's pretty good overall.'

'And what about our hacker friend. The one who was blackmailing our Manchester colleague?' Frank was amused to see the AC was wearing a smirk. 'Do we know who killed him?'

He wasn't sure whether she hoped it was ACC Frost or not, although for some reason, he suspected the former. Everybody liked a bit of juicy gossip and from Walsh's point of view, it would take another rival off the stage. But unfortunately, he had to disappoint her.

'Forensics are saying it was three powerful stab wounds to the abdomen ma'am. Not to get too sexist, but they're saying it's probably the work of a strong man, given how far the knife penetrated. And it looks like it's the same MO as the murder of the Macallan twin.'

The fact was, although it sounded callous, Frank didn't give a stuff about who killed Daniel Clarkson. He'd been given the task of finding the identity of Geordie, and that he had accomplished. Job done, tick in the box. Now he could turn his full attention to the upcoming interviews with Rory Overton and the very-much-not-dead Elspeth Macallan, who were being detained in considerable discomfort at New Gorbals police station.

And when he was done with *that*, he was shooting off to Loch Lomond to have dinner with Maggie Bainbridge. It was just a shame that his bloody brother and his bloody boss were going to be there too.

\*\*\*

They had gathered in a little lochside hotel for their now-traditional post-investigation debrief, and as had already become traditional, Frank was complaining about the prices.

'I mean, how can haggis, neeps and tatties cost twenty-seven quid, that's all I'm asking, even if it comes with a bloody whisky sauce? Christ, are they using a fifty-year old malt or something?'

'They call it fine dining mate,' Jimmy said, cracking a sardonic smile, 'not something you would understand mind you.'

'Don't worry,' Maggie said soothingly, 'Asvina's paying. Or the estate of Roderick Macallan, to be more exact.'

'And on that note, I assume we're going to hear the full gory Macallan saga this evening?' Jill Smart had driven down from police HQ at Tulliallen after her portentous interview with Brian Pollock and was intent, Maggie surmised with some bitterness, on continuing her pursuit of Jimmy Stewart. 'The whole story, without hesitation, repetition or deviation?'

'Aye ma'am, with none of the above,' Frank grinned. 'Maggie's compiled the entire story for us, from start to finish. But it's a long one, so we'd better order our food and get the drinks flowing first, don't you think?'

Of course, no-one disagreed with that, and there was general hilarity when Frank finally decided on the haggis, the young waitress merely raising a discreet eyebrow when he asked for an extra portion of the sauce on the side. Maggie gave him a fond smile. Once again, she reflected that Frank Stewart was one of life's good guys. Kindness had been baked into him from birth, and it manifested itself in every human interaction. It was just a shame he was so bloody hopeless when it came to matters of the heart. But later, when she was three or four chardonnays to the good, she might take matters into her own hands. She looked across the table to where Jill Smart had been careful to position herself next to Jimmy. Where it looked as if she too was planning to take matters into her own hands, and sod the near ten-year age gap. But all of that would have to wait until later. Three chardonnays later, minimum.

'Ok then,' Maggie said, taking a generous sip from her glass, 'let's start with Commodore Roderick Macallan, shall we? Not a nice man by any measure, and a man who liked to use his powerful position to his own advantage. A power he decided to use when he found out that Mrs Morag McKay was desperate for her husband to be given a shore-based posting. It seemed that after their daughter Isabelle had come along, she had been suffering from post-natal depression, made much worse by her husband's long spells at sea. So the predatory Commodore saw his opportunity. Quite simply, he offered to fix it for her husband in exchange for sex.'

'That's disgusting,' Jill said. 'What an evil man.'

'Yes he was,' Maggie agreed, 'and according to his wife, he had a long history of using his position to prey on vulnerable women. But it all started to unravel for him when Morag began to suffer terrible remorse for what she had done. That's when she decided for her own peace of mind she had to make a full confession to her husband.'

'And that's how our boy Geordie comes into it,' Frank said, 'or Communications Officer Daniel Clarkson to give him his proper title.'

Maggie nodded. 'That's right. He was the communications guy on board HMS Azure and because of the need for security, all comms to and from the submarine went through him.'

'Packet-encrypted technology,' Frank said, adopting a smug smile, 'at least that's what wee Eleanor told me they used. Basically a big bunch of coded stuff is sent to them about once a week and super-powerful encryption computers on the sub de-code it. It's a bit like that Enigma stuff from the war, but without the cogs and wheels.'

'I'm impressed,' Jimmy said, laughing, 'but you don't really understand a word of what you just said, do you?'

'Not a word,' Frank admitted, 'but in a nutshell, it means that Clarkson got to see all incoming comms traffic, which is how he found out about what Morag McKay and the Commodore had been up to, or to be more precise, what she had done for him.'

'Exactly,' Maggie said, 'and of course this information was absolute dynamite for a natural blackmailer like Clarkson. So we assume Macallan is surprised one morning to receive a communication from Clarkson on board Azure that says unless we can come to a satisfactory arrangement, I'm going to blow your secret.'

'Right,' Frank said, 'and that's when the Commodore sees his opportunity. By recruiting Clarkson, he was able to hatch the plan to silence Morag and frame her husband James for the murder at the same time.'

'Yes,' Maggie agreed, 'so he came to an arrangement with him. A hundred and twenty grand payment for keeping his mouth shut, a sum that would set him up very nicely when he left the service. But there were conditions attached.'

'That would be the falsifying of these e-mails between Morag and her husband?' Jimmy asked.

'Yes, exactly. Clarkson doctored the e-mail trail and instead of her confession, what James McKay learnt from his wife was that she intended to leave him and take little Isabelle with her. So of course he was distraught, and his anguish grew with every subsequent fake e-mail he received.'

'Until he finally lost it and threatened to kill her,' Jill said.

'Well yes ma'am, except we don't think he ever did make that *specific* threat,' Frank said. 'Remember, the whole conversation was being concocted by Clarkson. It was pure fiction. Both ways, to and fro. But what it did succeed in doing was to make sure that as soon as Azure docked in Ardmore base, James McKay would rush straight home to try and sort things out with his wife.'

Jill gave a rueful look. 'Where he was snared by that elaborate frame-up. I just can't imagine what it must have been like for him, walking into that scene of utter carnage.'

'Yes, it's impossible to imagine,' Maggie said. 'But of course, then he's apprehended at the scene and arrested, and when the police subsequently produce the email trail as evidence of clear motive, he of course denies having ever seen any of it before. Which naturally sounds ridiculous, even before Daniel Clarkson pops up at the trial as an expert witness and says it's impossible. Impossible that it was faked I mean.'

'Aye, the whole thing was brilliantly conceived by Macallan,' Jimmy said. 'Even down to him testifying that Lieutenant McKay had been suffering from mental health issues. The poor guy was stitched up good and proper.'

'But surely there was a chance that Macallan would be caught out by the forensic evidence?' Jill said, looking puzzled. 'Because the actual time of death was several hours' earlier, wasn't it?'

'Aye, that was a risk,' Jimmy said, 'but his reasoning was that since all the other evidence was so utterly convincing, it would over-rule anything that might point the other way. And that was before a pissed-up forensic examiner and a corner-cutting cop put the rubber stamp on the whole thing.'

'And so he got away with it,' Maggie said, 'although it didn't do him much good in the end, did it? Just four years before he got murdered too. In some ways, it's sweet justice, don't you think?'

Frank gave her an uncertain look. 'Aye, except his son Peter was killed too don't forget, and he was an innocent victim by all accounts. So I'm not sure about justice being served.'

'But were they connected?' Jill asked. 'The two cases?'

'One hundred percent,' Maggie said, smiling. 'And the connection was Daniel Clarkson, wasn't it Frank?'

He nodded. 'Too right. As you might expect, Clarkson had hacked Roderick Macallan's computer and that's how he got to know about him planning to change his will. It turns out Peter his son was doing such a cracking job of running the estate that the Commodore decided to hand it over to the boy before he died. At the same time, the twins were to be left only a small sum each. I guess he thought they were already well off enough and didn't need it.'

'Interesting that,' Jimmy mused, 'because when we met the twins, they both made a big thing about how badly the estate was doing and how angry the Commodore was with Peter.'

'They were lying of course,' Maggie said. 'To divert us from the truth.'

'So what really happened that night at Ardmore House?' Jill asked quietly.

'More drinks first,' Frank grinned, 'and maybe have a wee look at the pudding menu? Jimmy, see if you can catch the attention of that wee waitress.'

Maggie smiled at that. One thing Jimmy Stewart had no problem doing was catching the attention of wee waitresses and any other woman for that matter. Exhibit A being DCI Jill Smart, who she had just observed running an extended index finger down the back of his hand, an action that he had not seemed to notice. She knew why of course. Something had happened in the hospital, between him and Flora, when they'd gone to visit her. She hadn't meant to overhear, but she had, and now she feared what it might do to him.

The waitress appeared in response to Jimmy's beckoning, taking down their order with noteworthy efficiency before gliding off to the kitchen.

'Right then,' Frank said, 'on you go Maggie.'

'Ok. So what we think triggered the whole thing was when Geordie revealed to the twins that their father was planning to hand over the estate to Peter and to do them out of their inheritance.'

'So why did Clarkson do that?' Jill asked. 'What was his motive?'

'It was just the way he was,' Maggie said. 'A combination of power and mischief. He did it just because he could.'

'Aye, he was a right egotistical bastard,' Frank said. 'Really up himself. So it would be the sort of thing he *would* do just for fun. But I don't think he ever expected it would lead to murder.'

'Maybe not,' Maggie agreed, 'but by doing it, he set off the chain of events that resulted in these terrible killings. You see, Rory Overton was having an affair with his wife's sister, and when they discovered the terms of the will, they decided they had to act.'

'That affair was just so weird,' Jimmy said, shaking his head, 'with them being identical twins. Made me puke to be honest.'

'Yes it was seriously weird,' she agreed, 'but remember, Rory had been going out with Elspeth before they split. Before he married Kirsty and had their little girl.'

Jimmy nodded. 'So maybe at some point he realises that his new wife has an eye for other men and doesn't like it.'

'And you're speaking from experience,' Maggie said, giving Jill a pointed look. 'She had *you* in her sights didn't she?'

'Well maybe,' he said, evidently anxious to skirt round the subject, 'but whatever the circumstances, I'm guessing that Overton decided he'd made a mistake in marrying Kirsty and that's when he came up with his crazy plan.'

'That's right,' Maggie said. 'Rory Overton wanted so desperately to be the laird of Ardmore estate, and for that to happen, Roderick and Peter had to be got rid of. The plan was to stage the murder to look as if the Commodore had shot his son and then turned the gun on himself. And as far as they knew, they had got away with it, because the police investigation never challenged that narrative.'

Jill frowned. 'You say *they*?'

'Oh yes,' Maggie nodded, 'Elspeth was there that night too, we're pretty sure of that. Remember that Daniel Clarkson heard *two* car doors being slammed when they drove off. We learned that from the blackmailing messages he sent them.'

'So it was Overton's phone that was left behind at the scene,' Jimmy said. 'They must have been shitting themselves when they realised that.'

Maggie nodded. 'They would have been, but of course with Clarkson stealing it, it wasn't there for the scene-of-crime team to find. So in that regard, they were lucky. Except of course, it made them susceptible to Clarkson's blackmail demands. But Geordie-boy over-reached himself big-time when he decided to tangle with Rory Overton. A big mistake that ended up with him bleeding out in that cupboard.'

'So how did they find out who he was?' Jill asked.

Maggie shrugged. 'He was greedy Jill. He was asking for a hundred grand and more, and nobody hands over that sort of money to someone they haven't met. So we assume they insisted on a meeting, and then they forced him back to his flat, where Overton stabbed him to death.'

'Aye, in exactly the same way he had murdered his wife that terrible night in Fulham,' Frank said. 'Three stab wounds to the abdomen. See, that's the thing with murderers. When you find a method that works, you're going to repeat it, aren't you?'

'But what I don't get is why Kirsty had to be murdered at all,' Jill said. 'Why didn't Rory Overton just bring the relationship into the open and ask Kirsty for a divorce?'

'Don't you see?' Maggie said. 'It was because Kirsty Macallan *actually was* the elder twin. It was that which complicated the whole plan. Their original idea was to pay the twins' stepmother to testify that *Elspeth* was the elder and take their chance in court, but that was all thrown into disarray when Susan Priest entered the scene. Mrs Priest had read in the paper about the twins disagreement and got in touch with Kirsty to say that she would of course support her case, by simply telling the truth.'

Jimmy nodded. 'So that screwed it up for them good and proper. If they'd gone down the divorce route, then in any court case it would come down to Alison's word against Susan's. Meaning there was at least a fifty-fifty chance that Kirsty would inherit Ardmore House, and that just wasn't part of Rory Overton's life plan.'

'And so crazily, they decided that Elspeth would take her sister's place,' Frank said. 'So they arranged to have Kirsty killed that night Jimmy had dinner with Elspeth.'

'Aye, I see what was happening now,' Jimmy said. 'That phone she had on the table was a burner, and she was just waiting for that one text that told her Overton and Kirsty were outside.'

Maggie nodded. 'Yes, exactly. Remember I told you that Overton had arranged a secret dinner for Kirsty? I'm sure that's how it was done. He tells her they're going to *La Garrigue* and when they arrive outside the restaurant, Kirsty is bundled up the adjacent alleyway where Overton stabs her to death. He's made sure his wife is wearing the little black Dior dress, just like her sister. So then Elspeth becomes Kirsty and five minutes later they're in Chelsea having dinner with friends, having paid the Uber driver to conveniently forget about the five-minute stop-off en-route.'

Jill shook her head. 'But how mental was this whole thing? Did Elspeth really expect to be able to keep up the pretence for the rest of her life?'

Maggie shrugged. 'She was seriously nuts, a jealous woman who'd already been complicit in the murder of her father and her brother. And Overton was a cold manipulative bastard. They were made for one another really. So yes, I think in her warped mind she did think she could get away with it.'

'But surely they didn't have to do it?' Jill said, looking puzzled, 'Not after the hit and run on Susan Priest?'

'Yes, but remember it was Alison Macallan who was responsible for that killing,' Maggie said. 'She didn't know anything about Elspeth and Overton's crazy plan. All she saw was that if Susan vouched for Kirsty in court, then her agreement with Elspeth and the money that came with it would be blown out of the water.'

'God what a tangled mess,' Jill said. 'So I assume Elspeth and Overton didn't know that Alison had killed Mrs Priest?'

'I don't think so,' Jimmy said, 'and I'm certain Alison wouldn't have confessed. But of course now that they had decided that Elspeth would be faced with a lifetime of pretending to be her sister, they needed to get Alison out of the way,' Jimmy said, 'in case she eventually saw through the pretence.'

'She was lucky they didn't decide to kill her too, wasn't she?' Jill said.

'Aye, and I bet they considered it,' Frank said, 'but that would have got us police thinking about connections, and they didn't want that.'

'Yeah, but my Flora *did* see through it, right away,' Jimmy said. 'She and Kirsty and Morag had their pet names and their secret language when they were kids, remember? Flora was Flopsy and Kirsty was Mopsy, you know, like from Peter Rabbit. But when Flora addressed Elspeth at the funeral by her pet name, she got no response. Remember Maggie, we saw Flora's reaction?'

'Yes, but Elspeth realised it too and that's why they decided they needed to kill Flora,' Maggie said. 'To silence her. And if she had been drowned as they intended, they might very well have got away with it. Because her body would have been swept away to sea and never found.'

'Aye, and without a body it would have been another bloody Ardmore mystery,' Frank said ruefully. 'But thank god it didn't come to that, thanks to you Jimmy.'

'Yes, you were *so* brave,' Jill Smart said, squeezing Jimmy's hand and this time making no attempt to hide her action.

'Well, at least they confessed,' Frank said, grinning. 'Saved me a lot of time and trouble that did. *Seven* murders I've solved in total ma'am. Will I get a bonus do you think?'

To Maggie, it was lovely to witness his boyish enthusiasm, quite untainted by self-regard. 'Yes, go on Jill,' she said laughing, 'give the boy a bonus, he deserves it.'

Jill smiled. 'He's a public servant, which means that job satisfaction is meant to be its own reward. But I'll happily buy him a drink.'

'Now you're talking ma'am,' Frank said. 'Mine's a pint. Anybody else?'

But it seemed the lovely evening was drawing to a natural close.

'Naw, I think I'll give it a miss mate,' Jimmy said quietly. 'Been quite a couple of days and I'm bushed. I need an early night.'

But Maggie had heard the words that Flora Stewart had spoken during their hospital visit, and knew the real reason. As she recalled them again, it sent a searing pain through her whole being. *I'll always be grateful to you Jimmy for saving my life, of course I will. But it doesn't change anything. I've moved on you see. I'm sorry.* She'd watched as he'd kissed her gently on the forehead, and she'd watched as he'd walked away, his hopes dashed and his spirit crushed. And now she feared for him.

Looking across the table, she thought Jill Smart was about to remonstrate, but then almost imperceptibly, changed her mind. *She who fights and runs away will live to fight another day.* Maggie wondered if Jill had worked out what had happened with Flora and was silently pleased.

'Yes, that's a good idea,' Jill said simply. 'It's an early start in the morning. Good night all.'

\*\*\*

And now it was just her and Frank in the cosy restaurant, the clock barely past nine-thirty. By any measure the night was still young, and from nowhere, another of Jimmy's stupid ringtones filled her mind, one that he insisted meant nothing other than he loved the tune. From Frank she'd learnt it was co-written by Bruce Springsteen and performed by the Patty Smith Band, and was one of his favourites.

She couldn't quite remember it, but it was something about the night belonging to lovers.

A THANK YOU FROM AUTHOR ROB WYLLIE

Dear Reader,

A huge thank you for reading The Ardmore Inheritance and I do hope you enjoyed it! For indie authors like myself, reviews are our lifeblood so it would be great if you could take the trouble to post a star rating on Amazon.

If you did enjoy this book, I'm sure you would also like the other books in the series, A Matter of Disclosure and The Leonardo Murders, and the Aphrodite Suicides, all available on Amazon. Search 'Maggie Bainbridge'- or click here

Oh, and if you want to join the Maggie Bainbridge fan club, where you can get news of special offers on my books, please visit www.robwyllie.com


Thank you for your support.

Regards

Rob

Printed in Great Britain
by Amazon